Whistling Wings

A Whistling Pines Mystery

Books by Dean Hovey

Whistling Pines Cozy Mysteries
Whistling Pines
Whistling Sousa
Whistling Wings

Pine County Mystery series:
Where Evil Hides
Hooker
Unforgettable
Undeveloped
The Deacon's Demise
Family Trees

Coming in 2018
Stolen Past
(a mystery set in Arizona)

Whistling Wings

A Whistling Pines Mystery

———— ◆ ————

Dean L. Hovey

Cover art by Carrie Ayd
Author photo by Michelle Mero Riedel
Book layout by Nancy Koucky, NRK Designs

ISBN 978-1-938382-08-6

Dedicated to Natalie Lund,
my favorite (and only) sister-in-law

PROLOGUE
APRIL 1933

His father was a blacksmith for the local iron ore mine but even skilled mine employees could afford little more than groceries and a simple house. Alphonse (Alf) Paluzzo was lying awake on the thin mattress in the loft he shared with his two older brothers, Rudolpho (Rudy), and Angelo (Angel). A thick homemade quilt shielded them against the cold as sleet pelted the tin roof. Above him, a layer of newspapers provided the only insulation between the loft and the rafters. His parents' bed was directly below and some nights, when his parents thought the boys were asleep, Alphonse could hear the rhythmic creaking of bedsprings and soft whispers.

The boys attended the one-room school until they graduated from eighth grade. By then it was assumed they'd learned all a person needed to know to get a job in the mines. According to Alf's teacher, the northern Minnesota mines were an island of prosperity in a world mired in a depression. Mortgaged farms throughout the country were being seized by the banks. The stores in their little town survived only because of purchases made by the mines and miners.

The teacher said there had once been talk about unionizing, but Alf's dad said the unionists had been fired and none of the remaining workers were willing to risk their jobs by even whispering the word "union" in the local bar. His dad said the family had to stay on the good side of their neighbors and other miners because an irritated neighbor could leak false unionization rumors to the company. Talking about unionizing was enough to get a man fired.

As proud new Americans, his parents were emphatic that their children learn English but the family spoke a mixture of Italian and English at home. One night, with the boys tucked in bed, Alphonse could hear his parents arguing in Italian, which meant they were using words they didn't know in English. Alphonse understood a few of the Italian expletives his father used and the urgency with which he spoke.

"I've worked hard to save some gold coins and I will not turn them in to the bank for paper," his father said. "Gold will have value forever!" The argument was punctuated by the sound of the whiskey bottle hitting the table. His father drank whiskey only when he was very angry.

"But the government will come and take them," his mother pleaded. "The Italian taxmen came into our homes when I was a girl and took all our money and jewelry. When they thought people were hiding anything valuable, they searched and left houses in a shambles."

Alphonse was shocked to hear his mother arguing. In immigrant families, fathers ruled with an iron fist and arguments with a father usually led to a calloused miner's hand slapping your face or spanking your bare behind. "Go to the corner" or "Don't make me stand up" were paternal threats resulting in immediate compliance. He waited for the sound of an open hand slapping his mother's face or the more troubling thud of a blow from a fist that would leave his mother bruised in places that didn't show under her long dresses, but left her in obvious pain for days.

"My decision is this: You will turn in a few coins at the bank. If they're keeping records, they will show that we have given up our gold. The rest we'll keep so we'll have something of value in case …" The rest of the words were too soft to hear, but he knew both his parents lived in fear of a mining accident that would cripple his father … or worse. They all saw men with missing limbs in the store or going into the bars. Many people gave the men a coin or two knowing they weren't able to work anymore and that the mines paid them nothing when they were injured on the job.

Widows quickly remarried, usually to older men whose wives had died in childbirth or couldn't take the hard life and disappeared. Wives of crippled miners worked as domestic servants in the homes of the richer families, or sometimes were seen climbing the back stairs of the bars on Saturday nights, their faces hidden behind scarves. They did anything to keep their children out of the orphanage.

The next day Alf's mother came home from the bank and put a few bills in a shaving mug on the top shelf in the kitchen. In bed that evening, he heard the distinctive sound of coins being dropped into a canning jar followed by whispers. He never heard about the gold coins again, but he sensed that the family had a cushion if the unspeakable came to pass.

CHAPTER 1
TUESDAY

Alf Paluzzo was reading the *Duluth News Tribune* while finishing his lunch. The Whistling Pines dining room was nearly empty and he looked up at the sound of approaching footsteps.

"Alf, there's a call for you on my office phone," said Nancy Helmbrecht, the director of the senior citizen residence.

Alf sat frozen for a second, paralyzed by the fear of what news was so important someone would call the director in an attempt to contact him. He rose slowly from his chair.

"Who died?" Alf asked.

Nancy patted him on the arm. "I think you should get this news from the caller."

They walked the short distance to Nancy's office where she led him to her chair and handed him the phone before discreetly slipping away, closing the door as she left.

"Hello. This is Alf Paluzzo."

"Uncle Alf, this is your nephew, Ted."

"What's the matter with you?" asked Alf. "I don't hear from you for three decades and now you call up and interrupt my lunch."

"You probably wouldn't recognize me. Last time you saw me I was wearing sergeant's stripes."

"Yeah, sergeant's stripes and a purple heart. You Vietnam vets had it tough. We came home from the war to marching bands and people buying us free drinks at every bar. Hell, I was drunk for a month and never paid for a single drink. You Vietnam vets, you had it different."

"It was a different time," said Ted. "We're still fighting the war, but now it's with the Veterans Administration to get recognition of Agent Orange and other stuff we were exposed to, not to mention the PTSD."

"We still fight it too," said Alf. "I still have nightmares." He paused, then asked, "So, why call me now? I suppose Rudy is sick."

"Yeah, Dad had pancreatic cancer and he went fast. I thought about calling you, but he wanted to be remembered as he'd been." Ted paused. "I was going through Dad's papers when I came across a letter pertaining to Zim. Dad talked about coming back to share it with you but he ran out of time."

"I know why he never came here. Rudy always said that Two Harbors isn't the end of the world, but you can see it from here."

"Have you been out to the homestead lately, Uncle Alf?"

"Nah, there's nothing left of Zim anymore. Last time I was through, there were just a few abandoned houses and a green-house run by some yuppies. Besides, it's winter and no one goes out there this time of year except for some crazy bird people. I read in the Duluth paper that they take busloads of them from New York and California out to see arctic birds that spend the winter out at Zim. They're plain nuts."

"I sent a fax to Nancy, the director. It's a letter to Dad from Grandma Paluzzo, written before she died," Ted said, suddenly sad. "She told him to come back and that you two could find the money. Dad told me that Grandma and Grandpa hid a jar of gold coins."

Alf picked up the only paper on Nancy's desk. It was a fax copy of a letter written by a shaking hand. Alf recognized his mother's handwriting.

"Do you have a copy of the note, Uncle Alf?"

"Yes. It appears to be Momma's handwriting."

"Read what I underlined," said Ted.

"Rudy, I want you boys to split the money," Alf read. "Bring this letter to Alf and together you'll be able to find what I left for you. Remember where Angelo died. Look in the book."

"That's why I sent the letter to you," said Ted. "Dad stewed over this for years and couldn't make any sense of it. Grandma obviously thought the two of you together could solve the riddle and that you'd know what she meant. Read that other part again, the part about looking in the book."

Alf read the line again and closed his eyes. "I've got no clue. I don't remember anything Momma left behind. By the time we got home from the war Daddy was dead and Momma had moved into town. She didn't take much except the clothes on her back. I went to the Zim house and there was nothing there. Nothing. Even the cabinets and pipes had been stripped out. If something was left behind, the vandals took it long ago."

"We were thinking she might have meant something you left behind," said Ted.

Alf took off his glasses and closed his eyes. "I left behind a girlfriend who sent me a Dear John letter, and I left behind a set of hockey skates that were gone when I came home. Even the civilian clothes I left behind were gone. Momma gave them all to charity."

"Did the Marines send home a box of Angelo's stuff?" asked Ted.

"How would I know?" Alf replied. "I was in Italy getting shot at by Germans. Rudy was in England loading bombers. I never saw anything except for the telegram Momma got from the war department telling her that Angelo had been killed in action."

"Did Momma say where Angelo was buried?" asked Ted.

"Momma never said, so I thought maybe . . ." Alf teared up and looked at the ceiling.

"I did a little research," said Ted, "but most of the military archives burned in the '70s. I never found anything going through the military cemetery databases."

"He died somewhere in the South Pacific," Alf said. "Some guy called Momma after the war and said he was one of Angelo's buddies and he'd promised Angelo he'd call his mother. But that's all I ever heard and Momma couldn't talk about it."

They talked about life in Zim and what their lives had been since their war experiences. Rudy had gone to work for Boeing in Seattle and Alf had worked for the railroad in Duluth. Ted lived in a Twin Cities suburb working for a software company. After ten minutes the conversation lagged.

"Well," said Ted, "I've got to finish clearing out Dad's apartment."

Alf nodded, unable to speak.

As he hung up the phone, Alf said, "Bastard. Momma gives you half a puzzle to share with me. Instead, you spend sixty years trying to figure it out on your own. Then I find out you're dead and your son finally comes to me asking for my help." He walked back to the dining room and stared at the cold coffee grounds in the bottom of his cup.

Miriam Millam, the most compassionate of the dining room staff, poured fresh coffee for Alf. "I heard about your brother," she said, sitting down across from him. "I'm so sorry."

"My brother was always working an angle. They used to call us Alf and Rudy, the Catholic twins, because we were only nine months apart in age and were always in the same grade in school." Alf took a breath. "Rudy's had a letter from our momma with a puzzle for sixty years. She wanted us to work on it together, but I never heard anything about it until today. He kept it to himself all these years, and now that he's dead his son finally asks for my help."

"What kind of puzzle?" Miriam asked.

"My parents hid a jar of gold coins during the Depression. According to Momma's letter, something left behind is connected to where to my brother Angelo died."

"That seems pretty simple," said Miriam. "Where did your brother die?"

"He was killed during the fighting in the South Pacific and we're not even sure his remains were ever recovered."

"That's so sad. Is there some sort of clue?"

"It says to look at what we left behind. I left my home, my parents, and my naiveté," said Alf. "When I came home they were all gone. Daddy died in a mining accident and Momma moved into Two Harbors, a broken woman. I came home to a world that had changed. The mines were running out of ore and I was no longer the stupid kid who lived only for girls and hockey."

"Didn't you have a hidey hole," asked Miriam, "a place where you hid special stuff?"

"We lived in a two-room house. There was no privacy and no place to hide anything where the whole family wouldn't know about it." Alf shook his head. "We didn't have nothin', just the hand-me-down clothes on our backs and a new pair of shoes when school started. Hockey skates and shin pads were the only things that were really mine, and they were gone when I got home."

"Do you have a family Bible?" asked Miriam.

"I'm not sure. If we do I suppose it's stuffed in the storage room with the other stuff."

"Maybe your mother made a note in the Bible about your brother's burial place."

"I doubt it, but I suppose it wouldn't hurt to look." As Alf stood he cocked his head. "I think maybe there is a Bible. And Uncle Sal had a stamp collection. He told Momma I could have it, but I was more interested in hockey and roughhousing with the guys than boring old stamps. The kids probably boxed it all up when they made me sell the house and move in here. I'll have to find the key to the storage locker."

CHAPTER 2

I'm Peter Rogers, the activities director for Whistling Pines, an assisted living facility in Two Harbors, Minnesota. My job is providing entertainment for the 200 residents, activities that range from bingo to sing-alongs, movies, and trips in the Whistling Pines van. Some residents still drive cars, but for those who don't drive, the van trips offer them a chance to do some shopping, eat a restaurant meal, and have a change of scenery from the lodge-like décor of Whistling Pines. Although the dining room view of Lake Superior is spectacular, many residents prefer people-watching at any of the dozen Two Harbors restaurants, Shopko, or the Miller Hill Mall in Duluth.

Thursday afternoon we were at Judy's Restaurant eating desserts. On trips to Judy's, our van is always full and several of the residents also drive carloads of friends. Judy is a gem who welcomes our arrival after prepping the staff to expect a busload of demanding senior citizens who tip like it's still 1950.

Judy had blocked a parking spot for the van and our group was disembarking. Maddie Preston stepped off the van, and as she passed she said, "You should do something about the smell in the van. It smells like the cleaner they use when someone throws up."

"I'll see what I can do," I said. Several others also mentioned the odor as they headed toward Judy's. I made a mental note to check it out.

People migrated to their traditional spots with their usual group of friends. Although they're older, the groups are as cliquey as any school cafeteria. I pulled a chair up to a group of women who were sitting near the kitchen. The moment I sat the conversation stopped, making me wonder what secrets or rumors were being passed. Hulda Packer, a former teacher and the source of all misinformation, was dressed in a pullover blouse with large flowers that matched the slight tinge of pink in her newly permed hair. She stared at me with pursed lips.

"Peter, there are several other tables with open chairs. Why don't you move to one of them?"

"Are you having a secret conversation?" I asked, looking among the other three women for an invitation to stay. Millie Clay, Lorraine "Pete" Peterson, and Peggy Jones all sat with their lips sealed, unwilling to irritate Hulda.

"There are conversations that aren't secret, but are best discussed in smaller groups," she replied. The other women sat stoically, letting Hulda's comments stand.

"If you had a clique of students who chose to eat lunch at a table that excluded all others, what would you have done?" I asked.

I could see Hulda's ire rising. "First of all, we are not children!" she said sharply. "Secondly, the topic of our conversation is none of your business."

I thought about the usual topics: bodily functions, grandchildren, medical procedures, and food. Ventures into other subjects were brief and I decided to move on.

Howard Johnson, a retired Army colonel and the de facto mayor of Whistling Pines, was sitting at a table with Bill and Steven "Sonny" Nielson. Howard was dressed sharply in a plaid shirt and khaki trousers. As always, he sat with military bearing and the freshly pressed creases in his pants could cut a steak.

Bill and his brother, the former owners of Nielson's Clothing store, were dressed in suits and ties with freshly polished Florsheim shoes. It was rumored that Bill had even mowed his lawn wearing a suit and tie before moving to Whistling Pines.

Howard leaned over and pulled out a chair for me. "Please join us," he said with a smile.

"We were planning a trip to the VFW hall for pasties on Thursday." He pronounced pasty the proper way—rhyming with nasty.

Pasties are pie crusts folded over a filling of meat, potatoes, onion, and rutabaga, then baked. Pasties were a favorite lunch box item of the iron range miners, and their origins are claimed by virtually all the ethnic groups that worked the mines, from Cornwall to Finland and Slovenia.

"The VFW only serves pasties in the evening," I replied. "Most of the residents like to have their dinner meal at noon and then eat something lighter for supper."

"While our dining room is nice," Bill replied, "I sometimes like a glass of wine with my evening meal and I'm reluctant to drive after imbibing. It would be nice if we could ride the Whistling Pines van to a supper venue so we'd have a designated sober driver for the return trip. We can always bring the leftovers home with us."

"I'll talk to Wendy to see if she's willing to drive for the pasties next Thursday." Wendy, the assistant director and my duet partner when we performed for the residents, is not a morning person and I thought she might enjoy an evening shift.

"You could meet us there," Bill said. "Perhaps you could bring Jenny along and we could toast your engagement."

A few months earlier I'd filled in as the acting director for the Two Harbors City Band. The concert was interrupted by gunshots and the arrest of the shooter. After the adrenaline rush I was prompted to propose to my longtime girlfriend, Jenny, Whistling Pines' nursing director. I thought only our immediate families knew.

"I didn't realize our engagement had been publicized."

"You didn't think anyone would notice Jenny's engagement ring?" Howard asked.

"Oh," I replied, feeling sheepish for having overlooked the obvious.

"You been taking pre-nuptial classes from the pastor?" Bill asked.

"We had our last one Tuesday night. It's been a long haul."

"Ah, the last counseling session is the one where you're coached on physical love, as I recall. How did that go?"

"I'd rather not get into that," I replied.

"Touchy subject, or are you shy?" asked Bill. Howard just smiled.

"The pastor was as uncomfortable as we were with the topic, but said that he thought it was important to cover that ground with young couples. He said since I had been in the Navy, and Jenny is a nurse, he would assume we understood the mechanics and left it at that."

"So, being in the Navy apparently qualifies you as a sex expert?" asked Howard. "In the Army, we had to sit through movies showing the effects of venereal diseases and how to properly install a condom, but I don't recall any instruction in sex."

"Can we move on?" I asked.

"No," said Bill. "I really want to know what Navy training you had that made you an expert in marital love."

"I was a corpsman," I ad-libbed. "I was trained in everything from the diagnosis of venereal diseases to delivering babies."

"Ahh," said Bill. "And somewhere in there they taught you how to fulfill your future wife's needs. I can almost imagine that."

"Did you guys see the pie specials?" I asked, hoping to end the conversation.

The restaurant was filled with senior citizens and a few of Judy's regulars. The waitresses moved between the tables with purpose, obviously irritated when the senior citizens, who no longer understood urgency, asked repeated questions about the daily specials and the pie options. Lucy, who'd worked at Judy's for years, finally snapped when she had to repeat the available pie flavors for the third time at the table next to us.

"Really! Weren't you listening when I told the other two people?" she asked.

"You spoke so softly I couldn't hear what you said to them," Hedvig (Hedie) Judin said. "Please speak up."

Lucy rolled her eyes and repeated the lengthy list written on the back of her order pad.

"What was that second one?" Hedie asked.

"Raspberry cream, with a custard base."

"Oh, that wasn't it. Wasn't there a lingonberry?"

"We've never had lingonberry," Lucy said, clearly exasperated. "You might've heard me say lemon meringue."

"I don't care for meringue," Hedie replied, oblivious to Lucy's rising ire. "Do you have strawberry rhubarb?"

"Yes," Lucy replied, writing Hedie's choice. "Would you like coffee and cream?"

"A cup of decaf would be nice. No cream. The doctor told me to watch my cholesterol." I suppressed a smile at Hedie's choice to forgo the cream in her coffee to reduce her cholesterol when Judy's very best crispy pie crust was rumored to be made with lard.

"And what would you like?" Lucy asked the next diner.

"I think a caramel roll and coffee is all," Jeri Westfall replied, folding her menu and handing it back to Lucy. "Could you pop it in the microwave for just a second so the butter melts?"

"Oh course," Lucy said smiling, relieved that the fourth diner didn't need another recitation of the pie list.

I watched Lucy interrupt a huddled conversation between two Whistling Pines men at the next table. She recited the pie options and the men made their choices quickly — obviously anxious to return to their conversation.

Howard noticed that my attention had been drawn to their table. "It appears Alphonse is retelling his gold story to Maurie Coughlin."

"Alphonse has a story about gold?" I asked.

"I'm surprised he hasn't shared it with you," Bill replied. "He's told anyone who'll sit still for five minutes."

"I didn't think there was any gold mining around this region," I replied.

"The iron ore of the Mesabi Range was legendary, and during the peak of World War II virtually every piece of military hardware being shipped to the war front contained iron from the mines of northern Minnesota," Howard explained. "The mines were so essential to the war effort that the miners were all given draft deferments because their iron ore output was considered more essential than their service in the military."

"There were small gold and silver mines around the region," Bill added, "but most were low grade ore that didn't pay back the cost of mining. There were some pockets of higher grade ore that petered out quickly."

We were interrupted when Lee Westfall, a retired school custodian and recent addition to our residence, joined us. Turnover is a sad fact of life at Whistling Pines. People move closer to their children, need more intensive care, or die; new people move in and change the profile of the residents. Lee and his wife, Jeri, were younger residents who added some vitality to the mix. They both remained active in their church and community well into their retirement.

Jeri was sitting at a nearby table with three other women. She'd once been a secretary for the University of Iowa Medical School, then the town clerk, and the Methodist church secretary. She told me they'd moved to Whistling Pines because she no longer wanted to cook for two now that their four children were grown. I noticed Lee's gnarled arthritic knuckles and surmised that his life was also easier at Whistling Pines.

"Hi, Doc," Lee said as I pulled a chair to the table.

"I'm no doctor," I replied. "I'm just a guy who plays guitar and drives the van."

"The Marines don't hand out Silver Stars for good behavior," Lee said. "I appreciate the service you did for your country." Lee offered his hand.

"Thanks," I replied as I shook his hand. "I'd rather not dredge up those memories."

"We all understand," Lee replied, nodding to Howard and Bill, who were both battle-hardened Army veterans. "But you're in a small fraternity."

"By the way, I was a Navy corpsman, not a Marine."

"Worse yet," Lee replied. "You served under fire and didn't have a weapon to defend yourself."

Pie and coffee arrived as Lee chatted about his experiences as a shoe store owner, then later as a school custodian. I kept one eye on the residents to make sure everyone was happy, and the other eye on the clock to make sure we got the van loaded and back to Whistling Pines on schedule. The topic of Alf's gold was lost.

———— ◆ ————

After everyone was off the van I returned to my cubbyhole office. My workday was through, so I logged off the computer and grabbed my jacket, only to run into Wendy. Before I could ask her about taking a van load of residents for pasties, she said, "My band is playing at Hugo's Bar Saturday night. Do you and Jenny have plans?"

"I'm not aware of any plans for Saturday," I replied. "We usually crash at my place with Jenny's son, Jeremy, eat a pizza, and watch whatever movie is on television."

"You are like an old married couple," Wendy said, rolling her eyes.

"Hey! We like our stress-free lifestyle."

"Actually, I'd like to ask a favor. Our backup guitar player had an emergency appendectomy last night. I was hoping you'd be able to sit in with us." Sensing my reluctance, she added, "We'll pay you fifty bucks and give you a cut of the tips."

"Let me talk to Jenny," I replied. "She enjoys going to Hugo's for the music, but I know she doesn't like to sit alone at a table looking like she's trolling for a date."

"Who knows," Wendy said with an evil smile as she left my office, "maybe she'll be able to upgrade from you."

I walked to the nursing office where I found Jenny in a serious conversation with one of the aides. I hung back by the door, not wanting to intrude on a discussion about a resident's medical situation.

Nancy, the director, tapped me on the shoulder. "Peter, do you have a second?" I inwardly cringed because the director's requests for "a second" usually involved some modification of my plans.

"Sure," I said, stepping away from the door.

"I was in the dining room and a couple of the women commented on the odor in the van." Nancy glanced around to make sure no one was within earshot. "Please check it out. We don't want a replay of the unfortunate incident."

"You don't need to remind me," I said, shaking my head.

"Good," Nancy said, walking away.

Seeing her leave, Jenny stepped over and gave me a hug.

"What's up, boyfriend?" she asked.

I shook off Nancy's comments and refocused. "Wendy asked me to sit in with her band at Hugo's Saturday night. I told her I'd check with you because I know you hate sitting alone in a bar."

"Not a problem," she replied, holding up her left hand, flashing her diamond ring. "This ring is my 'creepy guy repellent.' They see the ring and they shy away. I wish I'd discovered that fact a long time ago. It would've saved me from enduring years of witty pick-up lines."

"I guess I'm not into pick-up lines. Give me an example."

"Honey, you must be tired because you've been running through my mind all evening."

"Really?" I asked, laughing.

"Oh yeah. Funny thing is, lots of guys seem to think they

sound even better after they've had half a dozen beers." Jenny looked at her watch. "You're off now. Can you stop at the grocery store and buy something for supper? I'll pick up Jeremy after I get off work and we'll buzz over." She hesitated, then added, "Try to find something in the produce aisle to go with whatever meat and potatoes you choose. I'll ask Mom if she can watch Jeremy on Saturday."

———— ◆ ————

I'm sure people in the South think Christmas in Minnesota is like living in a snow globe. In fact, December is cold, flirting with sub-freezing temperatures. Snow squalls come intermittently, often followed by days above freezing, leaving our roads full of potholes, our spirits dreary, and the landscape brown. Aside from the short few weeks known as deer hunting season, when the woods, restaurants, and hotels are filled with orange-clad people who drink, play cards, and sometimes actually shoot a few deer, life slows, like molasses in January. As we approach the winter solstice, the days are short and the lakes aren't fully frozen, so no one is ice fishing. Most often there is no snow. With no snowmobiling or ice fishing, the populace falls into an almost drug-like stupor driving to jobs before sunrise and home after dark, yards and fields a uniform brown when seen through headlights.

With groceries on the front seat and looking forward to an evening with my fiancée, I drove home through my Seagog neighborhood in Two Harbors. The winter solstice was only weeks away and the lingering twilights of summer were a distant memory. One of the three neighborhood deer was munching on shrubbery in my front yard, not far from the deer crossing sign erected the previous spring. The doe seemed unconcerned as I turned into my driveway, bolting only after I'd stepped out of my car.

"Peter! Yoo-hoo, Peter," Dolores, my elderly neighbor, called out as I approached my front steps.

"Hello, Dolores," I called back.

"When you get a moment, could you come over and look at something?"

"Let me put my groceries away," I replied.

Although well into her 80s, Dolores lived independently. Though I questioned some of her antics, particularly those that involve her discharging firearms at various critters in her yard, overall she was capable of caring for herself, and on those few occasions when something arose that was beyond her capabilities, she called on me for assistance.

With my lettuce and milk stowed in the refrigerator, I walked the short distance from my small bungalow to Dolores's sort-of-Victorian old house. It had been built by one of the people made wealthy by their investments in the railroad. It was a two-story with a wraparound porch and shutters for the windows. She's kept it up well, but it was now in need of paint and some of the shutters were starting to sag. She'd lived there first with her husband, then as a widow, for close to sixty years.

I crossed the creaking front porch, past the wicker chairs that saw scant use—we joked that a week-long Canadian fishing trip could cause you to miss the entire Two Harbors summer. Before I could knock, Dolores pulled the door open, leaving me with raised knuckles.

"I was afraid you'd forgotten about me," she said as she grabbed my elbow and pulled me into her living room. As I shed my coat I was once again in awe of the beautiful carved oak furniture and the hand-tied Persian rug that lay under her dining room table. I'm sure the rug alone was worth more than a year of my salary, and the dining room set with its beautiful sideboard covered with Royal Doulton china was more than several years' salary. I didn't know specifics of Dolores's finances, but I was led to assume that anything she wanted was within her means.

"Peter, look at this," she said as she walked away before I could hang my coat on the ornate hat tree behind her door.

I followed her into a pantry I had never noticed hidden behind the dining room. In the light of the single bulb that swung from a cord attached to the ceiling, I could see the shelves were stocked with canned goods and quart canning jars. The Mason jars contained unidentifiable vegetables and fruit, all faded to an ugly shade of gray after years of storage. A few of the cans bore the label of a grocery chain that had gone bankrupt when I was a child in the 1980s. I flashed back to a meal she'd prepared for me when she commented that a can had leaked and was stuck to the shelf. Looking around the pantry I saw several other cans of fruit that stood in dried puddles of juice. I bit my tongue, fearing I'd either embarrass Dolores or I'd volunteer to do the cleanup.

Halfway down the twenty-foot pantry she stopped and pointed to the floor. "I think an animal has been gnawing at my floor-boards," she said.

I looked at the dark spot on the floor in the dimly lit room and tried to understand the problem.

The dark spot was nearly the width of the narrow pantry. In the center was an open hole the size of a softball with ragged edges. I looked at the ceiling and saw a huge, brown circular stain on the plaster, with spider-web cracks radiating from the center.

"Dolores, you have a leak," I said taking her elbow and leading her out of the pantry. "You have to stay out of there until the ceiling and the floor can be repaired."

"Can you fix it for me?" she asked, looking more flustered than when I'd taken her shotgun away one evening after she shot at a woodpecker that was attacking her eaves.

"Please show me the room above this," I said. "You may have a leaking pipe."

The trip up the stairs was painful to watch. Dolores favored her left leg and leaned heavily on the wooden railing with each step, the cane in her other hand steadying her. By the time we reached the top, she was wheezing from the effort. She pointed the cane at a closed door down the hallway. I opened the door into a museum of curio cases, all filled with porcelain figurines and teacups. Every surface was dusty, and the floor was covered with another Persian rug, this one dark in the middle and littered with pieces of plaster. I looked up and saw the lath behind the plaster.

"I think your roof is leaking and the water has been dripping down through here into the pantry."

"When can you repair it?" Dolores asked as she stepped into the room to get a closer look at the ceiling. I stopped her short of the Persian carpet, unsure of the integrity of the floor beneath.

"I'm not a carpenter," I replied. "If you don't have someone you trust to do the work, I can ask Jenny's father to recommend someone."

"I've never needed a carpenter before. If you can find someone trustworthy, please have them start immediately."

After walking back to my house, I called Jenny's home, where she lived with her parents and her son, Jeremy.

"Hello, Peter," Jenny's mother said, obviously checking the caller ID. "Jenny's not home yet."

"Hi, Barbara. I need the name of a reliable carpenter. Mrs. Karvonen has a roof leak and she needs someone to make repairs."

"Everyone uses Tim Webb for repair work," she replied. "He does electrical, plumbing, and carpentry."

"I'm really concerned that we find someone who is trustworthy and won't rip off Dolores," I replied.

"We've had Tim do a couple jobs for us and his price has been reasonable. We've been impressed with his workmanship. I wouldn't hesitate to refer him to anyone."

When I dialed the cellphone number she'd given I was surprised that Tim, not his voicemail, answered. After a brief description of the problem he agreed to come over after supper to assess the damage.

"Are you Mrs. Karvonen's son?" he asked.

"I'm her neighbor, and I try to look out for her."

"I have a white van with my name and phone number painted on the doors. I'll stop at your house and you can introduce me."

"Perfect!"

◆

A bowl of salad was placed in the center of my chipped Formica table when Jenny and Jeremy arrived for supper. Our routine had become alternating dinner at my house and dinner with Jenny's parents. Before our engagement, my acceptance by Jenny's mother, Barbara, who was always perfectly groomed, had been frosty. Since then, I'd seen her without her makeup a few times and once I'd seen her with wilted hair and a dirty t-shirt when I'd interrupted her fall whole-house cleaning. Jenny advised me that exposure to her mother's vulnerable moments, like those, qualified me as family.

Jeremy was first through the door, dropping his backpack and kicking off his shoes next to the door, then racing to my television. He thought it funny that I had a giant CRT television, which weighed close to two hundred pounds, when the rest of the world all had thin flat-screen televisions weighing less than ten pounds. I heard the hum as the television warmed up, followed by the sound of the "Gilligan's Island" theme song, a regular feature on the Nickelodeon network.

Jenny was close behind with the scent of Irish Spring soap preceding her entrance. She pecked me on the neck as I removed a pot of rice from the stove.

"You don't have to shower before coming over for dinner," I said as I fluffed the rice before putting the pot on a trivet.

"You have no idea what bodily fluids might be splashed on me during a day," she replied as she stirred the pot of stew simmering on the stove. "I'd like to believe there's nothing communicable on me, but I'd rather play it safe. I throw all my work clothes into the hamper as I walk into the shower."

I put another cast-iron trivet on the table for the stew pot and took out a carton of milk. Jenny watched me pour the milk and asked, "What's the expiration date on that carton?" She knew my bachelor's surveillance of refrigerated foods. She had poured lumpy milk down the drain on more than one occasion.

"No worries," I replied. "I picked this up on the way home from work."

The sound of clattering dishes brought Jeremy from the living room just as Jenny was ladling beef stew onto piles of steaming rice. He dove into his portion before Jenny was back at the table.

"It would be polite to wait for us all to be seated before you start eating," Jenny said as she drizzled French dressing on her salad.

"Mom, you guys are so slow," he replied with his mouth full. "If I waited for you, supper would be cold."

"We may be interrupted," I said. "Dolores has a roof leak and there's a guy coming over to look at it."

"How bad is the leak?" Jenny asked.

"Her pantry floor is rotting, so I'd guess it's been leaking for years."

Jenny mulled that information as Jeremy scooped out a second portion of rice and stew.

"Don't forget your salad," she admonished him.

He gave her an "Oh, Mom" look, and took a forkful of lettuce after carefully pushing the cucumber to the edge of the bowl.

"Is Dolores really safe living on her own?" Jenny asked.

I took another spoonful of stew and chewed while I weighed my answer. "She's healthy, her clothes are clean, she's appropriately dressed, she gets out to socialize at church a few times a week, she's only taking one blood pressure medication, and I know she has lunch daily at the senior center. Other than dealing with the occasional house maintenance issues, and trying to shoot a few critters, she's doing pretty well."

Jenny nodded assent as I checked off the issues that usually brought people to Whistling Pines from their homes. "I'm worried that she didn't detect a leak that's been dripping for a year or more."

"It's over a spare bedroom she doesn't use, and it was dripping into her pantry." I reflected on the old canned goods, knowing she wasn't using them for her meals and hoping she was relying most on her lunches at the senior center and the few groceries she kept in the kitchen. "She's not in the pantry much, and it's poorly lit, so she didn't notice the stain on the ceiling or the hole in the floor.

"Have you ever mentioned the possibility of moving to an apartment with all her rooms on one floor, or coming to Whistling Pines?"

"No. I've never brought it up. She's in control of her life and I don't think she's ready to relinquish that."

There was a knock on the front door as I took the last bite of stew.

Tim Webb was a slender man with curly dark hair and thick glasses. He wore a tan Carhartt coat over blue jeans and scarred work boots. I'd seen his van around town but we'd never actually met. He introduced himself, we shook hands, and I could feel callouses and the firm grip associated with a person who made his living through his craft and old-fashioned hard work. I noticed his van wasn't new, had a couple dents, and was caked with dirt from travel down gravel roads. He was a man of serious work, not into showy trucks, and I respected him immediately.

"I'll introduce you to Mrs. Karvonen," I said as I took my jacket off the hook and slipped on a pair of tennis shoes. Jenny was right behind me, putting on shoes and a jacket.

I knocked on Dolores's front door as I explained my relationship with Dolores and the evidence of leaking I'd seen. He nodded as he looked around the porch, assessing the house and the current state of upkeep.

"Nice old house," he said. "I don't see many of these around town." He paused, then added, "I'll be happy to look at the damage, but just to be clear, I don't do rats."

"Rats?" Jenny asked.

"I get all kinds of business and ever since I cleared a pipe that was plugged by a dead rat, I've declined any job that involved dealing with rats."

"Someone had a pipe plugged by a dead rat?" Jenny asked.

"I put a pail under the pipe and pulled a drain plug in the basement. Nothing came out, so I ran a sewer snake into the pipe and it let loose. In a whoosh the plug came flying out and the dead rat hit me in the face. Ever since that, I don't do rats."

I could see Jenny shudder just as Dolores opened the door.

"Hi Dolores, this is Tim Webb, a contractor who is going to look at your leak. Tim, this is Mrs. Karvonen."

Tim took her hand and gently shook it. She was wearing a sweater over her plaid wool slacks and she assessed Tim as they shook hands. "If Peter trusts you as a contractor, I assume you must be good."

"I have as much work as I care to do, and I've been a general contractor in Two Harbors for thirty-five years. Nearly all my work is repeat customers."

I led Tim to the pantry and showed him the stained ceiling and rotten floorboards. He got on his knees to assess the floor damage with a flashlight while Jenny inspected the food on the shelves. The expression on her face and subtle headshake said she questioned the quality of the canned goods, and by extension, Dolores's capability to live alone.

"Let's go upstairs," Tim said, rising from his knees.

Dolores let us make the trip without her, and when I opened the door to the spare bedroom Tim stopped inside the door and looked at the collections on the shelves. "This is some really old stuff. I see porcelain dolls like these in museums."

We looked at the plaster fragments on the rug before we rolled it back to expose the darkened wood floor.

"Repairing this damage is no small project," Tim said as he poked at the hardwood flooring with a pen. "I need to look in the attic because I suspect the biggest part of the project will be repairing the roof and any rotten boards there. Let's hope that the damage doesn't include the rafters."

The attic access was in the hallway outside the spare bedroom. While Tim went to get a bigger flashlight from his truck, Jenny examined the collections on the shelves. She picked up a few pieces and wiped the dust from them with her hand before turning them to look at all the sides and the bottom.

"I'm no antiques expert," she said, "but some of these figurines look like pre-war German Hummels. The ceramic doll collection is incredible. If Dolores can't afford to pay for the repairs, she could sell this collection. I'd say it's worth tens of thousands of dollars."

I heard the attic door creak and Tim's footsteps as he ascended the stairs. I followed him up the narrow dusty steps. "No one has been up here in a long time," Tim said as he stepped into the attic that looked like it might've been a maid's room at one time.

"Does she have more treasures up here?" I asked without going further into the attic.

"No treasures and no insulation," he said.

We spent about ten minutes in the attic. He closed the door behind us as we walked into the hallway.

"Well," he said, dusting himself off, "the bad news is that the roof has probably been leaking for years. I'll need to look, but I think we'll have to pull off at least a portion of her shingles to repair the boards underneath. If the roof is more than twenty-five years old the whole thing should be replaced. The good news is there is enough attic ventilation to dry the rafters. They're water-stained, but they aren't in bad shape structurally. There's hardly any insulation. If we blow in sixteen inches of rock wool the savings on heating will probably pay for the repairs in a year or two."

Dolores was waiting for us in the living room. "Is the news bad?"

"The leak is coming from the roof," replied Tim. "We'll have to start the repairs there and work our way down to the pantry."

"What's your estimate of the costs and can you get to it before there's more damage?" I asked.

"I'll write up a list of materials and time when I get home. I learned a long time ago that a quick verbal estimate isn't worth the paper it's written on," Tim said with a smile. "As for the timing, I'll call the guy I use to do roofing and see how soon he is free. The roofing business is pretty slow this time of year, so he may be able to start Monday. That way we can get everything patched up before ice dams form so we can stop additional damage."

Dolores looked distressed. "Are you okay with that?" I asked. "I assume this will cost thousands of dollars."

"The money will be there," she replied. "I'm embarrassed the damage went on so long before I saw it."

Jenny, who always knew what to say, reached out and hugged Dolores. I heard her whisper, "Peter and I will be living next door. We'll help you with the house. It'll be okay."

"If you don't need me anymore," Tim said, "I'll go home and start my estimate."

I gave him a nod and mouthed, "Thanks," walking him to the door.

We stopped on the steps and zipped our jackets. "I'll give you a fair estimate, but there's a lot of damage, some that's hidden under the hardwood floors. I'll use some old friends as sub-contractors, like for the roofing and insulation, but I'll do most of the inside work myself. I'm guessing I'll be here for a week to rip open the damage and then patch it up." He hesitated and asked, "Can she afford it?"

"I think so," I said with a shrug. "I've never had a money discussion with her."

"I'll get an estimate to you in a day or two. I suggest you ask if she can afford ten to fifteen thousand dollars in repairs."

As Tim walked back to his van I was concerned. I couldn't afford that cost, but I'd never seen Dolores flinch when she broke out her checkbook to pay for anything that came up. I thought about doing some of the work myself to reduce the cost and quickly dismissed the thought, knowing I lacked the skill and the time.

I went back inside Dolores's house and found the living room empty. Voices emanated from far back in the house and I found Dolores and Jenny discussing the contents of the pantry. Jenny held up a jar of beets and said, "I suspect these beets have lost all nutritional value, and most of the canned goods are past their expiration. Peter and I could sort through the shelves and throw out what can't be used."

Dolores put her hand to her mouth and shook her head. "This is very upsetting. I take great pride in my housekeeping but things seem to be going to pieces around me. How did this happen?"

Jenny steered Dolores out of the pantry and patted her shoulder. "We all lose track of things. Peter and I can help you through this."

I saw Dolores was upset so I tried to find a segue to another topic. "I took a van load of residents to Judy's today and there was talk about Alphonse Paluzzo and some gold coins that his family stashed when the government went off the gold standard. Do you remember anything about that?"

"That was one of the greatest bureaucratic money grabs of all time," Dolores replied, her eyes narrowing. "FDR had the country by the throat and he wanted to play Robin Hood. He took all the gold from the rich people, gave paper in return, and then spread paper money around to all the poor and unemployed."

"I thought the point was that the country was being choked because there wasn't enough money in circulation and by going off the gold standard the treasury could print the money the country needed to get the economy moving," Jenny said. "I heard there was so little money available that people were forced to barter goods and services."

"Hmph," Dolores replied. "We had money, real gold coins.

When the government was through, all we had was paper script that was worth little more than the paper it was printed on."

"So you turned in all your gold?" I asked.

"Not all," Dolores said, the twinkle returning to her eyes. "Everyone lined up at the banks to turn in their gold, but many of us held back coins because we weren't really convinced the experiment was going to work. I'm sure there were staunch Democrats who followed along like sheep and emptied their pockets, but most of the people who had caches of gold coins kept most of them tucked away in a mattress, so to speak."

"You think Alf's story might be true?" I asked.

"I once heard that after the country went to paper money the houses of ill repute on the Iron Range would only accept gold coins for services rendered."

"I thought they were accepting two-dollar bills for ser- vices, and that was why the government stopped printing that denomination."

"Not that I would know much about it," Dolores said, couching her comments, "but the nicer places wanted gold. The cheap girls, who were oftentimes addicted to opium and spread some unspeakable diseases, were accepting currency. You have to remember that left-wing revisionists wrote most of the history you were taught in schools and it's all slanted to make Roosevelt look like a hero. In fact, he was a socialist who embraced a lot of Stalin's ideology. He gave Eastern Europe to Stalin and took our country to the brink of communism. If not for Eisenhower . . ."

I interrupted. "Do you still have gold coins?"

Dolores started tapping her cane as she thought. "I suppose I might." She looked at the canning jars.

Jenny's eyes went wide. "There are gold coins in the canned fruits and vegetables? Are these jars that old?"

"Don't be silly," Dolores said. "There's a false wall behind the canned goods. I suppose we should move the money somewhere else before Peter's friend starts his repairs."

Jenny glanced at her watch. "That's not a project for tonight. Jeremy still has homework and it'll be his bedtime shortly after that. Can we leave the coins there and deal with them later?"

"They've been there for seventy years. Another night or two won't make a lick of difference."

CHAPTER 3
WEDNESDAY

The morning's clear skies meant the temperature had dropped overnight. We were well into the December-through-March weather pattern of clear, cold days, or cloudy warmer days with snow. The clear days as we approach January are killers when the polar express blows in high barometric pressure and arctic air. It's on those days that television reporters throw a cup of boiling water into the air to show viewers that the water instantly crystalizes into snowflakes. My dad told stories of the old logging camps where the cook spit out the back door while he was making breakfast. If his spit froze before it hit the ground, he'd announce that it was too cold to work.

I started the car then scraped the thick layer of frost from the windshield. KDAL radio announced the temperature at the Duluth harbor had risen to zero degrees Fahrenheit. Although the water in Lake Superior is too cold to swim, even in August, it cools slowly and often stays ice-free for the whole winter.

I'd barely hung up my jacket when Patsy Evans, a longtime resident, showed up at my office door. "Peter," she said with nervous excitement, "have you seen this article from the *Minneapolis Star Tribune*?" She eagerly pushed a half sheet of newspaper into my hand.

The headline read "Snowbirds Flock to Sax-Zim." I skimmed the article, catching the theme that hundreds of people from all over the globe were flying into Duluth, then taking buses to Sax and Zim, Minnesota, where arctic birds congregate to spend the winter. Bird-watchers, anxious to add elusive species that are usually dispersed across northern Canada and the arctic, travel to the Sax-Zim area to add those birds to their lifetime checklists.

"That's very interesting," I said, passing the article back to Patsy.

"Can we go?" she asked with a pleading look.

"You want to go to Sax-Zim?" I asked.

"I'd kill to add a dozen new birds to my lifetime list," she said, nodding her head emphatically.

"I've never heard of either Sax or Zim," I said as I opened the bottom drawer of my desk and took out the Minnesota state roadmap. I quickly scanned the Duluth area for Sax or Zim and struck out. Checking the index of cities, I found them on a tiny county road northwest of Duluth.

"The article says Sax and Zim were booming in the iron mining days but now they're mostly ghost towns," I said.

"Peter," Patsy patiently explained, "the towns are only locators for the area where all the birding occurs. It doesn't matter if they're collections of deserted stores. The focus is seeing birds that are here for a short time before they scatter across the far north. I've never seen a tundra owl, and this article says they are the stars of the show!"

I put my finger on the tiny intersection marked Zim and looked for roads between there and Two Harbors. It was a checkerboard of township and county roads often ending abruptly at old mine pits, lakes, or swamps. There wasn't a direct route to Zim.

"I don't know, Patsy," I said, "winter driving is unpredictable. It looks like the best route to Zim might be driving to Duluth, then catching highway 53 toward Eveleth. I think it would take us two or three hours to get there, then some time driving around to look for birds, then a return trip of several hours. It would be a full-day trip."

"Perfect!" Patsy replied. "We can stop at the Wilbert Cafe for pasties. I haven't been there for years. Start a sign-up list. I'll tell people we'll be going next week," she said, and walked away before I could object.

I looked at the map again and considered the hours of driving involved in such a trip. Logistics of our outings were meant to be invisible to the participants, but they often involved days of phone calls and reservations. I'd need a couple volunteer chaperones and there had to be several bathroom breaks on each leg, so I'd have to locate convenience stores that would tolerate a load of senior citizens. Lastly, I'd have to see if the Wilbert Cafe was open in the winter and if they'd be willing to accommodate sixteen senior citizens. I looked at the activities calendar, already full for the next week. The van wasn't in use on Wednesday, but if I drove I'd have to find someone to run the bingo game and set up the afternoon movie. I hoped Patsy would be the only bird-watcher interested in the trip and I'd be able to cancel due to a lack of interest.

I was printing the sign-up sheet for the birding trip when Nancy, the director, walked into my cramped office. As always, she was dressed in a neatly pressed blouse and khaki slacks. Her graying blonde hair was perfect and she wore a tasteful touch of makeup. Most often her presence meant I had overlooked or forgotten something. Her smile caught me off guard.

"Patsy Evans was showing people the article about bird-watching up by Zim, and said you were putting together a sign-up sheet. Which day were you planning to make the outing?"

"If I can get someone to cover the other activities for me," I said as I took the sheet off the printer and held it out to her, "I can take the van out on Wednesday."

"Next Wednesday," she said, apparently in thought. "That would work for me. I'll be one of your chaperones and I'll be able to tick a few more birds off my lifetime list."

"What's a lifetime list?"

"Every serious bird-watcher keeps a list of birds they've seen during their lifetime. To qualify as an official 'spotting' you need to take a picture of the bird or there has to be at least one additional verification of the sighting."

"Really," I said with surprise. "How many birds do you have on your list?"

"I have over two hundred," Nancy replied, "and the potential to add another dozen arctic birds is a big deal."

"The logistics are complicated," I replied, hoping to quash her sudden interest. "I'll have to find rest stops and find a café for lunch that'll accept a load of senior citizens who tip poorly."

"Look on the positive side," she said, smiling. "It'll be really cold and there's not much chance of repeating the unfortunate incident."

"Crap," I said to myself as she left.

I was almost out of my chair when a cherubic face popped in the door. "What's the range of a tuba?" Without waiting for an answer, Brian Johnson, the tubist from the Two Harbors City Band said, "About fifteen feet if you get a running start."

I grimaced, acknowledging another of his sad tuba jokes. "To what do I owe the honor of your visit?" I asked.

"I just came by to ask why you haven't been at band practice," he said, sitting in the chair without invitation.

"I figured I was through once my director's stint was over," I replied.

"Nope. Once your name is on the roster, you're a member for life. Hey, did I tell you about the Memorial Day parade in Duluth? It rained all day and by the time we finished the parade route my wool uniform was so wet that my pants were falling down. My tuba filled with water so it sounded like I was gargling."

I laughed at the mental image.

"Just keep us in mind," Brian said, jumping up. "We could use another woodwind player."

"Thanks, but I don't see that happening," I said to his back.

CHAPTER 4
THURSDAY AFTERNOON

I herded everyone to the door for our field trip to the North Shore Brewery, then pulled the van to the front door. I opened the van door and helped the residents up the steps.

"It's cold in here," Hulda Packer said in her outdoor voice. "Why don't you warm it up before you load us?"

"It's against the law to leave an unattended vehicle running," I replied.

"You used to warm it up for us," protested Hulda as she shuffled down the narrow aisle while supporting herself on the seatbacks.

"Well, I'm smarter now," I said idly.

"You probably got a ticket," said Alva Pruitt. "I saw you talking with the police chief. He probably gave you a ticket because you left the van running."

I nodded without comment.

"It's because of the unfortunate incident," said Howard Johnson with a knowing smile.

I didn't answer.

The brewery offered public tours on Saturday afternoons, but agreed to a special tour for Whistling Pines because the brewmaster was the grandson of one of our residents. They had no idea what they were getting into with a group of senior citizens roaming the place. The brewery was located just over a mile from our residence, so the van was barely warm when we arrived. I left the van idling while the residents disembarked. By the time I'd parked, the brewmaster was already into his presentation to the group.

"We'll be walking into our warehouse," said Dan, our guide, "and the brewing is underway, so please stay together and ..."

"When do we get the free beer?" asked Hulda. "Do we have to wait until the end of the tour?"

"That's Dan, my grandson," I heard Esme Brady whisper loudly. "He's the brewmaster," she added proudly.

"You'll each get a complimentary beer sample at the end of the tour," Dan explained with great patience. "Are there any other questions before we begin?"

"Do we have to go on the tour to get the beer?" asked Alf Palazzo. "Can we just sit here while you walk around and then get the free beer when you get back?"

Dan cast a look at me that said, "Really?" He smiled at Alf. "If you don't feel like walking through the facility, you can wait here until we return."

"Do you have anything to eat while we wait?" asked Hulda.

"We don't have restaurant facilities," Dan said, his façade starting to crack.

"How about some pretzels?" asked Alf.

"I'm afraid we don't have any."

"What kind of pub are you running?" asked Hulda. "Everyone knows you sell more booze when you serve pretzels."

"We aren't a bar, ma'am, we're a brewery. We don't sell glasses of beer. We just offer samples when the tour is through."

"Is it at least a decent-sized beer?" asked Alf, as the other residents started to fidget.

"I think it's time to start the tour," I said, much to Dan's relief. "You take the group and I'll stay here with Hulda and Alf, and anyone else who doesn't want to walk."

"Isn't he something?" asked Esme as she passed. "He took classes in Germany and now he's back here!" She followed behind the pack.

"But I have more questions," blurted Hulda.

"I'm sure Dan will answer them after the tour," I said, helping some of the residents to their feet and guiding them toward Dan.

"Hmph," said Alf, after everyone else was gone. "If I'd known we were getting little beers with no food I would've stayed home."

"I doubt that," I said. "I think you'll take a free beer even if it isn't sixteen ounces."

"Oh, I'll take it," said Alf, "but I'd prefer to drink enough to get a buzz."

"It's hardly worth drinking at all if you don't get a buzz," said Hulda.

"It's a free sample. We have to take what they offer."

"At my age, I'm not afraid to ask for whatever I want, and I want a big beer," said Alf. "When I came home from the war I got a lot of free beer."

"That's just not going to happen," I replied.

Hulda started looking around the room. "Can you tell where they keep the stash of pretzels? I'd really like a pretzel."

"Dan said they don't have pretzels."

"That's just a ruse. Bette Weske was here with her daughter last Saturday and they were served pretzels with their beer. You check behind that bar and see if there isn't a bag of pretzels. I'll bet you can find one."

"I'm not going behind the bar," I said, searching for some way to change the topic. "Alf, what's this I hear about gold?"

"It's quite a story," he said. "My parents stashed a canning jar of gold coins in the '30s and my momma sent a letter to my brother Rudy telling him to contact me so we could find the coins. She gave him a clue, a piece of information so we'd have to search together. He was greedy and didn't share the clue with me for decades. My nephew called to tell me he'd died and he told me about Momma's letter."

"I'm sorry about your brother. Did you find the coins when you got the clue?" I asked. Hulda looked irritated but didn't interrupt.

"It's not that simple. I got Momma's clue, but I'm not sure what it means. She said it's hidden in something one of us left behind and it says to look where my brother Angelo was killed in the war. I'm not sure where Angelo died and about the only thing left behind was the family Bible."

"If you know when Angelo died, we might be able to correlate that date with where there was fighting," I suggested.

Alf reached for his wallet and unfolded a brittle yellowed telegram. "This is dated 27 November 1942," he read.

"There weren't a lot of places the U.S. was fighting that early in the war," I said, reflecting on my high school history and the Navy and Marine history that was drilled into us during boot camp. "The Army invaded North Africa, in Tunisia, and the Marines were fighting on Guadalcanal, Florida Island, and Tulagi."

"Angelo was a Marine, so he must've been on one of those islands. I don't know which one, or what that would have to do with the Bible."

"Those battles were in the Solomon Islands," I said. "They were brutal for the Navy and Marines. The Georgia Island bay had so many sunken U.S. and Japanese ships they call it Iron Bottom Sound."

"None of those places mean anything to me. I can't see how they'd show me anything in the Bible."

"They're in the Solomon Island group," I said again. "The Song of Solomon is a book of the Old Testament."

Alf's eyes lit up. "Yes! Of course! Take me home so I can look at the Bible."

"As soon as we're through with the tour, we'll go," I said.

"Nothing is going to happen to the Bible before we get back."

"I could've written the Bible in the time this tour is taking," said Hulda. "Will they be back soon?"

"It's not a long tour," I said. "They've only been gone ten minutes."

"We might starve if you don't find us some pretzels," Hulda grumbled.

"But I'm really excited about this," said Alf. "Take me back now and come back for the others after you drop me off."

"You'll just have to wait until the tour is over and everyone has a beer," I said patiently.

"After the beer, too? That'll take forever. You know how slow some of these people sip their wine."

To my great relief, Dan, with Esme beaming at his side, opened the warehouse door and led the group into the tasting room. The senior citizens toddled in while Dan held the door, maintaining a practiced, if not genuine, smile. When they were all seated he stepped behind the bar and set Pilsner glasses on the counter.

"Today, we've got India Pale Ale, Extra Pale Ale, and Stout on tap. Tell me which you'd like to sample."

The residents called out their requests and Howard Johnson helped Dan deliver the beer to the tables. Hulda had chosen the stout and looked at the dark brew skeptically.

"This looks like coffee with bubbles," said Hulda.

"Shut up and drink your beer," said Esme. "My grandson brewed it and I'm sure it's wonderful."

"Stout is a dark beer," I said. "Would you prefer something lighter?"

Ignoring my comment, Hulda took a sip, then spit it back into the glass. "Gak! That tastes as bitter as earwax! Your beer has gone bad," she shouted to Dan.

A dozen heads turned and stared at Hulda, who was wiping her mouth on a handkerchief.

Dan looked at me and mouthed, "Earwax?" He composed himself and took her glass. "It's pretty hoppy. Perhaps you'd be happier with an ale."

"I'd be happier with a beer that hasn't gone bad," she replied as Dan retreated with her glass, holding it away from himself, careful to not spill any of Hulda's backwash.

"Hulda's a drama queen," Esme whispered. "She does that whenever she doesn't like the dining room food, too. It gets quick service."

"Try this," Dan said, returning a fresh glass of amber beer in front of Hulda. The other residents were sampling their beers quietly and chatting.

Hulda eyed the glass suspiciously, then took a tiny sip. She puckered and shook her head. "This isn't as bad. Do you have any beer that tastes like Grain Belt?"

"No ma'am," Dan replied. "We make ale and we've never even tried to make anything that tastes like Grain Belt beer."

Hulda took another sip and shook her head again. "I can't drink this. It tastes like poison." She pushed the glass away. "I need a pretzel to get that taste out of my mouth."

"I'm sorry, but I don't have any pretzels."

Hulda picked up her purse and dug through it as Dan and I watched. "I saved some crackers from Judy's Café." She opened the package, spilling cracker crumbs on the tabletop. With her mouth now dry, she tried another sip of beer. "That's better. The salt cuts the bitterness. Do you have a salt shaker?"

"We don't recommend salting the ale," Dan replied.

"If you'd make a decent beer it wouldn't need salt." She took a second sip, shook her head, then dumped her cracker crumbs into the beer glass, making it foam. Dan was ready to say something, but words obviously escaped him.

"My beer is just fine," Esme declared loudly. She checked to see if Dan was buoyed by her comments, but he was totally off his game after Hulda's show.

Alf was already moving toward the door. I intercepted him at the entryway. "We're not quite ready to leave yet," I said.

He looked back at the roomful of people, willing them to be done. "I suppose I should pee before we go back out into the cold."

"That's a good idea," I said. "Loading and unloading the van always takes more time than we think."

He looked around for a restroom sign, then turned to me. "Add my name to the list of people going to Zim."

"I didn't know you're a birding person."

"I don't give a shit about the birds. Once I get that Bible I'll know where the gold is hidden and you can drop me off at our old house to dig it up."

"Alf, the ground is frozen. If you have to dig it up, you'll have to hire a backhoe or wait until spring."

"I can't afford a backhoe and I'm not waiting until spring. None of us know how much longer we have to live and we don't put things off that can be done today. Haven't you heard us say that we don't even buy green bananas?"

I watched him hobble to the restroom, thinking about his words. If the answer was really in his family Bible, and if the coins were buried at his old homestead, I wondered how I could help him recover them from the frozen ground.

Dan worked the room like a politician and answered inane and irrelevant questions with a smile. Esme finished her beer and linked her arm around Dan's elbow, beaming. Alf returned from the restroom and I saw him regaling Bud Bloomquist with his treasure story.

People were finishing off their beer samples and starting to stir. When Dan checked his watch and started guiding Esme toward the door, I took his cue and brought the van to the door. Alf was chatting with one of the other men, obviously excited about his new plan to find the family treasure. He was standing at the curb and gesturing as he spoke. I assumed he was telling everyone that he knew how to decode the clue left for him. Dan held Esme's arm until she was onto the first step.

"Thanks for the tour," I said. "I hope our residents didn't cause too much bother."

"Grandma warned me that some of the people suffer from dementia, so I had an idea of what to expect."

I slipped a folded $20 into his hand. "I hope we can take another tour someday."

He was apparently unaccustomed to tips, so he looked down at the paper in his hand as I mounted the steps and closed the door. He waved for me to stop, but I kept going. Twenty bucks was small compensation for his afternoon of stress.

Alf was standing in the aisle before the van stopped rolling and he rushed ahead to be the first person out the door. I watched him quickstep through the lobby as I assisted the other residents down the steps.

After everyone was unloaded and I'd parked the van, I went to Nancy's office and knocked on the doorframe.

"Hi, Peter. How was the brewery tour?"

"It went pretty much as expected. Hulda took a sip of stout, spit it back into her glass, told the tour guide it had gone bad, and made him bring her a glass of something else."

"Yup," she replied. "That sounds like Hulda."

"Have you heard about Alf's gold hunt?" I asked.

"Not yet."

"Alf said that his parents hid a jar filled with gold coins in the 1930s. When his nephew called about his brother's death, he also gave him a clue to the location of the gold that was left by Alf's mother. That hint seems to point him to his family Bible."

"Is that a problem?"

"Alf thinks the gold may be buried at his old family homestead in Zim, and he wants to come along on the birding trip. He said I could drop him off at the old house with a shovel and he'd dig up the gold while we're looking at birds."

Nancy's expression darkened. "I don't like the idea of a resident being dropped off at an abandoned house to hunt for treasure.

He could fall, break a bone, or worse."

"That, and the ground is frozen. He's not going to dig up anything."

"So, Peter, how are you going to keep him from doing that?"

Damn, she was good. I'd come to her office with a problem, and it came back to me so fast I didn't have time to dodge it.

"I'll work on it," I said. "Maybe the van is already full and there won't be room for him."

"You know that someone will cancel before the trip. You'll have to come up with another way to deter him from his plan to dig up the gold."

———— ◆ ————

I knocked on Alf's door and heard him tell me to come in. He was sitting in a recliner with a dusty box next to him on the floor. In his hands was a huge, leather-bound Bible and he was slowly leafing through the pages.

"Have you found the answer yet?" I asked.

"I just found the Song of Solomon chapter," he said. "It's been awhile since I've been inside a Bible and there's no table of contents in the front." He continued to flip through the pages as I watched.

"The Bible was in this old box?" I asked.

"It's stuff I moved out of Momma's house when she died. That's where I found the telegram about Angelo's death. I think she saved every card or letter she'd ever received. There are even a couple of love letters she got from Poppa."

"Do you need any help?" I asked.

Alf froze. "I don't intend to share my gold with anyone."

"I don't want your gold, Alf. I just want to make sure you don't get hurt."

"I'm fine," he replied, closing the Bible so I couldn't see inside it.

"If you need anything, let me know."

"You could find me a shovel," he replied. "I'll need it to dig up the jar."

"The ground is frozen, Alf," I said. "Let's talk when you find the clue and maybe we can come up with another plan."

"Don't worry about that," said Alf. "You just get me to Zim with a shovel. I'll take care of the rest."

CHAPTER 5
FRIDAY MORNING

My scraper wasn't effective against the morning frost until the heater finally started blowing warm air on the windshield. I was pulling out of the driveway when Tim Webb's van parked in front of Dolores's house. I stopped and rolled down my window.

"Hi, Peter," he said. "I'm going to start repairing the floor upstairs and then work my way down. My roofing guy will be here shortly. They'll get the shingles off today and should be able to do the repairs tomorrow."

"They're working Saturday?" I asked.

"Business is a little slow right now and they wanted to jump on the job as soon as possible. The bid they gave me is fair, and I don't really care whether they work the weekend or not if they don't charge extra for the overtime."

"Did you give Dolores an estimate?"

"She and I went over it yesterday. She seemed to understand what I was going to do and she wasn't disturbed by the cost. She can afford it, can't she?"

"I don't know the details of her finances, but if she understood that the repairs were going to cost thousands of dollars and that didn't seem to be a problem, then I'm not concerned."

"I've got to get started," said Tim. "Why don't you check in this evening. You can see what I'm doing and maybe you can talk with Mrs. Karvonen about the cost."

My heater was barely warming the frosty air when I pulled into the Whistling Pines parking lot. I was the first of the day-shift employees, so I parked among the frost-covered cars. The air was crisp and the thermometer mounted under the portico indicated 22 degrees. Cool, but hardly cold by Two Harbors standards.

The lobby was empty and the stuffed moose head hanging over the reception desk looked old and tired. He'd been rescued from a bar that was closing in an attempt to make Whistling Pines look more like a northwoods lodge than a senior citizens' residence. I thought it was time to replace him.

My small office was dark and cold. I turned on the computer, grabbed my mug, and walked to the dining room in search of coffee. With an infusion of caffeine, I studied the sign-up sheet for the Sax-Zim bird-watching trip. All sixteen lines were filled with names and after the last line additional names were crammed on the edges of the sheet. Not only would the van be full, there was a waiting list.

I heard a hinge creak and the sound of footsteps on the carpet. Howard Johnson was striding toward me.

"I see that you beat me to the coffee," he said. "Come sit with me awhile."

Howard was the liaison between all the residents who were too shy to express their feelings with the staff members. He had no official position, but by speaking clearly and confidently, he influenced many of the decisions in the residence. He set his coffee mug on the table, then sat carefully, crossing his legs in a way that left his pressed pants without a wrinkle. It was an impressive trick I never learned in the military, but something he had picked up as an Army officer. He, like many veterans of combat, rarely spoke of his experiences, but it was common knowledge that he'd been awarded several medals for bravery and a Purple Heart.

"I'm a little worried about Alf," Howard said, stirring a spoonful of sugar into his steaming mug. "He's been telling everyone about his family's stash of gold coins and how he's going to figure out where they're hidden and dig them up."

"I know. I'm concerned that he's going to fall down walking around his old homestead," I said.

"Beyond that, I don't think it's safe for him to be talking about the gold and how he now knows how to find it. There are people in Two Harbors who would beat the information out of him without hesitation if they thought he knew where it's hidden," Howard added.

"I don't think anyone in Whistling Pines would hurt him," I said.

"Everyone here has relatives and friends. Some of them are unsavory characters and if they happened to overhear a conversation about the gold, I think they'd act without hesitation."

"Have you said anything to Alf?" I asked.

"He's oblivious to the danger," Howard said. "He's like a kid on Christmas Eve and he wants everyone to share his enthusiasm."

"What do you suggest?" I asked.

"He needs someone he can trust. Someone who will help him tone down his enthusiasm and maybe help him recover the gold, if there is any."

"You don't think there's actually gold?"

"I think there was gold, but leaving it during the Depression and the war would take great restraint. I suspect his parents had to dip into that reserve at some point. Alf's father died in the mines. His mother probably had a hard time making ends meet on Social Security. I wouldn't be at all surprised if she had to sell a few coins to get by."

"I suppose you'd like me to step up and be that trusted person to guide him along."

"Peter, you're amazingly perceptive!"

"My platter is pretty full. I'm getting married next week, I have a full time job, I have an elderly neighbor with a crumbling roof who needs someone to make sure she doesn't get swindled. I don't know where I'd find the time."

Howard stood and patted my shoulder. "Responsibilities are only thrust upon the trustworthy and able. I think you qualify on both those accounts."

I sighed.

"At least this cold snap reduces the likelihood of a repeat of the unfortunate incident," Howard said with a smile as he walked away.

I tilted my head back and closed my eyes. "How can I help Alf with his gold fever and get through all the other stuff on my platter," I mumbled to myself.

"What gold fever?"

I snapped my head forward and was facing Miriam, the most outgoing kitchen worker, who'd taken the chair across from me. "Alf thinks he knows about a secret spot where his parents hid some gold coins," I replied.

"Oh, is that connected to his family Bible?" I'm always amazed how fast gossip travels.

"He thinks the clue is hidden in the family Bible. I'm sure he went straight to his room and started searching for the clue after the brewery tour."

The early breakfast diners started to arrive so I cut the conversation short and took my mug of coffee back to my cubbyhole. Looking at a Minnesota map, I drew a reasonable route to Zim, then started calling restaurants and gas stations to see who would accept a dozen senior citizens and their chaperones. It was nearly noon by the time I'd plotted out the stops and felt confident that we could make the trip with all the required food and bathroom breaks, spend two hours looking for birds, then make the return trip with the same stopping points. I thought we could be back at Whistling Pines in time for a late dinner.

I got up to stretch and walk around. I was near the front door when the fire alarm screamed. I threw myself to the floor and covered my head, awaiting the sound of incoming Iraqi rockets or artillery shells. A few seconds later, reason returned and I looked outside to see if the firemen were prepared to take a head count after the fire drill. Seeing no firetrucks, I realized that this was the real thing and I ran for the stairs.

In the event of a fire, each staff member has assigned duties. My responsibility was to assist the wheelchair-bound residents from the third floor. That meant either rolling them down the stairs in their wheelchairs or carrying them down. As I reached the second floor I caught the slightest whiff of smoke and when I reached the third floor a layer of smoke rippled along the ceiling and the hallway was hazy. I knocked on the first door with a wheelchair symbol, and found Millie Pederson just inside the door, ready to roll. She breezed past me, rolling toward the stairs. I saw smoke curling out from under the next door. I tested the door and door handle for heat, then pulled the door open.

Heat and smoke hit me in the face and I quickly turned and retreated a step to catch my breath. Taking a deep breath, I bent low and stepped into the apartment, scanning the floor for legs or a body. I turned toward the kitchen and saw flames licking out of the open oven. I kicked the oven door shut and stepped back into the hallway for another breath of air. An apparition moved toward me and I realized that Howard Johnson was leading a procession of residents toward the stairwell. Each person had their hand knotted in a long string of bedsheets that were tied together to make a long rope. Howard, still the hero, was helping others at the risk of his own life.

"Where's Opal?" I yelled, to be heard over the sound of the fire klaxon.

"Haven't seen her," he replied through the handkerchief held over his face. I motioned for them to keep moving. "Get someone to help Millie down the stairs."

I took a deep breath and stuck my head inside the door. "Opal!" I yelled. "Opal Mattson, are you here?"

Hearing no response, I fell to my hands and knees and crawled into her apartment, staying low where there was a bit of visibility. I was starting to feel like my lungs were about to burst when I got to the living room window. I pulled it open and drew in a deep breath. After a second breath I crawled toward the bedroom and literally stumbled on Opal, who was sprawled on the floor. She was a tiny woman and I grabbed her feet and easily dragged her into the hallway.

I threw Opal over my shoulder in a fireman's carry and duck-walked to the stairs. Past the fire door the air was clearer and I drew a few deep breaths as I stumbled down the stairs. My eyes and lungs still burned when we finally stepped through the outside door into bright sunshine. Two firetrucks and an ambulance were parked in the driveway and several firemen were standing next to the director, inspecting the alarm panel, trying to determine the source of the alarm.

I closed my eyes and concentrated on breathing. When I opened them, I headed toward the EMTs, who were administering oxygen to Marcy Albert, who had a very gray pallor. I laid Opal on the ground next to the nearest EMT and tapped his shoulder. I turned and grabbed the nearest fireman and shouted, "Oven fire in apartment 311!"

"Is anyone inside the apartment?" he asked.

I shook my head no, and pointed to Opal, who was being fitted with an oxygen mask by the EMT.

He gave me a thumbs-up and jogged over to the truck where he donned an air tank and picked up a huge fire extinguisher. He and another fireman ran through the open door and disappeared into the smoky stairwell.

I walked to the alarm panel and told the gathering group about the oven fire. The white-hatted chief spoke into a handheld radio, then thanked me.

"Sit down, Peter," said Nancy. She led me a few steps to a bench and I sat. "You look like hell," she said.

I nodded, trying to catch my breath and focus. I saw Wendy with a clipboard, walking among the residents taking a head count. Jenny was attending to one of the residents who'd apparently twisted an ankle. I thought, "If that was the worst injury, we were lucky." Miriam and the cooks were gathering the residents close together and throwing blankets and tablecloths over the shoulders of the shivering people.

When I focused again, Wendy was speed-walking toward Nancy and me, the clipboard pages flagging. She grabbed the fire chief as she approached. "We need the firemen to make another sweep of the building," she said. "I can't locate Alf Paluzzo!"

I stood but was frozen by Nancy's glare. "You are not going back in," she said with authority. "Your job has been accomplished and this is a job for the firemen."

Wendy showed the chief the roster and pointed to Alf's room number on the second floor. She then pointed to the floor plan. He spoke into his radio and then left to speak to the EMTs. Through the chaos a slender man in a blue parka emerged and walked toward us. Len Rentz, the Two Harbors police chief, was surveying the activity, but obviously aiming at Nancy and me.

"Peter, you look like hell," he said.

I was too short of breath to make a witty reply. Nancy said, "He carried one of the residents down from the third floor."

Len shook his head. "You can let someone else be the hero next time."

I shrugged.

"I just talked to the EMTs," he said. "Opal is loaded in the ambulance and she's breathing on her own. I spoke to the fireman who put out her oven fire. It appears she was pre-heating the oven but forgot she was storing Tupperware in there."

"Yup," I croaked, surprised at my raspy voice. "There were flames coming out of her oven. I closed it."

The fire chief and Wendy were having a discussion. They walked over to Nancy. "We've been through Paluzzo's apartment and all the public areas and there's no sign of him. We took Wendy's passkey so we can check each apartment and the utility rooms."

The fire chief and Len stepped away from the others to quietly converse, then Len joined me on the bench. "Oh dear," said Nancy. "Losing a resident is bad. Really bad."

"The fire is out. You can start bringing the residents into the lobby," said the fire chief.

I started to rise but Len put his hand on my shoulder. "Hang back a second, Peter." He sat on the bench next to me and took out a pipe and went through the ritual of packing it with tobacco and lighting it. By the time it was lit the crowd had all filed inside.

"What's the matter?" I asked. The adrenaline rush was starting to wear off as the cold was seeping in.

"The fire chief said that Alf's apartment looks like there's been a struggle. Have you seen it recently?"

"I was there yesterday. It looked fine."

"Let's walk up together," Len said. "You can tell me what looks out of place."

We wove through the clusters of people gathered in the lobby. Many had been on their way to the dining room for lunch, but others had been in their rooms in a variety of states of dress. Some were wrapped in blankets, still shivering from their exposure to the cold. The dining room staff were walking around with carafes of coffee and Styrofoam cups, pouring for anyone who wanted a warm drink. I grabbed a cup as we walked past, but Len passed.

The elevator ride to Alf's floor seemed to take forever and as we neared the second floor I started shivering uncontrollably, the hypothermia finally overcoming my adrenaline and resolve. Len took off his parka and threw it across my shoulders.

Alf's door was closed but not locked. Len took purple nitrile gloves from his pocket and handed me a pair. "I don't know that we'll be preserving much since the firemen have been in here at least twice, but it never hurts to be too careful."

Alf's recliner was in its usual place, but the table and lamp immediately next to the chair were tipped over and the floor was littered with newspaper clippings and coupons. The box that had been next to his chair was overturned. Yellowed envelopes, notes, and cards littered the floor in front of the chair. A black photo album was on the floor near the wall and an assortment of small leather-bound books were scattered as if they'd been tossed.

"I doubt this mess was caused by Alf's quick exit during the fire," Len said.

"Alf was pretty tidy," I said. "When I was here yesterday this box was alongside his chair and he told me there were old letters and cards inside that his mother had saved. It looks like someone opened all the envelopes and tossed the contents."

"Is anything missing?"

"I don't see Alf's Bible anywhere. It was a big old family Bible, leather-bound with gold lettering on the spine."

"Do you recognize the smaller books?" Len asked.

I picked one up and opened it, exposing pages and pages of European postage stamps. "It looks like the stamp collection Alf told be about. This volume is from Europe. Some of the stamps were issued by countries that no longer exist," I said as I flipped through a few pages. "These have tiny denominations. They must be from before the war."

"Leave the rest as it is," Len said, guiding me back out of the tiny apartment. "Lock the door until I can get the BCA here to do their forensic magic."

As I locked the door a wave of sadness swept over me. "We need to talk," I said, looking to see if anyone was within earshot. "Come down to my office. There's something you need to know about Alf and the Bible."

We rode the elevator back to the lobby and waded through

the mass of people gathered around the dining room entrance. Hulda Packer pushed her walker in front of me, blocking our path.

"Who made you a cop?" she asked, looking at Len's parka with the Two Harbors Police Department logo.

"I'm not a cop," I replied. "The chief loaned me his jacket." My emotional reserves were already thin and Hulda was starting to crack the little diplomatic filter that remained. "We're going to my office. Please let us through."

Hulda considered my request, then stepped aside. As we passed she added, "You should take a shower. You smell like a burned sausage."

My jacket was still on the reception counter, so I put it on and gave the parka back to Len. We broke through the crowd and walked to my cubbyhole office. I closed the door and took a deep breath, then told Len the story about Alf's gold, his mother's letter, the family Bible, and that he'd told nearly everyone in Whistling Pines about it all.

CHAPTER 6
TWO HARBORS

Risking the disappointment of those signed up, I talked with Wendy and cancelled the pasty trip to the VFW. I went home for a shower and a change of clothing. There were a few cars on the streets, but most people seemed to be staying inside to avoid the cold snap that had enveloped northern Minnesota. As soon as I turned onto my street I saw the line of pickups in front of Dolores's house. The crew on the roof was stripping shingles and feeding them down a chute into a Dumpster. They worked with ease on the steep slope of the roof. There was barely enough space to pull into my driveway.

When I opened the front door, which I never locked, I smelled a hint of perfume. I followed the scent into the kitchen where I found Dolores searching the cupboards.

"What are you looking for?" I asked.

Startled, Dolores spun around. "Where do you keep your coffee?"

"Take a seat at the table and I'll make a pot," I said, hanging my coat on the back of a chair.

I filled the coffeemaker with water, then inserted a filter and put a few scoops of coffee into the filter. When it started to gurgle, I sat across from Dolores.

"I don't mind you being here, but I was surprised to see you in my kitchen."

"I can't stand being at my house," she said. She was wearing a flowered housecoat over her heavy support hose and orthopedic shoes. Her hair wasn't quite as carefully brushed as usual. "I've been here most of the day reading the newspaper. I decided that I needed a cup of coffee, and that's when you showed up."

She looked at me, focusing for the first time. "What happened to you? You're all sooty and you smell like burned plastic."

"There was a fire at Whistling Pines today. One of the residents was preheating her oven and forgot that she was storing her Tupperware there."

Dolores nodded. "One of my friends did that with her cast iron. She stored them in the oven and she found them when she was putting sheets of cookies in. She dropped one of her frying pans on the floor and it melted her linoleum."

I heard the final gurgles of the coffeemaker so I filled two cups and brought them back to the table.

"The workmen are too noisy at your house?"

"Yes! They're pounding and using that infernal saw that howls like a banshee. I had to get out." She took a sip of coffee, then added, "I hope they finish today so I can go back to my normal life."

"I think it's going to take most of the next week to complete the repairs," I said. "They will only get the shingles stripped from the roof today, then they have to make the repairs before they put down a new roof."

Dolores's normally rigid façade started to crack and she reached for a handkerchief that was stuffed up her sleeve to dry a tear that had leaked from her left eye. "I just want to get back to my quiet house and my life. I had no idea making the repairs would be so . . . bothersome."

"It'll be over soon and things will go back to normal. Have you looked at Mr. Webb's estimate? Can you afford the repairs?"

"I looked at the bottom line, not the details," she said, regaining her composure. "I talked with my broker and he's going to sell some stock for me."

"I didn't realize you had stock," I said.

"My husband bought stock in the mines and the railroads when the mines were busy. After he passed, I spoke with his broker who diversified my holdings. We got out of the mining stocks before the ore ran out."

"What kind of stocks do you own?" I asked. I expected a list of blue-chip stocks that were stable and paid regular dividends.

"I used to be heavily into utilities that paid high dividends. I found that profitable but boring. Now I like to be speculative. I own quite a few foreign stocks because the dollar is strong and we're importing a lot of cars and electronics. Watching them grow is much more satisfying than just watching dividends pile up in my cash account."

"So you can afford the repairs?" I asked.

"That's petty cash," she said with a flip of her wrist.

I let out a deep breath, relieved that the repairs wouldn't put her in a financial bind.

"Jenny wants to go through your pantry and clear out the jars and cans that are past their expiration dates."

Dolores looked at the table, not meeting my eyes. "I didn't realize that things in there were that old. I don't cook for myself much anymore, so I don't go in there often. I'm frankly embarrassed that things got so out of control. Can you and Jenny make it right?"

"You do very well on your own," I said. "All of us need a hand from our friends and neighbors on occasion." I stood. "If you don't mind, I'm going to take a shower and put these clothes in the washer."

Dolores's nose twitched. "I think that's a good plan. You're a little gamey."

———— ◆ ————

When I stepped out of the shower I heard Jeremy's piercing voice. Freshly showered and wearing clean clothes, I found Jeremy rattling off an explanation of his Pokémon cards to Dolores, who feigned interest, but obviously had no idea what he was talking about.

"Are you okay?" Jenny asked as she hugged me. "I think you should have had some oxygen."

"The hypothermia from sitting outside was a bigger issue. I couldn't stop shivering for a while."

"Mom said we could go over to Mrs. Karvonen's house," said Jeremy. "I want to see what they're doing."

"Sure," I said. "Let's go."

———— ◆ ————

Dolores was silent as we walked past the piles of construction debris on the curb. The workers on the roof continued to slide shingles into the Dumpster, making a resounding "swoosh, boom" as each batch fell. Inside the house we could hear commotion on the second floor. We were at the bottom of the staircase when Tim Webb came down the stairs, wiping his hands on a rag.

"Oh, hello," he said. "Your timing is perfect. I've just glued down the last of the upstairs flooring. I'm going to start working on the first floor tomorrow and I need you to clear off the shelves before I start."

We walked to the narrow pantry and surveyed the four levels of shelving, most stocked with cans or canning jars. "I need at least the shelves close to the floor clear. It'd be better if all of them were empty."

"We'll get right to work on it," said Jenny. "Jeremy, get the boxes from the car and we'll load them."

Jeremy disappeared and Jenny explained, "We stopped at the liquor store on the way here and filled the car with sturdy liquor boxes that'll be perfect for this."

Dolores looked like she was in a trance as we talked. She stared into the pantry with a blank expression.

Jeremy came back with a half dozen boxes and set them outside the pantry door. "You guys can start. I'll get another load," he said, turning toward the door.

Jenny stepped into the pantry and started pulling Mason jars from the shelves and stacking them in the box.

"Are you okay?" I asked Dolores.

"I suppose all of these are garbage," she said. "I put so much effort into canning them and now they're just garbage." She let out a sigh as Jenny carried out one box and picked up another.

In ten minutes we had five boxes filled with Mason jars and Jeremy was loading cans of vegetables into boxes when he said, "Hey! There's a little door behind this shelf."

Dolores perked up and stepped into the pantry. The small wooden door was recessed into the wall, hidden behind the cans. She reached in and touched a hidden latch and the door popped open. "Bring one of the boxes," she said.

———— ◆ ————

We carried the box to the kitchen table and unloaded a pile of manila envelopes and a leather bag tied with a leather lace. The bag weighed several pounds despite its small size. I poured coins onto the table and stared at the pile of tarnished silver and gold.

"Look at all these old coins!" Jeremy said as he quickly dug in and started sorting them by denomination. I handed Dolores one of the envelopes and she opened it with shaking hands.

"I haven't been in these for a long time. I don't recall what's here, other than the coins." She flipped through sheets of paper and handed them to me.

"They're stock certificates," I said. "Most are mining companies, but there are a few railroad stocks too. I think most of these companies have been acquired by others. Some are thousands of shares."

"I suppose they're worthless now," said Dolores, slipping them back into the envelope.

I opened the second envelope and slid out bonds. Some were treasury bonds and others were corporate and municipal. "I'm sure all of these have been called, but I assume they retain their face value."

I closed the envelope and put it on the table. "I'm sure your stockbroker can determine the value of these."

Dolores was focused on Jeremy and the stacks of coins he was creating. When they were all sorted by denomination he stood back. "If I could have a sheet of paper, I could add these together and see how much they're worth."

Jenny handed him a pencil and notepad from a nearby desk and he started counting the coins in each pile and noting the denomination of the coins.

"He's totaling the face value of the coins," whispered Jenny. "I assume they have collector value beyond the face value."

"Some will probably be collectible," I said, "but the gold in those coins is worth over a thousand dollars per ounce. I have no idea what silver is worth today, but silver coins of that vintage are ninety percent silver."

Jenny pulled out her smartphone and was busy when Jeremy announced, "It's a lot of money. Four hundred twenty-three dollars and ninety cents."

Jenny tapped my elbow and held out her phone. "The twenty-dollar gold pieces are worth at least $1,200 each," she whispered. She flipped to a different website and showed me the auction prices for silver coins.

"Dolores," I said, "these coins are worth tens of thousands of dollars."

She reached back and felt the chair behind her and sat heavily. "I'm losing it," she said softly. "I'd forgotten what was in that cubbyhole and I can't take care of the house either." She looked deflated.

Jenny knelt beside her and patted her hand. "We all have lapses of memory. You hadn't been in that cubbyhole for decades. It's not surprising that you didn't recall exactly what was there."

"Thank you dear," Dolores said. "I really appreciate your kindness."

Jeremy had Jenny's phone and he calculated the value of each stack and added them together. "I don't know if I put in enough zeroes," he said, showing me his calculations. There were some multiplication errors and an addition error that we'd talk about later. I ran the total in my mind.

"The total is over forty-two thousand dollars, and that doesn't take into account any numismatic value that some of them may have."

Dolores watched Jeremy recounting the piles and smiled. "Put them back into the bag, please," she said.

Jeremy quickly slipped the stacks into the pouch and tied the bag shut. He held it out to Dolores, who didn't raise her hand to take it.

"Do you have a college fund, young man?"

Jeremy looked at Jenny who gave him a nod. "I have a coin bank and once a year we empty it and take it to the bank and sort the coins. Last year there was almost a hundred dollars. We put it into my savings account."

"Take these and add them to your savings account," she said. "I don't know what a college education costs these days, but if you invest it carefully, I suspect it'll put you through a couple years at a pretty good college."

Jenny took the bag from Jeremy and set it on the table. "That's very kind but I don't think we can accept this as a gift. You might need this money for your living expenses."

Dolores dismissed her concern with a flip of the wrist. "The banker said I'm going to outlive the cash I've got in savings, and he doesn't know about the investments I have. Take the coins and put them to good use. I can't think of a better use for them."

Jeremy looked at Jenny who was biting her lip. She hesitated, then carefully picked up the bag. "I promise that he'll put this to good use."

"Good!" said Dolores, obviously relieved. "Now stop wasting time and clean out the rest of the pantry so the man can work tomorrow."

We dove back into clearing the pantry with renewed energy, carefully stepping around the rotten spot in the floor. We had the shelves cleared after 15 minutes. Checking expiration dates as we went, Jenny located three cans of green beans that weren't past their expiration date. All the rest we set on the curb for the garbage truck.

We stood back and looked at the empty pantry and the dark spot on the floor that had started the whole house repair debacle. All three of us were tired and dusty. Most of the cans and jars had a thin patina of dust that had ground into our clothes and smeared on our faces.

"I suppose we should make dinner," I said, thinking fondly of the growler of ale I'd purchased in town.

"You'll do no such thing!" said Dolores, who popped up unexpectedly. "Wash your hands in the bathroom. The pizza should be here in a few minutes."

"Dolores, do you have some beer glasses?"

She considered the question, then said, "Sure. I think there are some glasses that would work. But I don't have any beer."

"Put out the beer glasses. I'll be back in one minute," I said, dashing for the door.

When I returned with my half-gallon jug of ale, called a growler, Jenny, Dolores, and Jeremy were sitting at the giant dining room table. Dolores sat at the head of the table. Beautiful china plates, silverware, and crystal goblets were set on the sides for the rest of us. Jeremy had a bottle of root beer.

"But, Mrs. Karvonen, I don't need a glass. I can drink out of the bottle," Jeremy explained.

Dolores gave Jenny a look that made her grimace.

"Jeremy," Jenny said sternly, "you can drink out of the bottle, and that's okay when you're just hanging out. But, at a nice dinner, you politely pour your root beer into the glass."

Dolores smiled and Jeremy stared at the bottle for a moment, then poured it into the goblet. I poured ale for Jenny and me, then asked Dolores if she'd like some, too.

"Of course!" she said, as the doorbell rang.

Jeremy ran to the door as I reached for my wallet.

"Sit down, Peter," Dolores said quietly, but with authority. "Jeremy has the money to pay the deliveryman."

Jeremy returned with two large pizza boxes.

"I ordered a house special and sausage with mushrooms. I hope those are to your taste," said Dolores, handing her plate to me. "I'd like two middle pieces of the sausage with mushroom pizza."

The melted cheese had fused all the pieces together, so I carefully separated them with my butter knife. "You don't strike me as a pizza and beer person," I said, handing the plate to Dolores.

She took the plate and smiled. "I'm a person of many mysteries."

Jeremy dug into the house special and was ready to pick up a slice when Jenny put her hand on his arm. "It's polite to cut your pizza with the knife and eat it with the fork."

"Mom. Really?"

Dolores laughed, picked up a piece and folded it in half, then took a bite. She wiped her lips with a linen napkin and said, "That's how I learned to eat pizza in New York. Pick it up, fold it, and then eat it."

We all laughed as we ate our pizza on china plates and drank North Shore Brewery India Pale Ale out of crystal goblets. Dolores told us about flying to New York for plays and shopping on Fifth Avenue. She'd led a full life and was full of interesting stories.

"You mentioned Alf Paluzzo's gold," said Dolores. "Then one

of the women at bingo mentioned it between games. I guess that's quite the talk at Whistling Pines."

I was stunned that Alf's story had spread as far as the church bingo game and I was reminded of Alf's disappearance.

"Excuse me for a moment." I stepped outside and called the director's cellphone.

"Hi, Nancy. I wanted to check on Alf Paluzzo. Did you find him after I left?"

"Len Rentz was schmoozing with the residents during dinner, but no one seemed to have any idea what happened. The Bureau of Criminal Apprehension mobile crime lab is here but I don't expect they'll know more until morning."

I dialed Len's cellphone and asked the same question.

"Peter, I just spoke with Sonny Carlson, one of the BCA techs. After getting a long verbal rundown of his Finnish/Swedish/American heritage, he told me they'd recovered some trace evidence they were taking to the St. Paul lab for analysis."

"I didn't see any blood when we looked in the apartment," I said.

"There wasn't a pool of blood. Just traces. Sonny said it looked like there had been a struggle and one, or both, of the people involved had some minor injuries. It appears that someone, presumably Alf, was dragged across the carpet."

"But where is he?" I asked. "There were lots of people around and it wouldn't be easy to carry Alf out without someone noticing."

"I suppose it could've happened during the confusion of the fire," Len said. "I wonder if the fire was set as a diversion."

"No way," I replied. "I was in the apartment where the plastic was burning in the oven. The fire was accidental."

"Well, it's certainly coincidental that we have a fire when one of the residents disappears and I don't believe in coincidences. You've got people going out of every exit, all of them coughing and partially blinded by the smoke. It would be easy for someone to slip out unnoticed."

"I think someone would notice a stranger carrying a body or

someone resisting. If nothing else, it would show up on the security cameras. I assume you've already reviewed the video."

"Oh, yes. I looked at the video. But there is one problem. Someone adjusted the camera that looks over the delivery door so it was looking at the ceiling a couple hours before the fire. I asked the kitchen workers if they'd seen anything unusual, but they'd just had their usual deliveries from the grocery and a coffee company. They thought the camera may have been jostled when they were unloading and stacking boxes."

"I assume it wasn't an accident," I said.

"I watched the grocery truck arrive, unload, and leave. The camera was moved after the food delivery truck left and before the coffee delivery arrived."

"We're having supper with my neighbor, and Dolores heard about Alf's gold coins at church bingo, so it's not like it was a secret. I suppose that half of Two Harbors has heard Alf's story by now. There are a lot of suspects beyond Whistling Pines."

"How is Dolores?" asked Len, changing the topic. "I haven't had any reports of her shooting at bunnies in her back yard in awhile."

"I think we've removed all her guns from the house," I replied. "I think her days of target practice are over."

"How goes the wedding planning?"

"As far as I know, we're still on track for a week from tomorrow, although I'm not part of the planning. I assume you're still willing to be a groomsman."

"I wouldn't miss it," Len replied. "It seems like every time you and Dolores show up at the same event there's gunfire and excitement. Are you planning to wear a bulletproof vest under your tuxedo?"

"I'm sure that won't be necessary," I said, suddenly paranoid. "But please check Dolores's purse before the ceremony. I'd feel more comfortable knowing that there's not a blunderbuss in her bag."

CHAPTER 7
SATURDAY MORNING

My hand was tingling, which woke me. Jenny was breathing softly, spooning, with her head in the crook of my elbow, cutting off the circulation to my hand. I smiled and silently thanked Jenny's father for offering to take Jeremy to a movie then back to their house. I carefully slid my arm out and flexed my fingers, trying to get the blood flowing.

I showered and dressed without waking Jenny, then started coffee. I searched my refrigerator and reflexively checked the expiration on the milk carton, before remembering I'd just purchased it. I pondered cereal and decided to keep digging.

I found a pound of bacon in the freezer, eggs in the refrigerator, and a box of pancake mix in the cupboard. I rarely made more than toast or cereal, but having Jenny stay overnight motivated me to make a real breakfast. I had bacon in the frying pan and was mixing pancake batter when Jenny wandered into the kitchen, yawning and stretching.

"I smelled bacon," she said, going immediately to the cupboard and taking down two mugs. She handed me a steaming mug and sat at the table, blowing on the coffee to cool it. She was wearing my terrycloth robe and a pair of moccasins that were too large, but warm. Her blonde hair was flattened on one side of her head.

"I'm making bacon and pancakes."

She turned her head and looked at me through sleepy eyes. "You do know that I'm trying to lose another three pounds before the wedding."

"Don't eat any," I said with a shrug. "All the more for me."

"You know that I can't walk away from crispy bacon. It's an addiction, second only to pancakes."

I poured batter into a cast iron skillet and brought a bottle of maple syrup to the table. I'd purchased the syrup and a jar of honey from a local vendor at the farmer's market.

I flipped the pancakes and put three strips of bacon onto a plate, followed by two golden brown pancakes. Jenny sat up and took a deep breath.

"Nope," she said. "I have no self-control this morning." She took a bite of the bacon and smeared butter on the pancakes as I poured batter for more cakes.

"So, what's the plan for today?" I asked as she mopped up syrup with her last bite of pancake.

"I have a wedding shower at Marie's house this afternoon, and you're playing with Wendy's band at Hugo's tonight. I have no plans beyond those."

"Hugo's," I said. "I'd forgotten about Hugo's in all the fire commotion. I should call Wendy to get their playlist so I can run through all the songs at least once."

"I assume you'll hear from Len if they get any leads on Alf."

The front door opened and Jenny quickly pulled the bathrobe around herself and tightened the sash. Dolores walked into the kitchen looking haggard.

"Can I sit over here for a while? The workmen have started and the noise is deafening."

"Sure," I said, pulling out a chair. "Would you like a pancake and coffee."

"That would be lovely," she said, sitting next to Jenny.

"I didn't have time to even brew coffee before the men were banging around on the roof."

"You're welcome to sit here all day, if you want," I said, setting a cup of coffee in front of her. "We're going to be busy with other things, but the house will be empty and quiet." I pushed my plate in front of her and poured more batter into the frying pan.

"Oh, Peter. I can't eat your breakfast," she protested.

"I'm fine. I've got more pancakes frying and there's plenty to go around."

"You were talking about Alf Paluzzo's gold last night," Dolores said as she poured syrup. "Did he find the gold?"

"Actually, Alf is missing," Jenny said. "After the fire at Whistling Pines we did a head count and he was unaccounted for. Last we heard, they hadn't found him yet."

"I suppose the wrong person heard about his gold and decided to take it," Dolores said. "There are always nasty people around who like to take advantage of others. That's why I like to keep a shotgun behind the basement door."

I froze. "Do you have a shotgun behind the door now?"

"Don't be silly," Dolores replied. "You took it away when I was shooting at the rabbit. If I'd still had the shotgun I would've shot at those deer that were eating our bushes yesterday."

Jenny was halfway through a sip of coffee. She snorted and coffee gushed out her nose. I rushed over with a paper towel as she gasped, choked, and laughed.

"Oh dear," Dolores said. "That must've gone down the wrong way."

Jenny nodded as she gasped to catch her breath. I dashed back to flip the pancakes that were now past golden on one side, but not yet burned.

"Do you have any other guns in the house?" Jenny asked.

"I don't think so. Peter and the police chief took them all away after the concert last summer. Len seemed very disturbed that I'd shot at the woman who was running at Peter with the gun.

He took that lap gun at the concert, then we walked through the house and he removed the others from the kitchen and bedroom."

I was just about to sit down when there was a knock on the front door. Tim Webb was standing on the front step holding a linen sleeve that appeared to contain a long gun. "I found this in the floor joists when I ripped out the pantry floor. It must've been right under the leak because it's badly rusted."

I took the sleeve and slid the gun out. It was a lever-action rifle. I tried to see if it was loaded, but the action was so corroded that the lever wouldn't move. "Thank you," I said.

"Too bad it's so rusty," he said. "It looks like a model 73 Winchester. They're quite valuable if they're in good condition."

I carried the gun into the kitchen and held it up for Dolores to see. "The contractor found this in the joists when he ripped up the floor." I set the gun in the corner.

Dolores cocked her head. "That looks like my father's deer rifle. I wondered what had happened to it. It appears that it should've been oiled."

Jenny quickly changed the topic to wedding plans while I ate. Dolores was excited about the upcoming wedding and asked about the details. They were talking about flowers while I poured more coffee and put the dishes in the sink.

"You'll have to excuse us," said Jenny. "I have to get dressed and Peter needs to practice because he's playing at Hugo's tonight."

Dolores dismissed us with a flip of her hand. "Yes, please get on with your lives. I'll just sit here and drink coffee."

Jenny was in the shower and I was gathering sheet music when the house shuddered from a blast, followed by the sound of breaking glass. I ran to the kitchen and found Dolores standing at the kitchen window with the rifle in her hands. She was struggling with the frozen lever when I took it from her. I heard shouting outside and a thud.

"That deer is eating my bushes," Delores said, pointing to her back yard.

"How did you get this to fire?" I asked, again failing to get the lever to cycle.

"I pulled back the hammer and pulled the trigger," she said. "It went off just like it's supposed to."

There was pounding on the front door, so I set the gun in the kitchen corner and ran to the door. The roofing contractor was standing there looking agitated.

"What happened?" he asked. "You scared the hell out of us and one of my guys fell off the roof!"

"Mrs. Karvonen was handling an antique gun when it accidentally fired," I said, hoping to calm the man.

"I don't think it was an accident. There's a dead deer in the back yard."

Tim Webb showed up, looking equally rattled. "What happened? Was there an explosion? All the windows rattled in the house."

In the distance I could hear a siren whine. Within seconds, a second siren started wailing, slightly out of sync with the first.

"I was a Navy corpsman," I said pulling on a jacket. "How's the man who fell off the roof?"

"He's lying in the yard. I called 911. He's hurt pretty bad, I think."

We ran to Dolores's house where one of the roofers was kneeling over a man who was writhing in pain on the ground.

"What's your name?" I asked as I knelt.

"Robert," he replied through clenched teeth.

"Can you move your fingers and toes, Robert?"

He clenched his fists and moved his boot. "Yeah, all the digits work."

"How did you land?"

"I twisted, so I landed pretty much flat on my back."

"Are you breathing okay?"

He started to take a deep breath, then grimaced and blew it out. "No. It hurts to take a breath."

The first siren stopped at the end of our block and an ambulance appeared in the driveway. I stepped back to let the EMTs do their jobs. The second siren stopped and a fire truck, rigged with rescue gear, stopped on the street. Two firemen, dressed in their bunker gear, rushed to help the EMTs. A third siren wailed in the distance and I wondered who else was on their way.

Tim moved next to my shoulder and whispered, "You might want to deal with the deer in the yard before the cops show up."

"We need to deal with the deer Dolores shot," I whispered to Jenny. I got *the look*.

"I deal with geriatric patients," she replied. "*You're* the expert in gunshots."

I caught Tim's attention and nodded toward the back yard. "I don't do rats or deer," he whispered with a smile.

I walked to the back yard and found a fork-horn yearling buck lying near the hosta bed. I approached him slowly, looking for a wound, but saw no sign of blood. I went to Dolores's garage and found an old sisal rope. As I walked into the yard I wiped the dust off and unwound the rope. I tied a loop in the end and considered whether to tie the rope around the antlers or rear feet. I looked at the long stretch of lawn I'd have to drag him across before I could get the deer into the woods. As I hesitated, his eye blinked. I took a step back and watched as he tried to lift his head. He slowly got to his knees and then stood, his legs wobbling like a newborn calf. He still had a forked antler on one side, but only a spike on the other side. When I looked closely at the spike I could see that it was splintered where the other antler forked. Apparently, Dolores hit the deer's antler and knocked him out. The buck stood for a moment, first considering me, then checking his surroundings. After a minute he slowly stumbled away.

"He's alive?" Tim Webb asked as he walked up to me. We

watched the deer disappear into the woods behind the house.

"Looks like he was hit in the antler. He probably has one hell of a headache, but otherwise he seems uninjured."

"I have a scrap of subflooring that would probably fit over your broken window," Tim said, surveying the bullet hole in the window and the glass shards on the sidewalk below. "I have a window guy, too. He usually has same-day service for emergencies, but that'll probably cost extra."

"That would be great," I replied.

I smelled pipe smoke and turned to see Len Rentz. "Let me guess," he said, "Dolores found another gun."

"Actually, I found it," said Tim. "I brought it over to Peter."

"And I thought it was rusted so bad the action was frozen, so I left it standing in the corner of the kitchen when I went to get dressed."

"And it wasn't frozen?" Len asked.

"Apparently. There was a shell in the chamber, and the hammer and trigger mechanism still work, but the lever won't cycle. Dolores shot once, but couldn't reload."

Len puffed on his pipe, considering his words. "You need to search the whole house, top to bottom, again."

"Why do I have to search the house?" I asked.

"You're the one who left Dolores alone with a gun," Len replied. "It would be less stressful to have you make a discreet search than for me to come through and tear things apart. But if I have to ..."

CHAPTER 8

After a couple squirts of penetrating oil, Tim Webb was able to loosen the action and eject the remaining five tarnished brass shells that had been in the gun's magazine. The rest of the roofing crew agreed to return to work after I demonstrated that the gun wouldn't fire another round.

Jenny had disappeared during the commotion. I found her in my living room sipping coffee and talking with Dolores. They both stopped talking and smiled when I came into the room, making me curious about the topic.

"We were just discussing the wedding plans," said Jenny. I thought her comments were contrived, but didn't press the issue.

There was a knock on the door and I met Len as he walked into the kitchen. "What can I do for you?" I asked.

"Put on some hiking boots and a warm coat. I've got something to show you."

"What's up?" I asked, digging a pair of insulated boots out of the coat closet.

Len looked over my shoulder at Dolores and Jenny and shook his head. He relit his pipe while I laced my boots.

With my boots and parka on and a pair of Thinsulate gloves in hand, we walked to Len's cruiser. Len started the engine and turned around in my driveway, puffing on his pipe.

"Let me guess," I said. "You didn't just happen to show up at Dolores's house after the shot was fired."

"We got an anonymous call about a dead body."

"I didn't think there was such a thing as an anonymous call in this age of caller ID."

"That's true to a degree. But people can buy disposable phones that aren't registered to a user. There are lots of stolen phones, and there are still a few pay phones around. This call came from a cellphone with a blocked number."

"But you can get the number," I said.

"We aren't CSI on television. Yes, we can get the number, but only after a judge signs a warrant and we present it to the phone company. It'll take a day."

I took a deep breath and looked out the side window, exhaling slowly and fogging the glass. "I suppose it's Alf."

"It's an elderly man," Len said. "We didn't find any identification with the body, but we don't have any other missing people."

"Where was he found?"

"A few miles out of town there's a place called Big Rock in the Little Stewart River. The place has been the town swimming hole for generations. There's a large rock where kids jump into the deep water where the current scoured away the bottom."

"How far away from Whistling Pines?" I asked.

"It's few miles down Highway 2, then down a side road a bit."

"Is there any indication why he would be there?" I asked.

"I suppose it has something to do with Alf's gold story. Someone chipped away at the frozen ground under the rock. At this point, it's unclear if Alf was there with a pickaxe and someone discovered him, or if he was forced to lead someone to the spot where they killed him and chipped away."

"Does it look like they found the jar of coins?" I asked.

"It's unclear. There's a hole in the ground, but I think the pick would've broken the jar and we would've found glass shards and maybe the lid. All we have is clumps of frozen dirt and a pickaxe that was apparently used to kill Alf."

We drove in silence until we saw the flashing red and blue lights of a Lake County Sheriff Office cruiser, the medical examiner's Suburban, and the BCA Winnebago parked outside a ring of yellow crime scene tape. I was surprised not to see a news van. The local stations monitor the police radios and sometimes have a crew at the site of the action within minutes of the police arriving. There are so few major crimes in the winter that I'd expect them to be chomping at the bit to get some video for their six o'clock newscast.

"Where are the news vans?" I asked as we lifted the yellow tape and stepped under it.

"All the discussions were done by phone," Len replied. "We might be able to keep the area secure and the newshounds away until the BCA gets through processing the scene."

Frost covered the grass and trees, but it was quickly melting as the sun's rays hit it. A group of people near the pond's shoreline huddled near the base of a boulder. Closer to the road we came upon a blue tarp covering a lump. Len led me to the tarp and lifted a corner, exposing a waxy face and wavy brown hair. Cloudy brown eyes stared back at us.

"Is this Alf?" Len asked.

I nodded and looked away. "I'll call Nancy and get the name of Alf's next of kin," I said. "I assume you need to make the visit to inform the family."

"If they're local, I'll drive over. Otherwise, I'll have the closest police department send an officer."

I pulled out my cellphone and called Nancy, who was at home. She promised to get the name, address, and phone number to me within fifteen minutes.

We hung back from the people who were working. The melting frost was trampled with footprints and I surmised that someone had probably taken pictures of them upon arrival on the scene. At that point there had probably been only prints from Alf, the killer, and the person who discovered the body. I wondered if that would be useful information. I looked at the tarp covering Alf's body and felt a sudden chill that had little to do with the temperature.

It's not like I haven't seen death and dealt with the dead bodies of people who'd been very close to me. But this wasn't Iraq. This wasn't a battlefield. Alf wasn't a casualty of a heated battle; he'd been killed by someone, probably just for greed.

A man with almost white hair and wearing a parka with a BCA logo was standing off to the side of the site making notes on a sketch pad. He carried a laser range finder mounted on top of a yellow tripod. He then measured the distance to Alf's body and set up to triangulate the distance from Alf's head and feet to the big rock and the "No Swimming" sign. Next he triangulated the spot where the pickaxe lay on top of the frozen ground. He made more notes and more sketches, documenting the location of all the pertinent evidence and its position relative to the rock and sign, all carefully recorded so the scene could be recreated at any time in the future.

"Who's that?" I asked Len.

"That's Sonny Carlson. He's a BCA crime scene tech who's known for his special gift. He can talk to anyone, about anything, at any time."

Hearing his name, Sonny walked over and shook Len's hand. "Hi, Chief."

"Sonny, this is Peter Rogers. He's from Whistling Pines, where the victim lived."

"That's quite a place," said Sonny. "Are you the house detective?" he asked with a grin.

"Not quite," Len said, before I could respond. "He's an inside resource for me."

Sonny held up his sketch pad. "No surprises. The body is here, as you can see."

The sketch showed the location of the rock, Alf's body, the

pickaxe, the area of frozen mud dislodged by the pickaxe, and the surrounding trees and pathway, all to scale.

"I had an aunt who lived at Whistling Pines for a while. Maybe you remember Helga Carlson. She lived on a farm down by Mahtowa until her husband Fred died."

"I'm not familiar with that name," I said. "She may have been gone before I started at Whistling Pines."

Sonny sized me up. "She died twenty years ago and you were probably in school then. It was a nice place even then. I remember Aunt Helga talking about going to movies and having sing-alongs. She said the food was better than she made at home and she put on ten pounds." He hesitated, thinking. "You might remember hearing about her. She was the woman who shot the horses that were standing in her barn when she came home after work one night. It was on all the news stations and there was quite a stink. The guy who owned the horses was mad, and Aunt Helga was mad because he didn't take care of his fences. He threatened to sue her but I think he finally gave up.

"You know, my other aunt, Edith, lived down the road from the Mahtowa dump. The bears would come and root around in their garden and her husband Gus used to shoot his 30-30 to scare them away. Well, one day Edith came home and Gus was all excited because he'd finally shot one of the marauding bears. They went out to the garden with a flashlight, Uncle Gus walking with his cane, and they found their neighbor's black angus bull lying dead in the garden. Those neighbors were none too pleased either. They took away Uncle Gus's gun after that."

"Peter has a neighbor who likes to shoot at rabbits in her yard," replied Len. "So far she's missed everything, but it's added a little excitement to the neighborhood. There's nothing like the sound of a ricochet to get your attention. Right, Peter?"

"Yeah," I agreed.

"Sonny," said the second BCA tech, with "J. Telker" embroidered on his parka. "Quit telling stories and finish the sketch."

"It's done," Sonny replied. "I was just telling Len and Peter about my aunts down in Mahtowa."

Agent Telker smiled. "Yes, there's nothing like seeing your relatives on the evening news after they've shot the neighbor's animals."

There was stirring among the workers around the base of the rock. Parka-clad bodies started straightening up and stretching joints that had stiffened in the cold. They were without identification other than the alphabet of letters stenciled on their jackets: THPD, BCA, LCSD, ME. They wore stocking caps, baseball caps with earflaps, and Rocky the Squirrel hats trimmed with fur. Their faces all had pink noses and cheeks, frosty eyebrows, and sad eyes that had seen too much death.

"What've you got, Jeff?" Len asked.

"Not much. The pickaxe was used to chip at the frozen mud. I don't see that it did anything but break loose some small chunks of mud. I don't think the excavation is even a foot deep. If he, or she, found something, it's not evident to me. There's nothing but chipped mud. No spot where something was dislodged. My guess is the digger got tired or heard a snowmobile coming and took off without whatever he was after."

Sonny returned carrying the pickaxe. "Man, it's cold. My relatives moved here when there wasn't anything but wool long johns and wool coats. I don't know how they lasted here. Of course, the Finnish side of the family was better prepared because the winters in Finland are about the same as here. But the poor Swedes, they had no idea what they were getting into. I suppose that's why they wrote home and told their relatives to bring warm clothes."

"You can identify him?" Jeff asked, nodding toward Alf.

"It's Alf Paluzzo," I said. "He was missing from Whistling Pines after a fire yesterday. Our director is driving to her office to get Alf's contact information."

"That's going to be tough on the rest of the residents," said Sonny. "I'm sure it's like a big family and when anyone is lost, everyone feels the pain. I remember when my uncle Eino died. The whole nursing home came to the funeral. It took hours to get all those wheelchairs and walkers into the church, and the buffet line after the funeral, whew, that was something to see."

"Sonny, why don't you bag the axe and start the Winnebago so it warms up," said Jeff. As Sonny walked away he added, "Sonny is a great guy, and he works hard. I appreciate his ability to hold both ends of a conversation on those long days driving backroads in the crime lab. He keeps me awake and makes me laugh."

A tall, almost anorexic-looking man approached us. "A. Oresek M.D., Medical Examiner" was embroidered on his jacket. He nodded to Len and Jeff, then stuffed his gloved hands into his pockets.

"I'll obviously do an autopsy after we get back to the office and get the victim defrosted," Oresek said, "but my preliminary observations lead me to believe that the victim died where he was found. The cause of death appears to be blunt force trauma to the head and the blood and hair on the pickaxe indicate that it's the likely murder weapon."

A bareheaded man wearing a medical examiner's jacket and sporting a salt-and-pepper ponytail was struggling with the body bag. Alf's arms and legs were bent, making it difficult to get the black plastic bag over the body.

"Excuse me," said Oresek, who left to help him.

My cellphone started playing the "Beer Barrel Polka," startling me and garnering irritated looks from the professionals working the crime scene. At first I didn't recognize the song as my phone ringing, then I remembered that Jeremy had been playing games on my smartphone and must've changed my ring tone.

"This is Peter."

"I'm back in my office and I have Alf's contact information," said Nancy. "Do you want me to tell you the name and phone number or do you want me to email it to you?"

"Len, Nancy has Alf's next-of-kin information. What's your email address?"

He handed me a business card and I read the address back to Nancy. "Send me a copy, too," I said.

"Did he die peacefully?" she asked. I realized that I hadn't told her where we were or what was going on. "I thought maybe he'd just wandered off and died of hypothermia."

"His body was found by Big Rock swimming hole," I replied. "The medical examiner said he likely died of blunt force trauma."

"Oh no! Who took him up there?"

"That's the question right now," I replied. "We assume whoever brought him here was the one who killed him. That person hasn't been identified."

"Why did they go to Big Rock?"

"Someone was chipping at the frozen mud under the rock. I assume he was looking for Alf's cache of gold coins."

Len made a zipping motion across his lips.

"That's all I can say. The medical examiner took his body away for an autopsy so I assume it will be a couple days before the family can start funeral plans."

"I just sent you and Len a scanned copy of Alf's next of kin. It lists his son, Gary, as the first contact. He lives in Woodbury, a St. Paul suburb. There's a secondary contact listed as his daughter, but that's crossed out. If I remember correctly, she and Alf had a falling out and he didn't want us to contact her."

Len opened the e-mail and studied the names and phone numbers, then made a call to the Woodbury Police Department, asking them to contact Alf's son, Gary Paluzzo.

We left the crime scene to one deputy sheriff. As we drove back to Two Harbors in silence, we met a white van with a satellite dish on top. The logo on the door said it was from Channel 10, in Duluth. Less than a quarter mile further we saw Channel 3's van.

"Aren't you going back to make a statement?" I asked.

"I'll leave that to the sheriff," he said. "He needs the votes.

I'm just an appointee who serves at the pleasure of the city council."

"That's an interesting way to look at your career," I said. "You make it sound like they could fire you tomorrow if you pissed them off."

"It'd take more than one pissed off councilman, but yes, I could be gone in one vote. But that probably won't happen as long as I don't screw up big time."

"What are you planning to do about Alf's apartment?" I asked. "I imagine his family will want access to Alf's belongings and Nancy will want to get the apartment cleaned up and rented."

"Once we get the autopsy results and the BCA is through processing the evidence from the crime scene, we should be able to release the apartment to the family. I'm reluctant to do that until we're sure every fingerprint and hair have been recovered."

"The Bible!" I said. "It was missing from Alf's room. Was it at the murder scene?"

"I didn't see it, nor did the BCA guys mention it."

We turned the corner near my house and could see that the road was choked with pickups, mostly the roofing guys and Tim Webb's people. A black pickup with a tiny badge on the driver's door sat blocking my driveway.

"Looks like the game warden is here," said Len.

"Why would the game warden be here?" I asked as I got out of Len's cruiser.

"I imagine he wants to talk about the deer," said Len as I closed the door.

A slender young man in a green parka and matching baseball cap was standing on my front step as I walked up. He turned as I reached the bottom step and I could see Dolores framed in the door. As I got closer I caught snippets of conversation.

"But I already have my Christmas wreaths. They're hanging on my porch railing," said Dolores.

The conservation officer's response was muffled.

"No, not popcorn either. The hulls get stuck under my plates. Why don't you just go next door? There are younger people who might eat Boy Scout popcorn. I'm not interested." Dolores was closing the door in his face when I reached the bottom step.

"I'm Peter Rogers. Come in and have a cup of coffee?" I said. "This is Mrs. Karvonen, my neighbor."

"Thank you," said the conservation officer, stepping aside so I could enter. We shook hands and he introduced himself.

Jared was very young, probably fresh out of college and the DNR training program. He was blonde, blue-eyed, with a baby face. His uniform looked like it had just come from the uniform shop. There were a few loose threads where the new patches had recently been sewn on.

Dolores had obviously mistaken him for a Boy Scout. My hopes for an amicable, no harm, no foul, solution waned. Young officers, no matter what department they represent, tend to be "by the book." More-seasoned officers often mellow and apply reason and experience more liberally.

Dolores stepped back so we could get into the small entryway, but she looked unhappy, nearing angry. I chose to ignore her displeasure as I hung my coat on a peg and took the officer's parka and hung it up. I led him to the kitchen with Dolores lagging behind. The carafe of coffee was still half full so I took down two mugs and poured, putting a cup for the officer across the table from Dolores's cup and spoon.

"How can I help you?" I asked as I sat.

"A tip-line caller said a deer had been shot behind this house. Do you know anything about that?

I sipped my coffee, trying to decide how best to frame my answer without lying.

"Why do the Boy Scouts care about deer eating bushes?" Dolores asked.

"Officer Paulson isn't a Boy Scout," I said patiently. "He's a conservation officer with the Department of Natural Resources."

Dolores scanned his uniform. "What merit badge are you working on?" she asked, her stare fixated on his badge.

"Ma'am, I'm a conservation officer and I'm following up on a tip about a deer shooting."

"It was eating my bushes" said Dolores, crossing her arms.

"Where are your bushes, ma'am?"

"They're in my yard, of course."

"Which direction is your yard?" Jared asked, taking out a small notebook and a pen.

"That way," said Dolores, pointing at the new plywood covering my kitchen window.

"And you shot the deer?" Jared asked skeptically.

"Yes."

"What did you use for a weapon?"

"I don't see it now," said Dolores, glancing around the kitchen, looking for the gun, which was carefully locked away. "It was in the corner." She pointed to the corner of the kitchen nearest the front door.

"Are you in the habit of leaving firearms in the corner?" Jared asked me.

"It isn't Peter's gun," Dolores said, starting to show frustration. "It's my gun."

Jared looked at me, but I was amused at the conversation, so decided not to say anything.

"What kind of gun is it?" he asked.

"It's my father's old deer rifle, a lever-action Winchester."

"Why did you bring it here, to your neighbor's house?"

"I didn't bring it here. The workman brought it over."

Jared's eyes started to dart between Dolores and me. I sensed his skepticism about Dolores's answers. I could easily see how he thought she had dementia.

"Why would a workman bring your rifle over here?"

"Well, that's simple enough," she replied. "It was in his way.

He's an upright man and he brought it here where it was out of his way but safe."

"Where did he find this gun?"

"In my basement rafters."

Jared pushed his pen and notepad aside. "A workman took a rifle out of your basement because it was in his way and he brought it over here, to your neighbor's house. Is that correct?"

"Are you dim?" Dolores asked. "I don't like repeating myself. If you can't grasp what I'm saying, please fetch someone who is bright enough to follow the conversation, maybe your scoutmaster."

"Oh, I'm following the conversation," Jared replied. "I'm just having a hard time understanding why the gun was here. I think I've got it now." He paused and sipped his coffee, considering his next question. "So, the gun was brought over by a workman, who left it in the corner, and then what happened?"

"I think Peter went to get dressed."

Jared closed his eyes and drew a breath. "What happened with the gun?"

"Nothing happened. It just sat there."

"At some point, someone discharged the gun. Who shot?"

"I did. I already told you that Peter went to get dressed," said Dolores.

"Why did you shoot?"

Dolores looked at me. "Is there some way I could make myself clearer to this Boy Scout, Peter?"

Paulson gave me a beseeching look. I shrugged and suppressed a grin.

"I already told you. The deer was eating my bushes."

"So," said Jared, taking a deep breath. "The deer was eating your bushes. Peter is dressing. The workman brings over a gun and sets it in the corner. You pick up the gun and shoot the deer. Is that correct?"

"No," said Dolores a little too sharply. "The workman brought over the gun before Peter took his shower. Peter checked to see if it was loaded, but the mechanism was rusted shut. What do you call it, Peter? Was it the lever that was rusted shut?"

"Okay, now I'm confused," said Jared, pushing aside his coffee cup. "The gun was rusted so badly that the lever wouldn't function?"

"Yes," said Dolores. "It's been in my basement a long time and I was very neglectful. I'd forgotten about it so it never got oiled and it was very rusty. My father would've had a fit if he'd known I'd treated a gun like that."

"So, the gun was rusted shut. Did you pretend to shoot the deer with it?"

"Of course not! I shot through Peter's window. That's why it's covered with wood."

Jared glanced at the plywood and looked back at Dolores. "How did you shoot through the window with a gun that was rusted shut?"

"I pulled back the hammer and pulled the trigger," she replied. "I couldn't cycle the lever for a second shot. It's a good thing I got him with the first shot."

"So, there's a dead deer in your backyard?" Jared asked.

"I don't know if he's there anymore," said Dolores, "but he dropped like a sack of potatoes when I shot."

Jared got up from his chair and nodded to me. "Show me the dead deer," he said, walking to the front door and taking his parka off the hook.

"There's no dead deer," I said, not moving.

"Mrs. Karvonen said the deer went down after the shot. I want to see the carcass."

"There's no carcass," said Dolores. "I think Peter dragged it off like the rabbits I shot last summer."

Jared took my jacket off the hook and threw it to me. "Show me the deer carcass."

"There's no carcass," I said, following him out the door as

I pulled on my coat. "She hit the deer in his antler and knocked him out. He got up and walked away."

Jared trudged ahead, ignoring my comments. I followed him to Dolores's backyard where the sound of hammers pounding roofing nails overwhelmed all conversation. We stopped where the grass was flattened. All other evidence of the deer encounter had been obliterated when the sun melted the frost.

"Where was the deer?" Jared yelled to be heard over the pounding.

"Right here," I said, pointing to the matted grass.

"There's no blood," he said.

"She hit him in the antler, not the body. He was knocked unconscious, but woke up and then walked away."

Jared stared at the plywood over my window and then at the matted grass.

"You're shitting me, aren't you? There's no way that little old lady shot from your kitchen, through the window, and hit a deer in the yard, here. What's the real story?"

"That's it," I said, holding my hands up. "Dolores finds old guns in her house and she shoots at things. She never kills anything. Ask the other neighbors. That's what happens."

"She said she shot rabbits."

"She shoots *at* rabbits," I corrected. "Her aim is so bad that they don't even run away anymore. She hits the dirt and chunks of sod fly up. The bunnies don't care."

"If that's true, someone should take her guns away."

"I have. Ask Len Rentz, the police chief. I've taken dozens of guns out of her house and she keeps finding more."

"C'mon," he said and we walked to the back edge of Dolores's yard where it turns to underbrush.

"See," I said. "No drag marks. No gut pile. No deer. He just walked off."

Jared opened his mouth, but said nothing. He just stared into the woods.

"I'm out of here," he said. "Please make sure she doesn't shoot anything else."

"Believe me," I said, "I'm not happy about my kitchen window, and I'm doing everything in my power to keep guns out of her hands."

Wendy pulled into the driveway just as the conservation officer pulled away. She hopped out of her car carrying a sheet of paper, waving as I stood ready to open the door.

"You wanted our set list for tonight," she said, jamming the sheet of paper into my hand.

"I don't know if I'm up to playing tonight, Wendy. They haven't notified the family yet, but they found Alf's body this morning. Len Rentz took me out to the scene and I'm pretty rattled."

"I heard about Alf and I feel this is just what we need. The music will take your mind off the bad things and put you in a better place. Besides, you're our last option for a guitar player."

I looked through the list of songs from the '60s, '70s, and '80s, chosen to appeal to the mix of Hugo's customers. I'd played all the songs I'd listened to while growing up. They were old friends and had been cathartic, getting me through my Iraq deployment and the PTSD afterward.

"Sure," I said with the opening lyrics of "Take It Easy" running through my head as I pictured Don Henley and Glenn Fry singing harmony.

"See you at seven for setup," Wendy said as she ran back to her car. "The first set starts at eight."

Dolores was still sitting at the table when I hung my coat.

"Am I going to be arrested?" she asked.

"Not this time," I said, refreshing her coffee. "But you can't shoot at critters in your yard. We live in town and the neighbors don't appreciate the sound of gunfire."

"I don't appreciate the rodents eating my flower gardens."

I was tempted to point out that neither deer nor rabbits were rodents but thought better of it.

"I'm going to practice my guitar for a while. I hope that won't disturb you."

"Please, go ahead," she replied. "Anything is better than that infernal pounding outside."

CHAPTER 9
SATURDAY EVENING

After inspecting the day's progress on the pantry repair and getting Dolores settled in her house, I picked up Jenny. She was bubbling over about the afternoon bridal shower and enumerated the games they'd played and the gifts she'd received.

"It was nice to see my aunts and cousins before the wedding when we could talk a little," she said. "The gifts were nice, but at some point I realized that we're getting married in a few days, which almost takes my breath away."

"But you knew we're just days from the wedding," I said.

"But having all those women hugging me and asking about the wedding plans, well, that made it real."

She continued to tell me details about the shower as I drove to Hugo's over dark county roads made continually treacherous by deer that like to bound out of a ditch without warning. We arrived a few minutes after seven. The band was already setting up their amplifiers when Jenny and I walked in.

Jenny joined some high school friends sitting at a table in the back. I unpacked my guitar and set it on stage. When last seen, Jenny had her left hand in the air and her friends were inspecting her engagement ring. Apparently approving, they all waved at me as we got the last of the equipment set onstage.

Hugo's dining room isn't large and every table was packed along with an additional dozen chairs — the fire marshal would not have approved. People lined the bar and those closest to the stage turned to watch. The first set opened with Wendy singing "I Don't Want To Set The World On Fire" sounding just like Linda Ronstadt. We moved to "Take It Easy" with Wendy and me on vocals. Within minutes the real world was a million miles away and Hugo's was the center of my universe. I became one with the guitar and contentment swept over me as I closed my eyes and played.

When we took a break after the first set a middle-aged waitress with tight jeans and one too many buttons unfastened on her western-cut blouse sauntered over and handed me a glass of beer. "Compliments of the redhead at the bar," she whispered.

I looked around for Jenny, who would only be confused with a redhead if she sat under a red lightbulb, but I couldn't see her. Scanning the faces sitting at the bar, I locked eyes with a redhead. Her hairdo reminded me of the country singer Reba McEntire. When our eyes met she set her beer on the bar, whispered something to the woman sitting next to her, then threaded her way through the crowd toward the bandstand. I checked for Jenny again to no avail. I put on my best smile and prepared to meet the redhead, who I hoped was a fan of the band.

"You're good, Peter" she said. "You're not just playing the guitar. You closed your eyes and the music flowed out. You have a gift."

"Thanks," I said, unsure of how to respond to the compliment.

"Do you remember me?" She was tall, slender, in western cut clothes, wearing tight jeans and snakeskin boots. She put her right hand on my chest as she spoke, violating my personal space. Her voice was deep and sultry.

"I'm sure I'd remember you if we'd met." I tried to step back but I was against the drum set with no route of retreat.

"It was a long time ago," she said, then waited for me to acknowledge our previous meeting.

"I'm sorry, I don't recall meeting you. Was I playing at some gig?" I asked. I'm sure her hand felt my heartbeat racing.

"We were partners in chemistry lab," she growled, leaning so close I could smell the beer on her breath. Her red lips were inches from mine and I could see brown flecks in her green eyes.

My mind flashed back to high school, my junior year, then chemistry. I remembered sitting in lectures, then running lab experiments in glass flasks. I looked into her eyes again and recognition swept over me.

"Bobby?" I asked.

"Roberta," she purred.

I tried to mentally peel away the big red hair, makeup, fake eyelashes, lipstick, plucked eyebrows, and female swagger. "Roberta. Huh. When . . . what?" The last time I'd seen Bobby, she had brown hair, braces on her teeth, was rail thin, wore glasses with Coke-bottle lenses, and was a better chemist than any guy in the class. Her yearbook statement said she'd be running DuPont by the time she was thirty and I believed it.

"I've seen this band a few times without you. Have they picked you up full time?" she asked, still standing in my personal space. She was so close I could see the edges of her contact lenses.

"The backup guitarist is sick so I'm just sitting in for the night. I have a regular day job. How about you?"

"I'm the newest emergency room doctor in the Eveleth hospital." I was pinned against the drums and she was reveling in my discomfort. "If you're ever sick in Eveleth, come see me."

"You're a doctor?"

"I can show you a business card with M.D. after my name. But enough about me. What are you up to when you're not singing with the band?" She glanced at my left hand, checking for a ring. "Are you playing the field?"

"I'm getting married on Saturday," I said.

"Hmm. Are you fully committed?"

"Yes, I'm happy and fully committed." I got slightly queasy

when I thought about Bobby, my high school lab partner, hitting on me.

Roberta put on a dramatic pout. "All the good ones are taken." She leaned forward and kissed me. She turned away and sashayed back to the bar, smiling at the guys in the band.

"Do you have a groupie?" Wendy whispered.

"An old friend from high school."

"I'd kill for that body. She must work out all the time to keep that trim. She's got hips like a twelve-year-old boy, although she could use a little more padding upstairs. Did she hit on you?"

"Nah, she's just an old high school friend who wanted to say hi."

"My old high school friends rarely kiss me when they say hello."

The drummer started a beat, signaling the end of the break. I ran to the bathroom where I read the sign over the urinal: "Procrastinators meeting Tuesday, or maybe Wednesday." I chuckled, then rushed back to the stage, strapped on my guitar, and took a sip of beer. As I played a few chords and adjusted the E string I scanned the crowd for Jenny. She wasn't at the table with her friends so I assumed she was in the bathroom or at the bar. I glanced at Bobby, who winked at me and gave me a grin with her mouthful of perfectly aligned teeth. It was amazing what braces, contact lenses, makeup, and adult hormones could do for a girl.

The second set was comfortable, mostly songs I'd played for the guys in Iraq. I scanned the room for Jenny again, but she still wasn't with her friends. I looked at the area around the bar. I was trying to avoid eye contact with Roberta but realized there was a short blonde next to the tall redhead. I missed a beat, but recovered after getting a scowl from Wendy. I focused on the music, casting a glance at the bar and affirming that Jenny and Roberta were talking, then laughing. They both looked at me and Jenny blew me a kiss. My mind reeled, wondering what they had in common besides me.

When we broke, I slipped the guitar strap off my shoulder and picked up the now warm and flat beer. I stepped off the bandstand and Jenny popped up in front of me after threading through the crowd.

"Hi, boyfriend," she said, with a slight slur. I wondered how much she'd had to drink. She pressed herself against me and gave me a kiss. She smelled like lemons and her lips were sweet. Her drink was rimmed with powdered sugar and the liquid was yellow.

"I was going for a fresh beer."

"The waitress is bringing one," she said. "You can have a sip of my lemon drop while you wait." She made a popping sound when she said, "drop."

I sipped her drink. "It reminds me of lemon syrup."

"I met Roberta," she said, getting pushed against me by the jostling crowd. "She's . . . interesting. She said she's known you since high school."

"Yeah, we were chemistry lab partners. I don't think I've seen her since then."

"She thinks you're cute and she's a little disappointed that you're engaged."

I tried to come up with a witty response, but just stood there with my mouth open.

"You should probably wipe the lipstick off your bottom lip. Your girlfriend might be . . . jealous."

Jenny disappeared into the crowd as my beer arrived, delivered by the same middle-aged waitress. "I don't see it," she said with a smile.

"What don't you see?" I asked, taking the beer and pressing a dollar into her hand.

"You've got two hot women fawning over you. I just don't see the attraction." She took a napkin off the tray, wiped the lipstick off my face, then turned and disappeared into the crowd.

I was taking a long drag of beer when I felt fingers in my front pants pocket. I almost blew beer out my nose as I jumped back, only to find myself against the bass drum again. A thirty-some-thing woman with bleached blonde hair showing brown roots was standing so one breast pressed against my arm.

"My number is in your pocket," she said with a smile, then melted into the crowd.

"What's with you and the women tonight?" Wendy asked. "Are you using pheromone cologne or something?"

"This is nuts," I replied. "The only thing different is that I'm engaged."

"That's it! They're attracted because you're safe. You can be a beefcake one-night stand and they know you'll go back to your fiancée so they have no long-term commitment."

"I thought women wanted long-term commitments."

"That's so twentieth century. Millennial women want mean-ingful jobs, excitement, sex if they can find a guy who knows how their equipment works, and solitude when they decide to take a break from the job, excitement, and sex."

"But Jenny . . ." I started to protest.

"Jenny is an anomaly. Having done the other stuff, she thinks it's superficial. She's really hung up on you and is ready to settle in for the long haul."

The drummer nudged me away from his bass drum and started a beat that brought the bass player back to the bandstand. We wrapped up the final set with another Eagles tune, "Tequila Sunrise." The waitress slid through the crowd and passed a bar napkin to Wendy as the last notes died. After reading the note on the napkin Wendy nodded toward the bar and leaned close to the drummer.

"We have a request for a Bellamy Brothers song."

The lead guitar player flew through a riff as the drummer set the beat. Wendy sang, "If I said you had a beautiful body . . ."

I hadn't played the song with them, but strummed the chords with a little concentration. After one verse I had the chord sequence and got into the rhythm. I saw Jenny threading her way through the tables, bumping into people, stepping on toes, and offering apologies. When she got to the stage she grabbed my hand and pulled me off the bandstand. I swung the guitar over my shoulder and onto my back as she pulled me close and started to dance in the couple square feet that opened by people pulling a table back. Jenny said quietly into my ear as we moved with the music, "If I were dying of thirst would your love come quench me?"

We were still dancing when the music stopped.

"Your friend Roberta is a hoot. She was flirting with all the guys, then telling them she was your girlfriend. When you played "Tequila Sunrise" she told me to call her if I ever decided to throw you back into the dating pool."

"She was so quiet in high school that I hardly knew she existed," I said as I packed my guitar. "She was on the A honor roll every quarter and tutored kids in math and science. She's probably the smartest person I've known. Well, except for you."

"Nice recovery Navy boy," Jenny said, pecking my cheek.

I loaded the guitar case in the trunk of my Toyota and was about to get into the car when a Land Rover with heavily tinted windows stopped behind me. I walked to the passenger window and knocked on the glass. The window rolled down and I was about to unload on the driver when Roberta leaned out the window.

"It was fun pulling your chain," she said with a grin. "I'm really pleased that you've found someone as genuinely nice as Jenny. I wanted to say . . ." she paused and her eyes started to tear. "I wanted to say that you were the one guy who treated me like a human being in high school, not a pimple-faced pariah. I had no self-esteem at all and was afraid to talk to anyone, but you were nice to me. I can't tell you how much that meant."

I shrugged. "You were nice and you were smart. Maybe I knew that you'd be the duckling who turned into a swan someday."

She smiled then said, "Jenny said you were decorated for your service in Iraq. I can see that. You always gave of yourself. Thanks for your service."

The window rolled up and the Land Rover pulled away. Somehow I felt like Alice going through the looking glass as I watched her taillights disappear into the line of cars pulling out of the parking lot.

When I got in the car Jenny asked, "Who was that?"

"Roberta wanted to thank me."

"Thank you for what?"

"She said I was the only person in high school who treated her with respect."

Jenny pulled me close and kissed my cheek. "You haven't changed."

We were barely out of Hugo's parking lot before Jenny was asleep. I was still cruising with the music and flush with adrenaline. "Why can't you make a living playing guitar?" I asked myself. "You're good. You like it."

Then the other voice in my head said, "Are you nuts? You're getting married in a week and you need a stable life for a wife and son. You've got responsibilities and you can't go running all over the countryside playing until midnight four or five nights a week, then coming home too wired to sleep. What are you thinking?"

I started singing "If I Said You Had a Beautiful Body" softly to Jenny while she snuggled against me.

I parked in Jenny's parents' driveway and nudged her. "You're home."

She looked around and stretched. "Can't we go back to your house?"

"The deal was that you'd spend most nights here until we're actually married. We're keeping up appearances for Jeremy until the ring is on your finger."

We got out of the car and I walked her to the front door feeling like a high school kid bringing his date home after a movie. Jenny pulled me tight and tucked her head under my chin and we stood there clutching each other until we were startled by the door opening.

"Are you going to stand out there all night?" Barbara asked. "You'll freeze to death."

She was in a heavy terrycloth robe and her hair was tied in some special wrap that kept it perfect throughout the night. Her makeup was gone, which made her look even more like an older version of Jenny. I usually saw her with copious amounts of makeup that made it hard to determine her natural appearance. Even without makeup she was pretty, with tiny crow's-feet at the corners of her eyes the main difference between her and Jenny.

Jenny gave me a peck and ducked inside. Barbara smiled at me and said, "I'll be happy when you can stop the subterfuge and just stay together." She stepped onto the porch and pecked me on the cheek, then patted my shoulder and went inside.

My house seemed cold and empty. I showered and climbed into bed, but the rush of the applause and music still had me wired. I got up and poured two fingers of Jack Daniels whiskey in a water glass, then dropped an ice cube into it before reclining on the couch.

I woke with a start when the glass tipped over and dumped cold liquor on my lap. After putting on dry boxers, I climbed into bed and tried to sleep. Alf popped into the back of my brain and I thought about his brother who might have died on Guadalcanal. My Navy and Marine Corps history painted that as one of the most desperate battles fought in the war. Most of the Marines were ashore, along with some of their supplies, when the Navy heard that the Japanese were steaming south to attack. With most of the supplies still on the ships, they weighed anchor and sailed toward New Zealand, leaving the Marines to fend for themselves with what was on hand. Those Marines experienced the first of the banzai charges of the war and were subjected to heat, humidity, malaria, dysentery, and repeated Japanese attacks for months before the siege finally broke. The fighting was horrific and only a prelude to the battles that followed, ending with Iwo Jima and Okinawa.

If Alf's brother's remains hadn't been found, his family was among thousands who never knew the exact spot where their sons died or where their remains were interred. The South Pacific campaign left a trail of dead American and Japanese, some in unmarked shallow graves and others buried by nature.

Now wide awake, I wandered to the living room and found the Bible I'd received in third grade. I opened it to the Song of Solomon and read. The passages were beautiful and lyrical. I read the entire Song of Solomon and saw nothing that told me where something would be hidden near Two Harbors, or even specifically where in a home something might be stashed. I read through it a second time and decided that whatever it was that Alf was supposed to find was something his mother had written or placed in their family Bible. Satisfied with that explanation I went back to bed and finally fell asleep.

CHAPTER 10
SUNDAY MORNING

The alarm rousted me from bed barely an hour before church began. I rushed through the shower, shave, and dress routine, grabbed a granola bar and a cup of coffee, and was out the door. The car was warm by the time I got to Jenny's house and I had barely stopped rolling when Jeremy stumbled down the steps and raced to the car. He climbed into the back seat.

"Grandpa bet Mom that you wouldn't get here in time for church," he said breathlessly as Jenny walked down the sidewalk. "Grandpa has to wash dishes the rest of the week because you were on time."

Jenny, wearing a long woolen coat over slacks, climbed in and squeezed my hand. "Dad was sure you'd be too wound up to be on time for church after playing last night."

"Well, he almost won the bet," I said as I backed out of the driveway. "I fell asleep on the couch, and then thought about Alf's clue, so I read the Song of Solomon twice."

"Did you figure it out?" Jeremy asked from the back seat.

"I'm afraid not. I think the answer must be something specific about his family Bible. Maybe a note or a map that his mother tucked into it."

"How much gold do you think he had? Was it more than

Mrs. Karvonen gave me?" Jeremy asked.

"I don't think Alf knew how much they'd put away. That was part of what excited him," I replied.

"Grandpa knows a guy who's into coins," Jeremy said. "We took Mrs. Karvonen's bag of coins to his house and he looked at each of them. He was really impressed with some of them. I think Grandpa was surprised by how much they were worth because when we left he took me to the bank and we put them in a metal box they keep in the vault."

"Did the guy say how much they were worth?" I asked.

"He wrote down the value of each coin and then added it all up. The number had a lot of zeroes."

"The total was over sixty thousand dollars," Jenny said quietly. "I'm not sure we can accept that large a gift from Dolores."

"Mom! She gave them to me for my college fund."

"I'm just saying that she might not realize how large her gift was and she may need some of that money for her house repairs or living expenses."

"Grandpa said they're safe now, anyway."

We arrived at the church just as the bell started ringing, signaling the start of the service. Jeremy ran to his Sunday school room while Jenny and I were the last people to enter the sanctuary before the doors closed.

Since it was the Advent season, part of the service was devoted to the lighting of a candle, followed by a long-winded sermon that didn't mesh well with the Bible verses. I struggled with the hymns, my voice still strained from the night at Hugo's. Because we were late, we were the last row to exit the church. Pastor Johnson, a middle-aged man who'd been counseling us prior to marriage, lit up when we got through the line to shake his hand.

"Jenny and Peter, it's nice to see you this wonderful morning. I'm so pleased that you're becoming regular attendees."

"That was the deal," Jenny said, leaning close to the pastor. "We can be married in the church if we become supporting members. We're keeping our promise."

He smiled. "The test isn't the weeks before the wedding, Jenny. What I want from you two are the years of attendance after the wedding." He shook my hand and whispered, "And maybe a male soloist and backup organist."

"I'm more of a guitar guy," I replied. "I can play some piano, but the organ is a whole different level."

"We'll get you some practice time with Marlys. You'll catch on in no time."

I started to decline the offer, but decided to defer that discussion.

"I'll see you Friday night for the rehearsal," he said. "Barbara has been in touch with me often. She's working with Pastor Redmond. It's very touching that you wanted to bring him back from retirement for this occasion."

Jenny's smile became forced and she bit her bottom lip. "Mother and Pastor Redmond have been working out the details," she said. "I think they're both rather strong-willed."

"Strong-willed," said the pastor. "That's such a perfectly polite way to describe their personalities. I think Pastor Redmond also has a bit of dementia that probably accentuates his strong will. But I'm sure everything will be perfect!"

"Mother wouldn't settle for anything less than perfect," Jenny said.

The pastor obviously wanted to say more but was weighing his words carefully when Jeremy raced up and grabbed my hand.

"Hurry! The Vikings play in half an hour! And Grandma made pot roast."

As Jeremy tugged on my arm the pastor leaned close and whispered in my ear. "Jeremy loves you as much as Jenny does. He prefers to show it rather than say it."

I smiled and nodded as I was pulled away.

I could smell the aroma of browning meat and caramelized onions from the driveway. Jeremy was out of the car and running for the front door the moment the wheels stopped turning. On cue, Barbara opened the front door as Jeremy hit the steps, so he never broke stride as he ran through. Jenny and I hustled to the door and were shedding our coats when my cellphone buzzed.

"Excuse me," I said, slipping off my shoes and stepping into the never-used ceremonial living room where white predominated. The caller ID said, "THPoliceDept." "This is Peter."

"Hi, Peter," I recognized Len Rentz's voice immediately. "The BCA techs have processed Alf's room. They've got bags of carpet residue and they lifted thousands of fingerprints. Most are probably Alf's, so they've requested a set of prints from the medical examiner so those can be excluded. As you know, it appears there had been a struggle, but they didn't find much blood in the apartment. It'll take them days to sift through all the hair and dust they sucked out of the carpeting."

"Has the Bible turned up anywhere?"

"No. Just the letters, cards, envelopes, newspaper clippings, a photo album, a postage stamp collection, and a few coupons, but no Bible," Len said.

"I assume the killer heard Alf talking about the Bible possibly holding the clue to finding the coins," I said. "He was telling anyone who would listen. Maybe the killer even heard it second-hand. There were a lot of people excited about Alf's story. It was big news in Whistling Pines, so I'm sure the story was retold, and probably enhanced, if not twisted."

"Yup," Len said with a chuckle. "If Hulda Packer was retelling the story, I'm sure it was twisted."

"I call her the fountain of all misinformation."

"I was hoping you'd tell me that Alf had one confidant," said Len, "so I'd have a trail to follow. You're saying that virtually anyone in Whistling Pines might've heard the story?"

"I think you can rule out any of our residents as the killer. I just don't think anyone would've been strong enough to swing the pickaxe to kill Alf or to chip away all that frozen mud. It must've been someone else."

"I hate when that happens," Len said. "I want my pool of suspects to shrink, not expand. What do you know about Alf's kids?"

"I've never met them. They've never volunteered to be chaperones at any of our functions. That's about it."

"Peter," I heard Jeremy whisper as he tugged on my sleeve, "Grandma says it's time to hang up the phone and eat before the roast gets any colder."

"Len, I've got to run. I'll call if I hear anything."

I followed Jeremy into the dining room where everyone was standing next to their chairs, obviously awaiting my arrival. Barbara was blushing. Her makeup hid most of it, but her ears and neck were red. She gave Jeremy a glare. I noticed a spare place setting had been set, but there wasn't a sixth person in sight.

"That's not what I said," she whispered through clenched teeth, sitting down.

"It's what you meant though," Jeremy replied. Unfazed, he sat down and started heaping potatoes onto his plate.

"Would you like some pot roast, Peter?" Barbara asked as she passed the platter.

"Thanks," I said, taking two slices and a spoonful of onions. "We seem to have a missing guest."

"I invited your mother. I hope to become more acquainted with her since she'll be a part of our family from now on. She wasn't sure if she'd be available but I put out a plate in case her situation changed."

"Was that Len on the phone?" Jenny asked as we started eating.

"Yes, but I'm not sure the topic is dinner table fare," I replied.

Barbara smiled, hoping that she'd been responsible for my sudden awareness of social norms.

"C'mon, Peter," Jenny's father said. "We're tough."

Barbara's smile became forced as she glared at Howard.

"The Bureau of Criminal Apprehension processed Alf's

apartment. They found lots of hair and fingerprints, but no real clues as to what happened."

"Was there blood?" Jeremy asked with too much enthusiasm.

"Very little blood, no knives, and no smoking guns. Just a lot of dust, hair, and fingerprints."

"Perhaps we can move on to a different topic," Jenny suggested. "How are the wedding plans going, Mother? Have you received all the RSVPs?"

Barbara chewed slowly, obviously weighing her words carefully. "About two thirds of the invitees have responded. I spoke with the caterers and they said we should plan for most of the others to show up." She paused, then added, "The ones we're missing are the kids. They apparently never learned social skills and think I put the stamped, pre-addressed envelope in the invitation just for fun."

Jenny suppressed a smile and looked at me. "The 'kids' being the people my age?"

I thought to myself that voting in three presidential elections, serving my country for four years, and being deployed overseas where I was both wounded and decorated, should qualify me as an adult.

Barbara realized her slip and the red crept up her neck. "The younger generation, or perhaps the term millennials, might have been a better choice of words."

I heard a car engine outside, then the slamming of a car door. Barbara wiped her mouth with her napkin and carefully set it next to her plate, then walked to the front door, arriving just as the doorbell chimed.

"Barbara!" My mother gushed, hugging my future mother-in-law. Mother didn't notice Barbara's reaction, which was less than enthusiastic. Barbara didn't hug. On the rare occasions that I received a hug it had been chaste, both of us leaning forward from the waist to minimize physical contact between our bodies. In contrast, Mother's hugs were full-body bear hugs.

Mother cruised into the dining room as Howard and I rose to

greet her. She jangled as she moved due to the half dozen bangles on her wrists and layers of necklaces. Howard got the first hug, which lasted a few seconds too long.

"Audrey, how nice to see you again," Howard whispered as he tried to catch his breath while in a boa constrictor-like hug.

I was next. Jenny was engulfed for a full ten seconds as Mother whispered something in her ear. Jeremy was still wary of Mother, so stayed in his chair, but got a hug from behind anyway. Unfazed by her obvious late arrival for dinner, Mother sat in the empty chair next to Jeremy and started scooping potatoes onto her plate.

"The traffic on London Road was terrible," she said, setting the potatoes aside and reaching for the platter of pot roast. "There were dozens of cars just tooling along at the speed limit, oblivious to anyone who needed to be somewhere. It was terribly rude."

Howard bit his tongue. He always drove the speed limit, although sometimes pushed it just a little if he was running late.

"Barbara, this is a lovely meal," Mother said as she covered her potatoes and meat with gravy. "You must've been up before dawn to get this into the oven. You're a gem."

"I haven't seen your RSVP yet," said Barbara, "but I assume you'll be at the wedding."

"Of course I'll be at the wedding. I probably set it aside with the other items I need to put on the calendar. It's this coming Saturday, right?"

"You're invited to the rehearsal on Friday, too, of course," said Jenny. "We're going to have a small gathering for the family and wedding party."

"There's a Friday night fund-raising dinner for the Duluth Flower Club and I'd volunteered to coordinate the quilt raffle, but I managed to find someone to cover for me."

"It's good that you could free up Saturday for the wedding," I said.

Mother missed the sarcasm entirely. "I had to move a few things around for that, too, but I made it a priority," she said.

"You were telling us about your call from the police chief," Howard said to me, trying to steer the conversation to a different, less contentious, subject."

"He just said that there is a ton of evidence to process and it will be days before they get anything back from the BCA. We agree that the supposed cache of gold coins was the motive, but the pool of suspects is huge because Alf had been telling everyone about his new clue and his plans to recover the coins."

"Someone had a cache of gold coins?" asked Mother.

I retold Alf's story about the hidden family treasure and the call from his nephew, that sent him off on a hunt for the coins. Everyone nodded, although I could see Mother's mind churning.

"Mrs. Karvonen gave me a bag of gold coins," Jeremy told my mother. "She told me to put them in my college fund."

"That was very generous of her," Mother said.

Dinner went on with forced small talk. Mother was uncharacteristically quiet with few comments about her political beliefs or her charity efforts. I could see her mulling something. I worried about what it might be.

Dessert was homemade apple pie with cinnamon ice cream followed by Barbara shooing everyone out of the dining room so she could clear the dishes. Mother tried to stay behind to help, but Barbara said it was easier to do herself.

I braced myself for an uncomfortable exchange between Mother and Howard, with my mother spouting left-wing political rhetoric and Howard politely nodding, but quietly disagreeing and occasionally correcting facts. Instead, Mother went to the hallway closet and took out her coat.

"I hate to eat and run, but I've got an afternoon meeting with the trustees who manage the rose garden funds. Thank you so much for the lovely dinner. I haven't eaten pot roast in years."

Barbara came out of the kitchen wearing an apron over her dress and doffing rubber dishwashing gloves before getting another unwanted hug. Howard and Jemmy once again got hugs that lasted a little too long. Jeremy had disappeared. No one feigned disappointment at her early departure.

I got the last hug and Mother whispered in my ear, "Your father left something for you that I was supposed to give you after you were old enough to appreciate its value. It's in my safety deposit box. I suppose you can consider it your wedding gift from him. Remind me to get it sometime."

With that unsettling bombshell, she was out the door.

"Your mother is an interesting person," said Barbara, donning her gloves and returning to the kitchen.

"What did she whisper to you?" Jenny asked.

"My father left something she was supposed to give me when I was old enough to appreciate it. She said I should remind her sometime and she'd get it out of the safety deposit box."

"What did he leave you?"

"She didn't say," I replied.

"We were talking about Alf's gold coins when she froze," said Jenny. "Do you think he left you some gold or coins?"

"I have no idea," I replied. "He set up trust funds for each of us, so I assume it's not cash or stock."

"Do you remember some family keepsake he might have locked away for you?"

"I have no clue," I replied. "He never mentioned any family treasures or hand-me-downs."

"Another mystery," she said.

When the dishes were washed, Barbara came into the study and spread papers across the top of the desk. "Here's a spreadsheet of the week's activities. Peter, your responsibilities are in blue, Jenny's are red, and mine are black."

I looked through the myriad items she'd listed and my head swam. I searched for blue print and found "Pick up tux," "Arrive at groom's dinner," and "Arrive at church for pictures one hour before the ceremony" as my only responsibilities. Jenny had about the same list and the hundreds of other items were all in black.

Barbara was going to have a busy week, but she'd laid them all out so each day was scheduled in half-hour increments.

"Can I help with any of the black items?" I asked. Howard gave me a discreet headshake, indicating I was on thin ice.

"I've got it under control," Barbara replied. "You and Jenny are busy working, so I'll dive in to get the other things done."

"She's in heaven. Let her be," Howard said after Barbara left with her spreadsheet. "Do you have plans for a honeymoon?"

"We're going to take a long weekend next spring and drive the loop around Lake Superior," I replied.

"We'd be happy to have Jeremy stay with us for a few days," he said.

"That would be greatly appreciated."

Jenny took my arm and walked me into the hallway.

"Your mother whispered another bombshell to me," she said, obviously irritated. "She's going to pay for the groom's dinner."

"Why is that a problem?" I asked. "I assume the groom's dinner should be my treat."

"She's reserved a restaurant in Duluth. There's no way we can have the rehearsal, then drag everyone to Duluth for dinner and drinks, then be awake and ready for all the morning prep. You'll have to talk to her."

My mouth opened, but no words came. "Sure," I finally said. "I should probably go home to check on Dolores, then dream up diplomatic words I know Mother won't like."

CHAPTER 11
SUNDAY AFTERNOON

My street was mercifully quiet, devoid of any contractors' pickups and vans. The roofing was about half completed, with the remaining shingles stacked along the peak, ready for Monday morning. I parked in my driveway and walked into the house, expecting it to be empty and quiet, but I could hear the television when I opened the door and found Dolores sitting on my couch watching football.

"Hello," I said as I hung up my coat.

Dolores shushed me.

I slid onto the couch next to her, surprised that she had chosen to sit in my house, and doubly surprised that she was watching the football game. The Vikings were losing, no surprise, but had the ball and were driving down the field with less than a minute left in the game. The ball was snapped and Matt Asiata broke through the line without being touched and was racing toward the end zone.

"He could take it all the way," Dolores said, shifting to the edge of her seat.

An opposing player came into view and the race to the end zone was on. The commentators were excited and Dolores was in a trance, much as I'd seen from Jeremy when "Get Smart" was on. The players were converging and at the five-yard line they met. Asiata put out his hand and the defensive player lunged, punching the ball loose. There was a mad scramble in the end zone as time ran out. The referees were trying to sort out the pile as whistles blew.

"I think Asiata recovered his own fumble," Dolores said without looking away from the television.

After much pulling and more whistles, the pile of players was slowly pulled apart and the referee pointed toward the other end zone. The Vikings had lost the ball and time had run out.

"Damn," Dolores said. "I thought they were going to pull it out." She picked up the remote and turned off the television.

"I'm surprised you're over here watching the game."

"I've become rather accustomed to being over here. Your house is much cozier than mine. I've also found that I enjoy Jenny and Jeremy coming and going with all sorts of excitement. My house is just quiet and rather lonely. Plus, your TV is bigger and easier to see."

"Would you like a cup of coffee?" I asked.

"That would be lovely."

Dolores followed me into the kitchen and watched quietly as I made a pot of coffee and turned on the machine. She was sitting at my small Formica-topped table in what was becoming "her chair."

"A drop of half-and-half would be nice if you have it."

I checked the expiration date on the carton and set it on the table, then took two mugs out of the cupboard.

"You used to be busy entertaining and doing things with your friends," I said, bringing the carafe to the table and pouring coffee.

"My friends are either dead or senile," she said, looking for a spoon to stir the coffee. "I'm a bit at loose ends. Besides, you're so comfortable and easygoing." She held up the carton. "How clever of you to just set the carton on the table and not waste half and half by pouring it into a creamer. I always felt compelled to enter tain more formally. You have a very down-to-earth, functional lifestyle." She sighed, then admitted, "I'm tired of cooking for one. It's just not fun."

"Perhaps you should consider changing your living arrangement," I suggested, hoping that she'd catch the hint that Whistling Pines might be an acceptable option.

"It's so kind of you to offer your spare bedroom to me," she said. I choked on my coffee. "But you're going to need that space for Jeremy once you're married." She paused a beat, then asked, "Are you okay? You seem to be choking. Did your coffee go down wrong?"

I waved my hand as I gasped for a breath while mopping coffee off my shirt with a paper towel from the roll.

"See," she said, "that's the kind of thing I mean about your casual life. I'd have linen napkins out and you'd have stained them with coffee. It would never occur to me to keep a roll of paper towels on the table. Your life is so much simpler."

I was unsure if I'd been chastised, insulted, or complimented. I decided to accept the comment as a compliment and moved on. "Perhaps you could come to Whistling Pines for lunch someday. You could tour the place. There are people there to talk with and your meals would be prepared for you."

"Peter, there are old people there. I enjoy coming over here because you're young and I draw energy from you and Jenny. Jeremy has a little too much energy, but he's fun to watch. Besides, when I get tired I can walk home and go to bed."

"You'd have an apartment at Whistling Pines. When people want to be alone they return to their rooms, but if they prefer being sociable or engaging in the activities, they can choose to stay in the lobby or in one of the activity rooms. The choice is yours."

"I suppose a tour would be okay. Can you arrange it for me?"

"Certainly," I said. "I'll talk to the director when I'm at work tomorrow and she'll have someone call you to choose a time."

Dolores stood, almost too quickly.

"Is something wrong?"

"No, the Packers play at 3:15. I'm going back into the living room."

"Are you a Packers fan, too?"

"Heavens, no! I cheer for whomever is playing against them."

I put the coffee mugs in the sink and joined her on my green nylon-covered couch. It was a garage sale deal. The owner told me she'd had it since the 1960s and the nylon was so tough it looked like the day it had been delivered. I bought it because it was comfortable and I didn't find the pea-soup green offensive. Jenny has threatened to set it on the curb the day she moves in.

My cellphone chirped halfway through the third quarter and I walked to the kitchen to answer it.

"Peter," Mother said, "I've reserved the back room at the Pickwick Restaurant for Friday night. What time do you think you'll be through with the rehearsal?"

"There isn't time for the wedding party to drive to Duluth, eat supper, and return to Two Harbors after the rehearsal. We're having a small get-together at the VFW so everyone can get home early and be up in time for their Saturday morning commitments before the wedding."

"But I've already put a deposit down."

"It's not going to happen. We're going to the VFW. You should have asked us."

"But the VFW is so ... I hate to say tacky, but that's the word that comes to mind," Mother said with disdain.

"That's where I eat and drink with my friends, Mother."

"Oh."

"You became very quiet when I told the story about Alf and his family's coins," I said. "Why?"

"It just reminded me that there are some things I need to see a lawyer about."

"Like what?"

"Um, I'd rather not get into them right now. Let's get the

wedding behind us and we'll have years to talk about things."

"Do you have a cache of gold coins?"

"I have some modern gold coins in the safety deposit box," she replied. "They aren't collectible."

"Is there something I should know about them?"

"Nothing special."

"You're not going to send me clues that have to be solved to find them."

"Don't be silly, Peter. They're in the safety deposit box with a bunch of other things."

"So, no surprises about gold coins," I said.

"No. Not about gold coins," she replied.

"Not coins, but there's a surprise about something else?"

"I don't want to get into it now," she said.

I had a sudden, scary thought. "Are you bringing a date to the wedding?"

"Don't be silly. I might have someone escort me, but it wouldn't be a date."

"Who is escorting you, Mother?"

"I said I *might* have an escort. I didn't say that I *had* an escort."

"Who, Mother? Is it someone who will embarrass me or offend Jenny's parents?"

"I'm sure you haven't met him."

"Who is it, Mother?"

"The governor owes me a favor for my fund-raising, and he's such a great conversationalist. I'm sure everyone will enjoy him."

I took a deep breath and let it out slowly. "Don't you think that bringing the governor of Minnesota to the wedding might upstage the bride a bit?"

"I hadn't considered that," she said.

"Generally, the wedding day is considered the bride's day and I think it would be highly inappropriate to do something that would blatantly distract attention from Jenny on her special day."

"He's a communist!" Dolores yelled from the living room.

"You don't want him anywhere near your wallet."

"Who is that?" Mother asked.

"Dolores is over watching football."

"Your neighbor, Dolores, is watching football at your house?"

"Yes. Can we get back to the governor? Please call and free him from this commitment. I'm sure he has better things to do."

"You don't know how many arms I had to twist to get his calendar opened for this event," she said. "He even called me personally to accept the invitation. I can hear him now, saying, 'Audrey, I would be delighted to attend your son's wedding as your escort.'"

"How much did you have to pledge to his campaign fund to get his commitment?"

"You are so negative, Peter. Politicians sometimes like to show kindness to their supporters."

"Either you call his office and cancel, or I will."

There was a deep sigh. "Don't call. You'd embarrass me."

"If I called, I would be sure he wouldn't show up unexpectedly."

"Trust me. I'll call."

As soon as I ended Mother's call I called Jenny. "Just to let you know, Mother was planning to be escorted to the wedding."

"That's nice. Is she dating someone?"

"Um, not exactly. She asked the governor to escort her."

"What?"

"Take it easy. After a little discussion I got her to agree that she'll call him and cancel."

"It would be a circus. He has a state patrol escort and body-guard. They'd come in a limo with state patrol cruisers. I mean . . ."

"Take a deep breath. I told her to cancel. It'll be okay."

"You're sure she'll cancel? She wouldn't lie to you and then show up with him?"

"It'll be fine. I just told you because I thought it'd give you a chuckle."

"It's not funny. Please don't drop bombshells on me like that." Jenny paused, then asked, "Did you talk to her about the groom's dinner?"

"Yes, she's canceling the Pickwick too."

"She'd reserved the Pickwick. That's such a nice gesture, but it's just not workable."

"Yes, she knows."

"And to be clear, the Democratic governor of Minnesota is not coming to my wedding. Correct?"

"The governor is not coming."

"He's a communist!" Dolores yelled from the living room.

"Why is Dolores at your house?"

I lowered my voice. "She's watching football here because her house is too quiet and she likes the drama we provide."

"Oh dear. Please tell me this isn't the new reality of living there."

"I suggested that she take a tour of Whistling Pines. She asked me to set it up."

"That'd be better than having her camping out at our house. It's not that she's not kind and thoughtful, I just don't . . ."

"I know. It's taken care of."

CHAPTER 12
MONDAY MORNING

I slept in until 7:30, then made coffee. As I ate a bowl of cereal I heard slamming pickup doors and the rattle of aluminum ladders. The roofers had started their day. As I dressed I heard the banging of pneumatic nail guns on Dolores's roof. Seconds later, I heard the creak of my front door.

I'm sure there's a key for the front door somewhere, but I've never felt the need to lock it. My hair was still damp when I walked into the kitchen and found Dolores sitting at my kitchen table, tapping her fingers and looking irritated. She wore a long gray dress and black orthopedic shoes. Her permed blue-gray hair hadn't been brushed, making it flatter on one side.

"Would you like a cup of coffee?" I asked.

"That would be nice," she said. "I appreciate that the workmen are eager to get their work on my house completed, but I wish they'd wait until a decent hour before starting that infernal racket."

"They are trying to get your roof done before it gets colder or we have more snow. The weather often cuts their work-year short."

Dolores stirred cream into her coffee as she considered her words. "I suppose that's true. Just the same, this is not a decent hour. The sun is barely up."

"Do you like the work Tim Webb is doing inside?"

"He's a craftsman and is very picky. I like that in a workman. The pantry looks very nice, although he's going to have a hard time matching the dark shellac on the boards around his patch." She paused. "With all the food gone, it's so bare in there, it doesn't feel like my pantry anymore. I suppose I'll have to go shopping and restock some of the food staples when he's done. But I just don't have the energy to cook with all that clatter."

I answered a knock on the door and found Tim Webb holding my newspaper. "I thought I'd save you a trip," he said, handing me the paper.

"Would you like a cup of coffee?" I asked.

"I rarely turn down free coffee," he said with a smile. "Good morning, Mrs. Karvonen. I suppose the roofers woke you this morning."

"I was awake," she replied. "I just wasn't ready for the hullabaloo."

"They'll have all the shingles on today and they'll finish off the trim tomorrow."

"I suppose I'll stay here, at Peter's house." She picked up the newspaper and started reading.

"How are you doing on the inside?" I asked.

"I've removed the rot and completed the replacement patches. I need to put a finish on the wood, which is why I'm here." He turned to Dolores. "I think what would look best is if I have my flooring guy sand down the whole room and then I'll put down urethane. That way the whole room will look the same."

"Do whatever you think is best," Dolores said with a flip of the wrist, not looking up from the paper.

Tim looked at me and I nodded. "Do what you think is best."

"It's hard in these old houses," he said, sitting at the table. "Anything you patch doesn't match the area around it, so you redo lots of things. Ideally, I'd suggest sanding down all the wood flooring throughout the entire house so everything looks the same, but that's an expensive and messy process." He waited for Dolores to say something, but she just flipped to the next newspaper page. "So, I suppose we'll just do the two rooms with floor patches and cut off the refinishing at the door."

When Dolores didn't answer I said, "Okay."

"Your replacement window is here," he said. "I'll put it in after I get the flooring guy started. That'll brighten your kitchen up." He drank the last of his coffee and left.

"I just want them to be done so I can have my house back," Dolores said, looking up from the newspaper. "I'll gladly write them a check and bid them adieu."

"Are you certain you have enough in your checking account to pay them?"

"The banker says I do, and I don't argue with him. He seems to have a good grasp on my accounts and is trustworthy."

When I left, Dolores was working on a crossword puzzle. At Whistling Pines I checked the signup sheet for the birding trip. No one had cancelled due to Alf's death. I knocked on Nancy's door and stuck my head into her office. She set aside a stack of invoices and smiled.

"What can I do for you, Peter?" she asked.

"In light of Alf's death, I think we should cancel the bird-watching trip."

"Are people cancelling out?"

"No one other than Alf."

"Then let's go! It'll help people take Alf's passing off their minds."

"My neighbor, Dolores Karvonen, is thinking about moving out of her big house. Please call her and set up a tour so she can see Whistling Pines."

"I assume you also think it's time for her to move out of the house," said Nancy.

"She's struggling with upkeep and meal preparation, so Whistling Pines seems like a natural transition for her. She's spending the days at my house while the workmen finish her roof, so you can probably reach her there rather than at her house."

Breakfast was in full swing as I got a cup of coffee in the dining room. The staff was busily serving food and clearing tables. Miriam winked at me as she rushed past with a platter of hot caramel rolls. The most recent dining room hire, a middle-aged Korean woman named Soon Jung, moved among the tables with precision. Despite having English as a second language, she joked with the residents, quickly winning over their hearts.

Conversations, interspersed with laughter, filled the room. "Life goes on for the living," I said to myself. I saw Howard Johnson, Bud Bloomquist, and Lee Westfall sitting at a table. Howard pulled out a chair for me.

"I was just telling Howard and Lee about my new tattoo," said Bud. He had a large piece of gauze taped to his forearm. "It's going to be a couple of days before I can leave it uncovered," he said. "Say, you were in the Navy. Where's your tattoo?"

"I'm not a tattoo kind of guy," I replied.

Soon Jung leaned on my shoulder, "Can I get you some cream or sugar?" she asked.

"No thanks," I replied and she rushed off.

"I thought everyone in the Navy got tattooed, a rite of passage on your first shore leave. I heard everyone gets drunk and gets a tattoo."

"Peter was a corpsman," Howard explained. "He was with a Marine unit."

"What's a corpsman do?" Bud asked.

"I went with the Marines when they were on patrol. Mostly I bandaged blisters and treated heatstroke," I explained, not wanting to expand further.

"How many medals did you get for treating blisters?" Lee asked with a sly, knowing grin.

"They don't give medals for treating blisters," Bud said, then recognition swept his face. "You were with a combat unit and you were decorated. Funny, you don't look like the hero type."

"How is our junior sleuth today?" asked Howard, apparently trying to change the topic.

"That's how Howard has portrayed you," said Lee. "I expected you to be wearing a Dick Tracy secret decoder ring."

"Thanks for your votes of confidence," I replied. "But as long as we're on the topic, have any of you picked up any talk about who might've murdered Alf?"

Bud leaned forward, like he was going to tell me a secret. "I haven't heard a thing."

"It's like Alf was never here," said Lee. "People were a little subdued the day they found Alf's body, but it's like taking a scoop of water out of a lake — the hole fills in immediately and no one notices the loss."

"I suppose some miscreant overheard Alf bragging about his stash of gold," said Lee.

"It's not like he was trying to keep it a secret," said Bud. "He was telling everyone and asking opinions on the meaning of the clue."

"Tell me about Big Rock, the spot where they found Alf's body," I said.

"That's right," said Howard, "you're not from around here. Well, it's a well-known swimming hole that kids have been biking to for decades. The pool is actually a wide spot in the Little French River. The river has scoured away the riverbed below the rock, making a deep area where it's safe to dive. Everyone in town knows about it and I'd guess that three quarters of us have been there."

"Can you think of a reason why someone might hide a treasure there? It seems like it would be an awfully busy spot with a risk of someone finding it accidentally. Wouldn't it be safer to bury it in the woods somewhere?"

"Burying it in the woods would certainly be more secure," said Lee. "But how do you describe the spot so your children could find it? And, what happens if the woodsy hiding spot is sold and you don't have access to the land? I think it's brilliant! You're hiding it in a public area that's easy to describe and that any local person would be able to identify."

"So we can rule out anyone who didn't grow up here," I summarized.

"Unless Alf guided them to that spot," said Howard.

"So we haven't ruled out anyone."

"I heard he was killed with a pickaxe," said Lee. "That would rule out any of the female residents I would think."

"Don't be so quick about that," said Bud. "I think Mary Nielsen could swing an axe if she was mad."

"Only if you tell her she's fat again," said Howard, which brought guffaws from the trio.

"She clocked me good for saying that," said Bud. "I didn't know she was so touchy on the subject."

"Have you ever met a woman who wanted to hear someone say she was fat?" asked Howard.

"In Hawaii it's a sign of prosperity," said Lee.

"I'm pretty sure Mary's not Hawaiian," I said.

Wendy pulled out the fifth chair at our table and set down her crossword, ignoring the conversation.

"Good morning, Wendy," Howard and Lee said, in unison.

"I need a three-letter-word for pismire," she said.

"Ant," replied Howard.

She looked at me and I nodded.

She wrote the answer, then asked, "What's a four-letter word for old-style?"

"Dost," replied Howard.

"Home of the Cyclones?" asked Wendy.

"Ames," said Lee.

She looked at the three of us with a scowl. "What's with you guys? Was I sick the day they covered stupid trivia in high school?"

"Lifetime learning," replied Lee. "I also had two children and three grandchildren who graduated from Iowa State, which is the home of the Cyclones—Ames, Iowa."

"Peter, the police chief is in with Nancy," Wendy said as she wrote A-M-E-S. "I heard your name in passing."

"My cue," I said, rising from the chair.

"Don't forget your secret decoder ring," said Lee.

Len was sitting in one of Nancy's guest chairs when I knocked on the doorframe. Nancy waved me in and pointed to the other chair.

"I just told Nancy that the BCA is making slow progress on the evidence they collected," said Len. "Of the thousand fingerprints they checked in the AFIS database, ninety percent were Alf's and nearly all the rest were probably housekeepers or aides, who we would expect to be there. They're halfway through the prints, but their expectations are low that the killer left a fingerprint behind."

"What about the vacuumed samples?" I asked.

"You're learning," Len said with a smile. "Most of the recovered material was house dust and fibers from Alf's carpeting. Plus crumbs, paper fibers, and hair. There are two fibers that don't match anything in the apartment and they're trying to identify the source. They could be something innocent that Alf carried in on his feet, or something the killer left behind. I was talking to Jeff Telker, who is doing the fiber analysis, and he said that, on a microscopic level, every criminal leaves something behind, and *always* takes something with him or her.

"I spoke with Sonny, too. He's always . . . chatty. He kept working the whole time he was talking. He seems to know something about everything," Len said with a smile, "and, he's happy to share it all with anyone. I got the impression that his job is often solitary and he savors the opportunity to actually talk with someone."

"I didn't get five words in during our conversation," I said, then paused. "Chatty. I like that."

"His partner is not quiet either," said Len. "Jeff gets in his share of conversation. I don't think they have many quiet moments."

"On a different topic," said Nancy, "I had a call from Alf's son. We talked about removing Alf's furniture so we can paint the walls and scrub the carpeting. When can he get into the apartment?"

"I'll double-check with the BCA," said Len, "but I got the impression they were done with the crime scene. If that's the case, I could take down the crime scene tape and release the apartment to the family."

CHAPTER 13
MONDAY AFTERNOON

The aroma of pipe tobacco preceded Len's rap on my door. He walked in without invitation and cleared a chair by setting the stack of papers on the floor.

"I spoke with the BCA. They'll be back this afternoon. They want to get carpet fibers from all the other areas in Whistling Pines, and the van, so they can set aside fibers matching those that are known. They also want fingerprints from the staff who had access to Alf's room so they can be excluded."

"That's reasonable," I said. "I don't know why any of the staff would refuse to supply prints."

"Where else had Alf been in the days before the fire?"

"I took him on a couple of outings," I said, reflecting on the previous week. "He went with us to Judy's and on a tour of the North Shore Brewery. Those are the only ones I'm aware of. He may have gone somewhere with his family or other residents. We can check the sign-out sheet for that."

"I don't suppose the killer happened to sign in when he came visiting or signed Alf out when they left the building. Let's look at the guest register."

We walked to the lobby and located the guest register and sign-out logs on the reception desk. One of a rotating crew of high school students who answered phones and called residents when visitors came in was the receptionist of the moment. She was new and her temporary nametag said Amber. She nervously looked at Len, who was paging back through the visitor log.

"Is something wrong?" she asked.

"We're just checking to see if Alphonse Paluzzo had any visitors last Thursday or Friday," I replied.

"Friday was the day of the fire, right?" she asked.

"Right," I replied. "Did you work Friday?"

"Yes. That was really scary. I walked outside with a whole bunch of people from the dining room. I was lucky because I grabbed my coat before I went outside. There were lots of people who didn't have coats or jackets and they got cold really fast."

"No one for Alf in the guest register," said Len, setting the binder aside and flipping through the sign-out log.

"Would you recognize Mr. Paluzzo?" I asked.

"Not really," she replied. "There are only a few men, but the only names I remember are Howard Johnson and Bingle. He's the maintenance man." She paused, then blushed. "I remember you, too. You're Peter, right?"

Len spun the sign-out log around toward Amber. "There seems to be a page missing," he said, flipping the loose-leaf pages back and forth.

Amber stood and looked at the log. "The last person on this page left at 4:27 on Thursday afternoon," said Len. He flipped the page. "Then, the next entry is 7:55 Saturday morning. Where's the Friday page?"

Amber looked, then shrugged. "It's not a big deal. The sheets tear loose once in awhile. We usually put them back in, but they get out of order."

Len quickly flipped through the pages, looking for the missing page. "It's not in here," he said.

Another teenager walked into the lobby wearing a parka that looked suitable for the North Pole and UGG boots rimmed with fur. She walked to the reception desk and started peeling off layers. Her laminated name tag said Mindy.

"Hey, Mindy," said Amber. "Do you know what happened to the sign-out page for last Friday?"

"I have no idea," said Mindy, with a shrug. "That was the afternoon of the fire and it was just nuts in here. I'm surprised more stuff didn't get lost."

"Do either of you remember any strangers who came in that day?"

They both shook their heads. "Just the usual people coming and going," said Mindy as she slipped off her boots and put on a pair of tennis shoes.

"Uh uh!" said Amber. "There were lots of strange people here. There were firemen all over the place, and cops, and an ambulance with EMTs. It was chaos."

"Chaos," Len shook his head. "The perfect diversion. Peter, are you sure the fire wasn't set as part of a diversion?"

"Opal was pre-heating her oven. She almost died from the killer Tupperware smoke. I doubt the fire was deliberately set as a diversion."

"Did she have cookie dough sitting out, or did someone slip in and start the oven?" asked Len.

"I didn't notice any cookie dough," I replied. "I just assumed."

"I heard she had toffee in her oven and it leaked through the pan," Hulda Packer pushed her walker to the reception desk. "Everyone knows that toffee melts. You don't just put it on the oven racks."

"Hulda, it was Tupperware," I said patiently.

"What idiot bakes in Tupperware? You can't bake in Tupperware," Hulda stopped to think. I hoped she realized her mistake and we could move on. "You know, that's funny. Boy Scouts boil water in a paper cup over an open flame. I suppose you could bake in Tupperware."

I took a deep breath and blew it out slowly while I counted

to ten. Len clenched his pipe between his teeth and was using it to hide his smile.

"Where are you going, Hulda?" I asked.

"I'm not going anywhere. I'm talking to you about Tupperware."

"Would you go somewhere?"

"Why? I'm trying to help you understand the fire in Opal's oven. You said she was baking in Tupperware and I don't think it would start a fire if you baked in it."

"She wasn't baking in Tupperware. She pre-heated the oven. The Tupperware melted and started to burn."

"What was she going to bake? Was it chocolate cake? I like chocolate cake."

"I doesn't matter. Whatever she was going to bake never got into the oven because the Tupperware started to burn."

"Um, Peter," Amber said, tapping my shoulder. "My shift is over. Can I leave?"

"Sure," I said. "If you think of anyone unusual who was here before the fire, please let me know."

"I saw a stranger before the fire," said Hulda. "He carried a box in from the dock."

Hulda's memory and credibility were both questionable. "What kind of box?" I asked.

"A brown box," she replied.

I bit my lip. "Was it a big box, a medium box, or a small box?"

Hulda cocked her head. "No."

"No?"

"What don't you understand about no?"

"I asked how large a box the man carried in. You said no."

"It wasn't large, medium, or small," she replied.

"Tell me, Hulda. What size box was he carrying?"

"It was tiny."

"Was he wearing a uniform, like UPS or FedEx?" I asked.

"He was just wearing street clothes."

"Did he drop off the box at the reception desk?" I asked.

"No, he walked to the elevators and went upstairs."

"How long before the fire did that happen?" Len asked.

Hulda thought. "About a day. Yes, I think it was Wednesday," she replied.

"The fire was Friday," I said.

"Well," she said in a huff, "he probably had nothing to do with the fire." She spun her walker around and joined a group of women waiting for the mailman to finish dispensing mail.

The BCA mobile crime lab pulled under the portico and Sonny and Jeff got out. Sonny was carrying a toolbox. Len and I met them at the door.

"Hi, guys. Thanks for coming back."

"We need to fingerprint the staff to exclude them," Jeff said. "Where can we set up?"

"We're between meals, so we can use a table in the dining room. Come this way," I said.

"Doing this is fun," said Sonny. "I get to talk to innocent people, which beats the heck out of dealing with lying felons."

He opened the toolbox and took out a stack of fingerprint cards and an inkpad. "Bring on the staff. I can start with you, Peter."

Within five minutes there were four people in line and Nancy was chasing down the rest of the staff members. Sonny was chatting up everyone who came through.

"Your last name is Peterson?" he asked Roger Peterson as he printed information on a card. "I'm related to the Petersons in Mahtowa. There were five Peterson brothers who moved here from Sweden and they had lots of children and grandchildren. Every time I meet someone named Peterson I assume we're related."

Jenny stepped up next and gave her name. "Well, I'm pretty sure we're not related," he said as he inked her fingers and rolled them on the card. "Wait, you're Peter's fiancée! You guys are getting married this weekend. That's great! I've been married to the same woman for thirty-eight years and I wouldn't trade a moment of it."

"Sonny, are we done? I need to get back to my patients."

"Sure," he said. "Good luck Saturday. Next!"

Jeff and Len were standing next to the dining room door. "It's good that you got here during the shift change so we can catch virtually all the staff in an hour," I said.

"Take me out to the Whistling Pines van so I can get a carpet sample," said Jeff.

I put my coat on and led Jeff and Len to the van. Jeff took out a pair of tweezers and pulled a few fibers from the van's floor.

"Is this the site of the unfortunate incident?" Jeff asked as he dropped the fibers into an evidence bag and labelled it.

I glared at Len, who was smiling.

"Yes," I said, "but that has nothing to do with the murder investigation."

Jeff sniffed the bag before taping it shut. "You can hardly tell," he said with a smile. "Did Alf have a car?" he asked.

"He didn't drive anymore," I said. "His son took it away about a year ago."

Back inside, I led Jeff around Whistling Pines where he pulled a few carpet fibers from each of the common areas. Sonny was packing up the fingerprinting supplies when we returned. He had just finished alphabetizing the cards and was ready to leave.

"Okay," he said, closing the toolbox. "I've got to compare these to our unknown prints and narrow down the list of subjects."

"The victim's son asked if he could pack up the apartment," said Len. "Can I release it and remove the seal?"

"Sure," said Jeff. "We got everything we need."

After the BCA guys left, I walked to Alf's room with Len. He removed the tape on the doorjamb and unlocked the door. The apartment was too hot and smelled musty. I opened a window and let the cold wind blow in for a minute. Len stood at the end of the hallway and stared at the living area. His pipe was clamped between his teeth. I arranged Alf's bills in a stack while Len packed his pipe bowl. I started collecting the assorted holiday cards, which were harder to arrange because they varied greatly in size.

I heard Len's lighter strike and looked up. He puffed on the pipe several times before he was satisfied that it was lit.

"I know it's not allowed," he said, putting the lighter back in his pocket. "I thought the pipe smoke would smell better than the stuffy apartment."

I found a wad of plastic shopping bags under the kitchen sink and put the letters and cards in separate bags, then set them on the kitchen table next to salt and pepper shakers. I took the cardboard box that had been next to Alf's chair the last time I saw him and gathered the stamp albums and put them in the box.

"Did Alf strike you as a stamp collector?" Len asked.

"No. I think he said it was his uncle's collection," I said, setting the box on the table next to the bags of cards. I thought for a minute. "Alf said he was only into hockey and girls before the Army. Those don't seem to mesh well with stamp collecting."

I took out a stamp album and opened it on the table. "These are pages and pages of stamps, from Eastern Europe, many from countries that didn't exist after World War I. The denominations are tiny, some just fractions, and the paper is yellowed."

Len watched as I opened another album filled with Colonial African stamps. They all appeared to be very old. I opened each of the albums and flipped through the pages. Each was dedicated to a different region of the world: Asia, Europe, Africa, Australia, New Zealand, and North and South America. One album was only U.S. postage stamps. Inside the front cover was written "Salvadore Rizzo, Hibbing."

"Who do you suppose Sal Rizzo was?" Len asked. "Whoever he was, he's probably dead. Most stamp collectors start as kids, and the owner of this collection was probably a kid very early in the 20th century."

I took out my smartphone and searched for the name Rizzo in

Hibbing. The search didn't yield any results. I flipped through the envelopes, looking at the return addresses.

"Here's a letter to Anita Paluzzo from Carmen Rizzo. The postmark is from Hibbing." I flipped through more envelopes and found a square one, apparently from a card. It too was addressed to Anita Palluzo with a Hibbing postmark.

I quickly sorted through the cards and found cards the same size as the envelopes. "This one says to 'My daughter, Anita.'"

"So, Alf's mother's maiden name was probably Rizzo," said Len. "I suppose the stamp collection belonged to her brother, Alf's uncle. Not a big mystery."

I loaded the albums back into the box and straightened the furniture so the room looked much like it had when I'd last seen Alf.

"The search seems to have been focused on the living room. Everything else seems to be untouched," Len said, looking into the bedroom. He turned back toward the living room and sucked on the pipe, which had burned out. "No way to know what's missing."

"Other than the family Bible. We know that's gone," I said.

"Other than the Bible, and that's where Alf thought the clue was hidden," said Len. "Do you know if he ever found the clue?"

"Last time I spoke with him, he'd been through the whole Bible looking for a note, then read the Song of Solomon and hadn't found anything. He said he was going back through the chapter, and if he didn't find something he was going to go through the whole Bible again, page by page."

"He must've found something," said Len. "Otherwise, why would the killer drag him out to the Big Rock?"

I shrugged and looked at my watch. "I've got to run back home. The guys should be wrapping up Dolores's roof."

"Does she appreciate all you do for her?" Len asked.

"Jenny found a hidey hole in her pantry with stock certificates and a bag of old coins. Dolores gave the coins to Jeremy for his college fund. I think they're worth sixty grand."

Len whistled. "That's a nice start on a college fund."

"She's been very kind to me since I moved in. She used to bake casseroles and desserts. Luckily, that's stopped."

"Why is that lucky?"

"Most of them were inedible," I replied. "But her intent was good."

CHAPTER 14
MONDAY EVENING

When I pulled onto my street, I could see that the Dumpster of roofing materials was gone and the crew was loading their tools and ladders onto their trucks. Tim Webb's van was still in Dolores's driveway but there was no sign of him. Inside my house I found Dolores watching "Dr. Phil." I stepped into the kitchen, which was now brighter with the new, clean window.

"The roofers are done. They're packing up their tools."

"Yes, the foreman was over and I gave him a check."

"Was it for the amount of his estimate?" I asked.

"That nice Tim Webb assured me it was fair. That's all I needed to know."

"Did that tap out your finances?"

"I don't believe so," she replied. "I took those stock certificates we found in the pantry to the broker and he said it would take some time to determine their value, but he was certain that legacy corporations exist and they have value."

"What's a legacy corporation?" I asked.

"Could you make a pot of coffee? I could use a jolt of caffeine."

As I made coffee she explained, "When companies are acquired, their stock doesn't go away, it becomes a part of the parent company and the old company is a legacy. The acquisition usually results in cash or parent-company stock. In some cases, it appeared that the companies represented by my stock certificates were acquired by even bigger companies and it'll take a while to determine which fish ate which minnow and how many dollars or shares resulted from each of those transactions."

"But he felt they did have some cash value," I said, putting cups on the table.

"He followed one of the train companies through several mergers and he thought my shares were probably worth several thousand shares of Union Pacific Railway. Some of the mine ownership was harder to trace. There have been many changes of ownership and bankruptcies. It's harder to say if those shares have any value."

"Would you like to tour Whistling Pines tomorrow?" I asked, changing the topic.

Dolores took a deep breath and let it out. "That nice Nancy called, but I'm not sure I'm ready to move out of my house."

"That's fine. A tour commits you to nothing. It's just information and a free lunch."

"Do you think I could bring Etta Parker along? She enjoys free lunches."

"I'm sure they'd be happy to have both of you. I'll call and set it up."

"No, Peter. You're busy. I'll have to talk with Etta to see when she's available. I'll call Whistling Pines after we compare calendars." Dolores stirred cream into her coffee and asked, "Are your wedding plans all set?"

"I guess a bunch of people haven't returned their RSVP cards so we're not sure how many people are coming."

"People have no manners anymore. I returned mine the day it arrived." She paused. "Yes, I'm sure I returned it. Could you call Jenny and make sure they know I'm coming? I suppose it might've gotten lost in the mail somewhere. I'd hate to have your new in-laws think I was a slacker who couldn't return an RSVP card."

"I saw your name on the list," I lied.

"Good! I haven't lost my mind."

There was a knock on the door and Tim Webb walked in without waiting for me to open the door.

"Coffee?" I asked.

"Certainly," he said. "I thought I smelled it from next door."

"How much do I owe you for the window?" I asked.

Dolores waved the question off. "I broke the window. I paid."

Tim nodded, then said, "The flooring guys will be here tomorrow to sand. It'll be very dusty and noisy. Is there a place you could go for the day, Mrs. Karvonen?"

"I imagine Peter wouldn't throw me out if I came over and watched television on his couch."

"That's fine," I said. "I have to work all day so I won't even know you're here unless you leave crumbs."

"I've had a bit of a cold," she said. "Every time I sneeze I squirt a little. You might have to get the couch cleaned after I've gone."

I spun around with Tim's cup, slopping coffee and apparently looking shocked. Dolores was smiling. "Gotcha."

"Could you top my coffee off?" Tim asked, smiling widely. "I think you slopped half of it on the floor."

CHAPTER 15
TUESDAY MORNING

The morning was silent. No roofers banging ladders and no pounding of nails. I showered, shaved, and made coffee. The expiration date on the milk should have been okay but I sniffed it and poured it out. It was time to move on to toast. I found a loaf of bread in the refrigerator, but it too was evolving into a new life form. I chucked it too.

No eggs. No bacon or sausage. I found a box of Pop-Tarts left behind from one of Jeremy's visits. I didn't bother to check the expiration date. Pop-Tarts are indestructible and will survive in landfills forever alongside Twinkies. I picked up the newspaper from the driveway while the coffee brewed.

The headline on the front page of the *Duluth News Tribune* was about the future of the Duluth Central High School building. Below the fold was a small article about Alf's death with quotes from the Lake County sheriff and an unidentified source in the BCA. The sheriff said they were following several leads. The BCA said they hadn't finished analyzing the evidence and wouldn't speculate on suspects until their analysis was complete.

At Whistling Pines I found a note Nancy had left on my chair. Alf's son was driving up and she wanted me to take him up to the apartment and help him if needed. I checked the calendar and realized I had to put gas in the van and reconfirm all the planned stops before our Wednesday trip to Zim.

I kept my coat on and took out the van keys. The van was cold, balked at starting, and felt like it had square tires until it warmed up. I briefly considered leaving the engine running when I paid, but decided it was officially illegal and I'd never hear the end of it if someone took it while I was inside. That would be more than I could face. I didn't need another unfortunate incident since the first one was apparently still fresh in everyone's minds.

Amber, the receptionist, flagged me down as soon as I walked into the lobby. "Peter, there's a man waiting to see you. I sent him into the dining room for a cup of coffee."

Breakfast was winding down, but there were still several tables of residents sipping coffee and chatting. A lone middle-aged man sat at a table scrolling through screens on his smartphone. I drew a mug of coffee and sat down across from him. He was so engrossed in his phone he didn't acknowledge me.

"I'm Peter. The receptionist said you were looking for me."

The man who looked up bore a vague resemblance to Alf — younger, red-rimmed eyes, a jaundiced pallor to his sagging skin. I assumed he was in his fifties, but he looked like he was closer to seventy. He was wearing a plaid shirt stained with several varieties of food and green work pants that were stained with grease or oil. The clothes were all baggy, like he'd recently lost weight.

"Oh. Sorry," he said, pushing the phone into his pocket. "I'm Gary Paluzzo." He didn't offer his hand for a handshake.

"I'm sorry about your loss," I said, feeling stupid for not coming up with a more original line.

"Whatever happened wasn't your fault," he said, picking up his cup and tipping it back, only then remembering it was empty.

"Would you like a refill?"

"Naw. I drank a Big Gulp Mountain Dew on the way up. I don't need more caffeine."

"Would you like to go up to your father's apartment?" I asked.

"How bad is it?" he asked.

"How bad?" I asked.

"I heard he was attacked there. Is it bloody?"

"It appeared there was a struggle but there's no blood. I picked up the papers and set the furniture in place. It looks like it did before."

Gary steeled himself and stood. "No time like the present."

We rode the elevator and walked to Alf's apartment in silence. I unlocked the door and held it for him. Inside, he looked around like he was seeing it for the first time.

"Did you visit Alf often?"

"I helped him move in and came up for Christmas the first couple years," he said, looking around without stepping into the living room. "Things got busy and he wasn't a happy man. It was easier not to drive up to listen to an hour of prattle over supper at Betty's Pies."

"Your dad had been going through a box of material he'd brought up from the storage locker. I put it on the table over here." I led him to the table. "Letters here. Cards in this bag. Stamp collection in the box."

Gary slid the bag of letters closer and flipped through them idly. "The medical examiner said Dad might've been killed over some old coins."

"There was the rumor of some old coins," I said. "Your dad got a call from one of your cousins, who said he had a letter from your grandmother telling her sons to cooperate on the recovery of some money. There was a clue that was supposed to have meaning to your father. He was digging through your family Bible trying to find the clue."

"I don't see the Bible."

"It disappeared with Alf."

"So the killer has the clue and probably knows where the coins are," he summarized.

"I suppose so," I said. "Although he tried digging at the site of your dad's murder and it doesn't look like he found anything."

I pushed the box of stamp albums toward him. "These are interesting."

He opened the cover of the first album and looked at the name inside. "Dad had Uncle Sal's stamp collection? I didn't know that." He threw the album idly back into the box.

"You seem surprised."

"Grandma talked about it when I was a little kid, but I never knew what happened to it."

"Alf didn't strike me as a stamp collector."

"The stamps were a family joke. Grandma tried to give them to everyone, but none of us were interested." He paused. "I guess I'm still not interested."

"They're really old," I said, opening the European album. "Half of these countries don't even exist anymore."

"You sound like you care," he said, picking up the box. "They're yours." He handed the box to me.

"But they might be valuable," I protested.

"Knock yourself out if you can figure how to make a buck out of them. I don't want to deal with them."

"Maybe your sister . . ."

"My sister lives in a starter mansion with her banker husband. They aren't into anything antique. In her words, 'Antique means something past its life expectancy.' Her house is a showplace of modern architecture and art. Old stamps don't fit her lifestyle."

He looked around the apartment. "Can you arrange for some charity to pick up the furniture?"

"I'm sure some group will want it."

He picked up the bags of letters and cards and tucked them under his arm. "That's it, I guess. Can you take me back to the lobby? I forgot to drop breadcrumbs on the way here."

"Sure," I said. I locked the door and led him to the elevator. He appeared to be on the verge of tears, but held it in at least until he was out the door. I watched him walk to his car. He sat in it for several minutes and appeared to be sobbing while reading through the letters.

"Who's that?" Jenny asked as she stood next to me.

"Alf's son is in the parking lot reading through his dad's old letters and crying."

"When is he coming back to pack up the apartment?"

"He's not coming back. He asked me to find a charity to pick up the furniture."

———— ◆ ————

Back in my office I looked up charities online and found the Disabled American Vets. Their website said they picked up clothing and household goods. The man I spoke with sounded like he was a very old smoker. He seemed excited about an apartment full of furniture and said they'd have the truck stop on Thursday.

CHAPTER 16
WEDNESDAY MORNING

I was out the door without bothering to brew coffee or even eat a Pop-Tart. I scraped the thick layer of frost from my windshield and the middle sections of the side windows, then headed for work.

I rushed to the dining room for a cup of coffee, then raced to my office to get the van keys, the sign-up list, and the travel itinerary. The first residents were coming down for breakfast when I grabbed a second cup of coffee. Howard Johnson cornered me near the aviary.

"You're really going ahead with the bird-watching trip?" he asked, with the lovebirds cooing their approval in the aviary behind us.

"That's the plan," I said.

"It's going to be a long day with a bunch of cranky old ladies."

I looked at the sign-up list and verified that Alf had been the only male resident on the list.

"I have the trip all plotted out and the residents are lining up." I pointed to three women standing near the door with binoculars hanging from their necks. Nancy emerged from her office with her own binoculars, and locked her door.

"Oh," said Howard seeing Nancy. "Your options are limited. I hope there isn't a repeat of the unfortunate incident."

I started the van and drove it under the portico. When I returned to the lobby nearly all my passengers were gathered around the door. I got their attention and announced, "Okay, the first leg of our trip will be about two hours. We'll stop to stretch our legs and use the restrooms. The next stop will be at Eveleth for lunch. We'll spend two hours driving around Zim, then we'll stop again for stretches and restrooms, then the last leg home in time for supper in the dining room. Are there any questions?"

"Where are we eating lunch?" a voice asked from the back.

"We'll stop at the Wilbert Café."

"Oh, dear. They only have one women's bathroom and it's barely big enough to turn around."

"They're willing to accept a van full of senior citizens and the food is good. Work with me."

"We can go there, but I won't be happy."

I held up my hand to get everyone's attention. "Give me your name as you board and I'll check you off the list."

One by one, the passengers loaded, with Nancy boarding last. "I hope this goes better than the last field trip I went on," she whispered to me.

"What happened on that trip?"

"We went to a church luncheon and everyone got food poisoning." She smiled at me and climbed the steps.

We drove south, through Duluth, with the ladies happily chatting among themselves. The first two hours flew by and we were at our first bathroom stop in what seemed like no time. The group unloaded as I put gas in the van. A school bus full of adults, all armed with binoculars, was gassing up on the opposite side of the pumps.

"Are you going to Zim?" I asked the driver.

"Second trip this week," she replied. "I've had people from all over the world riding with me. It's funny to hear people shouting out in three or four languages as they call out the birds they're seeing."

"I'm not sure exactly where to go when we get there," I said. "I figured that we'd just drive the roads around the area and hope for the best."

"There'll be a few buses there. Just fall into the caravan and stop when we stop. That usually means there's something to see."

There was still a line at the women's restroom when I paid. I tried the men's room door and found it locked. I waited and waited. Three women came and went from the ladies' room before I finally heard the toilet flush in the men's room, followed by the sound of running water.

I was surprised when Blanche Brown walked out of the men's room door. "Weren't any men in line when I went in," she said, before pushing past me. Nancy was the last person in the women's line and she laughed out loud.

I took a head-count as people straggled out of the convenience store, many with coffee in Styrofoam cups and some with pastries. The line ended with Nancy but I was still one person short. "Was Skipper Swanson in the restroom?" I asked.

"I'll check," she said, trotting off.

She returned unaccompanied. "I looked all over. There was no sign of her."

"We can't leave without her," I said. "Can you make another trip through, just in case she's hunkered down in an aisle?"

"I'll stay here and you look this time," she said.

I wandered the aisles of snacks, beverages, food, eggs, and fresh baked goods. I knocked and rattled the door on the men's and women's restrooms and found nothing. I walked out the back door and looked at a field leading to woods.

When I came out the front door, trying to formulate a plan, Nancy was waving to me.

She pointed to the yellow school bus pulling out of the parking lot. "Blanche got on the wrong bus," Nancy said. "They brought her back and we all laughed."

I wasn't laughing. We'd lost half an hour and we'd be hard-pressed to return to Two Harbors before the dining room closed.

———— ◆ ————

As we unloaded at the Wilbert Café, I warned the group that we only had half an hour. I could tell my words were falling on deaf ears as the chatting riders trooped into the restaurant. There were only two other cars in the lot and they apparently belonged to the cook and a waitress. My ladies quickly found tables and ordered. While waiting for their meals, an orderly line formed at the restroom.

I ordered a pasty. "Can I get gravy with it?"

"They normally come with ketchup," the young waitress replied. "I can ask the cook if she has any gravy."

The waitress disappeared and I took out my map and reviewed the route to Zim. From the kitchen I heard commotion followed by a loud voice. "I haven't got any gravy. Tell him to eat it like any good Catholic boy, with ketchup."

The waitress returned, looking sheepish. "Um, there isn't any gravy. Will ketchup be okay, or would you like to order something else?"

"Ketchup will be fine," I replied. The cook was still muttering in the kitchen and I could hear snippets of her grumbling about people from offbeat religions wanting gravy. "Gravy! Who in hell would ruin a pasty by putting gravy on top of it? His mother obviously neglected his training. Gravy! Where in hell would I find gravy?"

Nancy returned from the restroom and took a chair alongside me. "I hear you stirred up a hornet's nest with the cook."

"I like gravy on my pasty, but I can live with ketchup."

"You'd better hope she isn't so pissed off that she spits in your pasty," said Nancy, smiling.

"Thanks," I said.

The food orders started coming out almost immediately and the

conversations waned. Nancy's cheeseburger and fries smelled wonderful and juice was running out of the bun. My pasty was the last
item served and the waitress set a ketchup bottle on the table.

"This is really okay?" she asked.

"I'll live with it. Thanks."

Although senior citizens generally tend to eat slowly, the
first people were through with their lunches moments after my
pasty arrived. More passengers lined up for the single bathroom
and they soon began to fidget as I wolfed down the last bites of
a lovely crusty pasty. The women started paying their bills and
the waitress was soon swamped and confused. Arguments broke
out about who had ordered which meal, and about the cost of
the meals. After everyone paid and left their tips I went out and
started the van. As it idled the women lined up and I checked
the head count against the list of riders and was relieved when it
came out correctly. I watched Nancy thank the waitress and cook
before jamming an extra twenty dollar tip in each of their hands.

We were back on the road in thirty-five minutes, a new record
for people who like to linger over their meals.

As we approached the Sax/Zim area on Arkola Road the
houses started to thin and the patches of woods became forest.
I fell in behind a slow moving school bus and followed past the
Sax Greenhouse, which appeared to be the only remnant of the
original town. We turned left onto County Road 28. From there,
we turned onto a smaller gravel road and the bus slowed. When
it came to a stop I was tempted to pass, but then saw the bus
leaning to the right and realized what was going on.

"Look on the right side," I called out.

"Where? What are we looking at? I don't see anything."

"There's a hawk-owl! In that pine tree."

"Which pine tree? I only see pine trees!"

"On the bare branch of the tallest tree. On the right side."

I was amazed as the ladies gasped at the sight of the owl.
The bus started to move, but my passengers were still trying

to spot the owl and get pictures. The owl decided to move on and he spread his barred wings and flew right at the bus, passing overhead by a few feet.

"Wow! Did you see the brown stripes on his belly?"

Convinced that everyone had seen the owl, I drove ahead, trying to catch up with the bus. It was still a hundred yards ahead when it stopped and the passengers shifted to the left. I got close and watched a ruffed grouse walking under the boughs of a nearby balsam fir.

"It's a damned partridge. I've seen a thousand of them," someone called out.

"The official name is ruffed grouse," someone corrected.

"Partridge or grouse, it's all the same."

"Look! There's a black-backed woodpecker in the tree just right of the grouse!"

I heard murmurings and felt the van shift as my passengers took turns moving to the windows so everyone could check that bird off their lists. The bus started moving again and I followed. It stopped abruptly and I had to jam on the brakes, generating a round of grumbling from my passengers. The bus shifted left again.

"Look on the left, ladies," I said.

"What are we looking at? I don't see anything."

"There's a black-billed cuckoo! It's flying ahead of us!"

Conveniently, the bus moved ahead slowly and I followed, keeping the cuckoo in sight. We stopped again and the bus kept leaning left.

"The cuckoo is gone. Why are we stopped?"

There was a gasp from the back and I turned to see if someone had fallen. The whole group was looking out the windows through binoculars. A couple of women were snapping pictures with their digital cameras.

"I can't believe it! There's a great gray owl!"

The scenario played out over and over through the next two hours. The bus stopped and we'd search the trees for whatever bird the bus riders had seen. Birds were being checked off lifetime lists quickly.

"I haven't checked off this many birds in one day since I bought my *Field Guide to the Birds of North America* when I was nineteen," someone said from the rear.

After two hours we'd checked off seventeen birds and we'd come to Zim Road.

"Okay ladies," I said, "we have to turn here and go back to Two Harbors."

There was a collective groan, but no arguments as I turned the van east onto the blacktop road. We drove a mile and Ginny Johnson slid into the seat behind me.

"Do you want to see Alf's family home?" she asked.

"Do you know where it is?"

"I grew up near the sod farm and we used to wander these back roads. Every old house was known by the name of the last family who lived there."

She directed me to a narrow, poorly maintained road within sight of Highway 53. The trees had overtaken the few deserted houses on the road, indicating their abandonment had been decades earlier. A single set of tire tracks were visible in the gravel.

"That next house, on the right," she said.

There was a path with fresh footprints leading from the road to the house. I stopped the van and got out.

"Where's the bird?" someone asked as the van shifted to the right.

I followed the footprints through the weeds to the house. Stepping through a broken door that lacked a knob I nearly fell on my face. I pulled back. Someone had recently pulled up all the floorboards. The wall covering and insulation had been pulled down, exposing the outside boards, as had the ceiling. A bedspring lay in one corner, resting on the bare floor joists covered in the debris torn from the walls. I couldn't see anything of value. I followed the footprints to an old outhouse that had been tipped over.

There were marks where someone had tried to dig in the pit. The tracks went no further than the outhouse, so I retreated to the van.

"What did you see?" asked Nancy when I returned to the van.

"Someone stripped the house to the studs," I said, closing the door to warm up.

"I've heard about people stealing the pipes and wiring out of old houses," said Evelyn Sampson.

"This was more than that. Every space that could hide something had been ripped open."

I pulled out my cellphone and dialed Len's number. I stepped outside as the phone rang.

"What's up, Peter?" he asked, apparently checking the caller ID for my name.

"I'm at Alf's house in Zim. Someone has stripped it to the walls."

"Those old houses are always getting stripped. It's sad."

"No, Len. There are fresh tracks and the floorboards were recently broken out. I think someone has been treasure hunting. They even tipped over the outhouse and dug in the pit."

I heard Len sigh. "What are the odds that it's Alf's killer?"

"Do you believe in coincidences?" I asked.

"You're in Zim?" he asked.

"On a township road about a quarter mile off Zim Road," I replied.

"I'll call the St. Louis County sheriff and ask him to send a squad, then I'll see if I can pull the BCA techs in again. If this is just vandalism I'll be eating crow."

"I don't think crow is on the menu."

"Can you stay there until the county gets someone out?"

"I'm in the van with a load of bird-watchers who need to be back in time for dinner." I looked at the van and could see the ladies were already restless. "Tell you what, I've got an orange cone in the back. I'll set it at the edge of the driveway."

I drove to the gas station on Highway 53. The ladies rushed for the convenience store and the bathroom while I put gas in the van. I was paying inside when a St. Louis County cruiser parked in front of the door. A deputy who was tall, trim, and sporting a military haircut stepped into the station. His face was deeply tanned. He looked around before locking eyes with me.

"Are you Peter, from Whistling Pines?" he asked.

I offered my hand, "Peter Rogers, the recreation director from Whistling Pines."

"Tom Norton," he said, shaking my hand.

"Freshly returned from the Far East?" I asked.

"Iraq," he replied. "Does it show?"

"Your tan has the same pattern I saw on my own head when I was wearing a helmet all day."

"Army or Marines?" he asked.

"Navy corpsman."

He cracked a smile. "One of the crazy idiots who went into combat without a weapon."

Evelyn Sampson came around the corner and froze when she saw the deputy. She edged forward slowly. "Is he here to talk with you about the unfortunate incident?"

"No, Evelyn," I replied. "I think Deputy Norton is here to talk about the vandalism at Alf's house."

She nodded and wandered down a different aisle, looking over her shoulder.

"I take it that Whistling Pines is some sort of retirement place."

"It's called assisted living. We provide independent living with people preparing their own meals or eating in a dining room."

"Tell me why the recreation director is interested in a vandalized house in Zim."

I explained Alf's treasure hunt, his murder, and how the vandalism to the house looked like someone was searching for something.

"The dispatcher said the BCA was sending a team. They asked me to watch the scene until they showed up." He looked at the line of women at the cash register, each with a cup of coffee and about half with a pastry from the homemade selection in a case next to the register.

"Are these your passengers?" he asked.

"Yes. I brought them here to go bird-watching."

"You're shitting me. Bird-watching? I know some people are into that now, but I think it should be a summer sport."

Evelyn edged up to us and whispered, "We were looking for arctic birds that winter here. I added eleven new sightings to my lifetime list." She sidled away and slipped through the door to join the line forming next to the van.

"I've seen the buses, but I thought they were schoolkids taking field trips. I'll be damned. Adult bird-watchers."

Nancy tapped my shoulder. "Give me the keys and I'll start the van so we can load our passengers." She took a step, then turned. "Don't worry. I won't allow another unfortunate incident to occur."

"She's the second person to mention an unfortunate incident. What's that all about?"

I waved off the question. "It's an inside joke and wouldn't make any sense to you."

He shrugged. "So, how likely is it that I'll see the vandal again?"

"I think the house is totally trashed. If there was anything to be found, it's gone. All you can do is make sure someone doesn't mess with it before the BCA gets here."

"It's cold out. Whoever did the damage was wearing gloves. What evidence do you think they'll find?"

"I don't know. Just give them a chance before anyone else messes with it."

———— ◆ ————

I pulled under the Whistling Pines portico at 6:15 with a van full of tired women and one tired driver. Some went directly to the dining room while others returned to their apartments to stow their coats and binoculars. Nancy was the last one off the van.

"Long day," she said, "but I'd say it was a success. Most of the women were very pleased with the trip and the chance to check so many birds off their lifetime lists."

"Evelyn seemed rather taken with the deputy at the gas station," I said.

Nancy leaned close. "She told me she put her phone number in his pocket."

"You're kidding."

"I think she was serious."

I was speechless.

"Park the van and go home," she said, patting my shoulder. "And thanks. I had a good time too."

———— ◆ ————

When I turned onto my street I could see the lights burning in my house and thought Dolores was probably waiting for me. When I got closer I could see Jenny's car and I smiled. I could smell bacon frying as soon as I stepped out of the car.

"Hi, honey, I'm home," I called out as I hung my coat and kicked off my shoes. I turned the kitchen corner and saw Jenny at the stove and Dolores sitting at the table. My heart sank.

"Dolores called me at work and asked if she could stay here tonight," Jenny said.

The table was set for three and the toast, lettuce, and sliced tomatoes told me the menu was BLTs. I sat across from Dolores, who looked grumpy.

"My house stinks," she said.

"Did they put the urethane on the floor?" I asked.

"I don't know what they did, but it stinks and I can't stand to be in there."

"I'll go over and get some night things for you," said Jenny as she piled bacon onto a paper towel. "You can stay in Peter's spare bedroom as long as you want."

I glanced at her, knowing that she was doing the kind thing, but dreading the outcome. I looked at Dolores, hoping that her fierce independence would come through and she'd refuse the offer.

"Thank you, dear," said Dolores. "That would be very nice."

"How was the bird-watching?" Jenny asked as she assembled a sandwich for Dolores.

"Evelyn Sampson gave her phone number to a St. Louis County deputy."

"No way!" Jenny exclaimed.

"She put it in his pocket when I was talking with him in a gas station."

"What's the matter with that?" Dolores asked. "It's a new century and the rules have changed."

"Evelyn is close to eighty," I explained, "and the deputy was maybe thirty."

"What do they call that?" Dolores asked. "Oh yes, she's a cougar!"

We all laughed.

After dinner I washed dishes while Jenny took Dolores next door to pick up some unmentionables. They came back with a small suitcase that they took to the spare bedroom. After a few minutes Jenny returned and took me by the hand to the kitchen door.

"Dolores apologized, but she's too tired to socialize anymore tonight."

I put my arm over Jenny's shoulder and pulled her close. "Do you think this is a short-term arrangement, or do you think she'll never go back again?"

"It's too early to tell," she replied. "It really does smell at her house and I don't blame her for wanting to be out of there for the night. On the other hand, she's not happy living alone either and she's concerned about her ability to keep up that huge old house."

"She's touring Whistling Pines. I think she'd enjoy the socialization if she moved there."

"She's afraid of losing her independence," Jenny said. "But she also told me that most of her friends are gone, either dead or moved closer to their children. I think she's depressed and the two of us are her only friends."

"But we're getting married. I love her and don't mind helping her, but I don't want to be her butler while you're her private nurse. I'm sure having Dolores move in would cut into the time we could spend with Jeremy."

"I know," she said, putting her head against my chest. "Let's take this one day at a time."

"Are you sleeping over?" I asked.

"Mother is getting bogged down in the details and feeling overwhelmed. I need to get home and smooth her feathers. I may have to take vacation the next two days so I can be her gofer and take some of the load off her," she said, putting on her coat.

I waved goodbye to Jenny and listened to her car drive away. I closed the door and heard Dolores snoring.

"Great tradeoff," I said to myself.

CHAPTER 17
THURSDAY MORNING

Dolores was still snoring when I got up, so I showered and shaved as quietly as possible, then started a pot of coffee. I opened the refrigerator and was delighted to see it had been restocked with fresh food. I filled a bowl with cereal and poured milk on it without checking the expiration date. "You're living on the edge," I said to myself.

I was halfway through my cereal, a cup of coffee, and the newspaper when Dolores shuffled out in slippers and a flowered housecoat. She looked tired and older than usual. Then I realized that I usually saw her with her carefully applied makeup.

"Coffee?" I asked, taking down a cup without waiting for her answer. I put out the half-and-half she called cream and set a spoon on a saucer. "Can I get anything else for you?"

"Some toast with strawberry jam would be good, as long as it's not too much trouble."

"No trouble," I said, feeling like I was already late for work. I put bread in the toaster and took butter, peanut butter, and strawberry jam from the refrigerator. When the toast popped, I put it on a plate and was ready to dash for the door.

"Um, Peter. Do you have any other jam? There seems to be mold on top of this jam."

I took a deep breath and ran options through my mind. "I'm sorry, there's no more strawberry jam," I said, thinking that I'd just scrape the mold off and use what was underneath, but I couldn't suggest that. "I have a bottle of honey. Would that be okay?"

"I don't really care for the taste of honey," she replied as I checked my watch. "Do you have some grape jelly?"

"Sorry," I said. "I'm out of all other jam and jelly options."

Dolores considered that while I stood ready to bolt for the door. She pushed the toast aside and wrinkled her nose.

"Maybe a fried egg and a strip of bacon would be okay," she said. Then she added, "If it's not too much trouble."

I blew out a deep breath and took bacon and eggs out of the refrigerator. While the bacon was frying Dolores sipped coffee and watched.

"Have you made an appointment for a Whistling Pines tour?" I asked, thinking that someone there might we willing to be a short order cook for Dolores.

"Actually, Etta and I are meeting with someone named Nancy at eleven this morning. She seemed very pleasant."

"Nancy is very nice," I said, carrying the two strips of bacon and one fried egg, over easy, to the table. I set them in front of Dolores and stepped toward the door.

"Peter, I hate to be a bother, but I prefer my bacon well browned and my egg yolk firm."

I put the bacon back in the pan and turned on the heat again.

"I know it's a throwback to when I was young. Everyone was concerned about trichinosis, so we cooked pork until it was dried out and tough. The eggs caused food poisoning, so we never ate an egg with a runny yolk or, heaven forbid, a runny egg white."

I ate the first egg while I refried the bacon, sopping up the yolk with the dry toast Dolores had refused. I flipped the second egg and cooked it until there was no bounce to the yolk, then slid it onto a plate with the bacon.

"I hope that does it for you," I said with a forced smile.

"Actually, I like buttered toast with my egg. If it's not too much trouble."

———— ◆ ————

By the time I arrived at Whistling Pines the staff parking lot was nearly full. I dashed for the front door and passed a few residents lined up near the dining room. The smell of fresh-baked cinnamon rolls nearly had me drooling.

"Peter!" I heard a young woman call out. When I turned, I saw Amber waving at me from the front desk.

"What's up?" I asked, after going upstream against the flow of diners.

"There's a woman here who wants to talk with you."

"I'll hang up my coat and . . ."

"I'm afraid she's terribly impatient. I promised to send you into the dining room as soon as you walked in the door."

"What does she look like?"

"She's the only redhead in the dining room," Amber replied. She leaned close and whispered, "I think it's a dye job, but it's very recent. Her roots are red too."

The redhead was alone at a table, sitting near the windows overlooking Lake Superior. She had a cup of coffee in her hands. She wore a striking green dress that complemented her red hair, which was pulled back in a bun. Her legs were crossed, and one foot was bobbing, indicating her level of impatience. Soon Jung was replacing table linens and setting the next table but I could tell she was invisible to the redhead. I immediately disliked her. I've long believed that you treat the janitor with the same respect as the CEO and the redhead was making it clear just by her body language that she felt superior.

"Good morning, Soon Jung," I said as I passed. She smiled, nodded to me, then went on with her work.

I sat across the table from the redhead. "I'm Peter." I offered my hand, but she chose to ignore it and continued staring out over the lake."

"I understand my brother was here yesterday. I assume he removed anything of value."

"And you are?" I asked.

"Judy Paluzzo," she replied, tersely.

"There wasn't much of value. Your brother took a bag of old letters and cards, then told me to have a local charity pick up everything that was left."

She let out a sigh and turned toward me. At first glance I would've guessed her to be about forty years old. On closer inspection, I could see the crow's feet at the corners of her eyes. The taut skin on her face made me think she'd had some plastic surgery and she was closer to sixty.

"My brother is a lazy lout. Sell the furniture and send me the check."

"I'm sorry, but I'm the recreation director. Furniture sales are outside my span of responsibilities."

She sniffed and stared at me. "I see. Who is your supervisor?"

"Nancy Helmbrecht is the director. She is the person I report to."

"To whom I report," she said. "Don't let your participles dangle. I know it's a Minnesota thing, but it's not proper English."

I bit my tongue, but my mind said, "She's who I report to, bitch," which would've removed the dangling participle. Instead, I said, "Would you like me to see if Nancy is available?"

"Please," she replied. "The receptionist gave me the impression that you take care of most matters related to the residents. I suppose she was mistaken."

I left the dining room and found Nancy in her office having a conversation with Jenny. "Excuse me. Alf's daughter is here, and she's asked to speak with my immediate supervisor."

"Is there a problem?" Jenny asked.

"She told me to sell Alf's furniture and send her the check. I replied that furniture sales aren't my responsibility."

Nancy's head bobbed and she stepped out from behind her desk. "Lead me to her," she said.

Nancy patted Soon Jung on the shoulder as she passed. I like and respect Nancy for those very personal touches that take so little time and effort, but mean a lot to the people who work for her.

"I'm Nancy Helmbrecht, the director of Whistling Pines. I understand you wanted to speak with me." Nancy and I remained standing. Judy Palazzo looked up with a glare.

"Your lackey isn't very cooperative," she said. "I made a request and I got a snotty response."

"Peter isn't a lackey," Nancy said, sitting down so she was eye-to-eye with the redhead. "He's the recreation director. I understand that you asked him to sell your father's furniture. I agree with him; that is not his responsibility. The disposition of the furniture is the responsibility of the family of the deceased. I can show you the lease agreement if you'd like. Peter was doing your brother a favor when he offered to call a charity to pick it up."

"I don't have time to deal with it," the redhead said.

"Perhaps you'd like to contact a moving company to have it packed and delivered to your house," Nancy suggested.

The woman stood. Although she projected herself well, Judy Paluzzo was five-three in high heels, hardly a physically impressive figure. "Please take me to my father's apartment."

"I think the door is unlocked," Nancy said. "You can go on your own."

Under the makeup I could see her blush. "I'm afraid I don't recall the way."

"I suppose that's because you've never visited in the seven years that Alf was here," Nancy replied as she stepped back and guided the woman toward the lobby. "I've seen your brother a few times, but he indicated that you were unavailable."

"I have a lot of job responsibilities," Ms. Paluzzo said as the three of us waited for the elevator. "Two Harbors is a long drive from my Minneapolis office."

"What type of job do you have?" I asked.

"I have a career in a marketing firm," she replied. "I've been a senior partner for several years and the job requirements are daunting."

"That's interesting," said Nancy as she opened Alf's door. "Alf showed me the postcards you sent when you were on a two-week Panama Canal cruise."

"That was business," the redhead said sharply. "As if it's any of your business."

We stopped at the end of the short hallway that led past the bathroom and kitchen, looking at Alf's living room area.

"Where's the other part of his suite?" she asked.

"You're looking at the whole thing," I replied. "Alf used to sit in that recliner and watch *The Price is Right*."

The woman stood silently, her eyes darting around, glancing at all the furniture and every corner. "This is all he had?"

"This is it," said Nancy. "This is the same apartment floorplan that most of our residents live in."

"But it's tiny," the woman said. She put her hand on the back of the recliner, then withdrew it like she'd touched a piece of shit. "This furniture isn't worthy of a garage sale. I think it should go into a Dumpster."

"Actually," Nancy said, "the furniture is dated, but it's well-made and there are a couple local charities who clean and repair donated furniture, then give it to families who are in crisis."

"They'd take this?"

"I'm sure they'd be happy to have it," I said.

The redhead shuddered. "Then let them have it. Where are Father's valuables?"

"His wallet is at the medical examiner's office," I said. "Other than that, I'm not aware of any other valuables."

"Where is his safety deposit box?" she asked. "Who is his stockbroker?"

"I'm not aware of any stocks or valuables," Nancy said. "His apartment rent was subsidized by the county and I've helped him fill out an annual declaration of assets to qualify. He's got a checking account, but there isn't more than a couple hundred dollars in it."

"My brother took the other valuables?" she said.

"I packed up the bags of letters and cards and handed them to your brother. They are quite literally everything he carried out of here, and I was with him the whole time he was in the apartment," I said.

"My brother said there were gold coins. Where are they?"

"That's probably what got Alf killed," I said. "He claimed that his family had stashed a jar of gold coins somewhere. A call from one of your cousins gave him a clue to the location, but the last I saw, Alf was sitting in his recliner, right here, looking through the family Bible trying to find that clue."

"Where's the Bible?" she asked. "I don't see it."

"The Bible was gone when we came to look for Alf," said Nancy. "As far as we know, the killer has it."

Judy Paluzzo turned and faced Nancy. "There's going to be a lawsuit. This should be a secure facility and you allowed an elderly man to leave with a kidnapper. There is negligence involved."

"Why don't you come down to my office," Nancy said, guiding the redhead to the hallway. "I'll give you the name and contact information of our attorney."

I felt sad again. Alf had been a nice enough guy. He didn't deserve a bitchy daughter who was too busy to come visit him. As I stepped into the hallway, I thought I should tell her about the stamps. Then I reconsidered. Her brother had given me the stamps. They were probably worthless anyway. No need to stir the pot.

I took the stairs down to my office where I found a note taped to my office door that said, "Meet me in the dining room." It wasn't signed, but the handwriting looked like Wendy's. I checked my email, then grabbed my cup and wandered to the dining room. Wendy was sitting in the back corner hovering over a cross-word with the pencil eraser clamped in her teeth. I drew a cup of coffee from the urn and sat down across from her.

"You left me a note," I said.

She was in such deep concentration that she literally jumped when I spoke. "Don't sneak up on me like that!" She took a deep breath and blew it out slowly. "So, Alf is dead, no one knows where the Bible is, but the killer hasn't found the gold yet. Right?"

"I don't know if the killer's found the gold or not," I replied. "It didn't look like he'd found it at Big Rock or in Zim. That doesn't mean he hasn't figured out the clue and found it some-where else."

"I think we should rent a metal detector and drive up to Zim," she said, with a sparkle in her eye.

"No way. It's a long drive and I don't think there's any gold there."

"Why?" she asked, leaning close. "Did you get a look at Alf's Bible before it disappeared?"

"No. It's a treasure hunt and by definition, they usually end in frustration and spending more than you ever recover. I'm not interested."

She looked unhappy, but I didn't care. I wasn't going off on a treasure hunt with, or without, a map. I stood and she put a finger up.

"Before you go, I need eight letters. The clue is 'He said nevermore.'"

"'The Raven,' by Edgar Allen Poe."

Her expression brightened, as she started penciling the answer while making motions to shoo me away.

Back in my office, I was surprised that there was a voice-mail from the North Shore brewery. My first thought was that someone had left a glove or something behind. My second thought was that we were going to be permanently banned from the facility. But I called.

"Hi, Peter, I wanted to say thanks for the tip. It really wasn't necessary," said Dan.

"You put up with a lot while we were there. It's the least I could do."

"Um, Grandma told me that one of the old guys who was on the tour died. That's sad."

"He was murdered, which makes it even sadder. But life has to go on for those of us who remain."

"I feel a little bad. I was kinda abrupt during the tour, but Grandma said everyone really enjoyed the outing. If you'd like, we could do another tour, maybe this spring before sales pick up. I'd be happy to host your group again."

"Thanks. Everyone had a good time. I'll call you when I do the April schedule and see if we can find a date that'll work."

"That sounds good. I'll look forward to your call."

I was barely into planning the movies for the next week when Esme's head popped into my office. "Did Dan call you?"

"I just got off the phone," I said. "We're going to schedule another tour in April."

"Oh, good," she said. "It's been a little slow for them and I hope we can help stimulate some business."

"You know," I said, "senior citizens aren't known for being the kind of spenders who will keep any business afloat."

"I know, but still, we should try to help him out. Thanks."

"Esme, how much do you have invested in the brewery?" I asked.

"I have more money than I'll ever spend," she said as she stepped away.

"Thousands?" I asked myself. "Maybe tens of thousands?" I was grateful that my job had little to do with the residents' families or finances.

◆

I was carrying my late morning cup of coffee back to my office when Hulda Packer rolled her walker onto my foot.

"Peter, you're a cop. You've got to arrest Ronny's grandson for murdering Alf."

"First of all, I'm not a cop," I said, then ran through the list of residents in my head. "Secondly, we don't have a resident named Ronny."

"In the apartment almost next to mine, 232," she replied.

"Vivian Swanson lives in that apartment," I replied.

"Of course she does," said Hulda.

"You want me to arrest Ronny's grandson in apartment 232."

"Try to keep up," Hulda said sharply. "Vivian's grandson, Ronny, is a thief from long ago. He killed Alf for the gold. We were discussing it this morning."

"I'm sorry, but breakfast discussion is hardly the basis for arresting someone. But I'll mention Ronny's name to Chief Rentz."

I tried to slip away but Hulda was undeterred. "Peter, he's been stealing things since he was a kid. Everyone knows that criminals just elevate their crimes."

"Who's been stealing?" asked a woman's voice from somewhere behind Hulda.

"Ronny Swanson," replied someone else, who'd been closer to the discussion.

I took two steps toward my office before I was frozen by her next comment. "If you won't arrest him, I guess we'll have to make a citizen's arrest," Hulda said.

I walked back, hoping to lower the tone of the conversation, but it was getting out of control.

"I'll talk to Chief Rentz and pass along your suspicions. He'll know about Ronny. Criminals tend to escalate their crimes, not elevate them."

"That's what I said!" replied Hulda.

The crowd awaiting the opening of the dining room for lunch

was growing and someone bumped my elbow, slopping coffee onto my shirt and pants. I controlled the spill so the only victim was me.

"You ought to be more careful," said Hulda. "Coffee stains. I hope you have another shirt to change into so you can get this one soaked before the stains set."

"Yes, I'll do that."

I tried to step away from the crowd but was accosted by Bud Bloomquist, who tapped my shoulder. I saw the gauze was gone from his tattoo. It looked crusty.

"Bud, I think you're supposed to keep that tattoo covered for a few days, then keep lotion on it until it's healed."

He looked at the tattoo. "I suppose that's what they said, but I can't work the tube of lotion with one hand."

"Talk to Jenny," I said. "One of the aides would be happy to apply lotion for you."

"I'm not so sure about that. They're pretty busy. Besides, I want people to see it. Who knows if I'll be alive long enough for it to heal."

I looked at the three-inch-long character. "What's it mean?" I asked.

"It's Japanese for samurai," he replied proudly. "My grandson just opened his tattoo shop in Duluth, and I wanted to give him some business, so I got this tattoo. He knew I'd been a soldier, so he suggested I get this samurai symbol."

"Very nice," I said, nodding politely. "Did you want to talk to me?" I asked.

He pointed to a quiet corner away from the crowd, and I followed. He leaned close and whispered, "It wasn't Ronny Swanson who killed Alf."

"Who do you think did it?" I asked.

"I don't know who did it," he replied. "But I know it wasn't Ronny. He's locked up in Stillwater for a robbery he did over in Eveleth. He's been there for a couple years."

"Thanks," I replied. "Why didn't you tell me when Hulda was there?"

"Oh, no," he said, shaking his head. "You don't cross Hulda Packer. She's got a mean streak as big as her mouth."

I nodded and returned to my office.

I kept a spare set of clothing hanging behind my door. In a place full of senior citizens there were routine incidents involving spilled liquids, food, or bodily fluids.

I switched shirts and was contemplating the stain on my pants when I smelled pipe tobacco. Len Rentz stopped at my office door and took in the scene.

"Looks like you had an accident," he said, looking at the coffee stain that was suspiciously close to my crotch.

"Coffee spill," I said.

"Nasty stain. Coffee sometimes doesn't come out."

I waved him into my cubbyhole office and closed the door before changing into clean pants. I doused the stains with bottled water and threw the clothes into a plastic shopping bag.

"Any progress in the investigation?" I asked as I tied the bag shut.

"I spoke with Jeff and Sonny. They finished processing Alf's old house," he replied. "They said that the tire pattern was a truck tread, but it was a Goodyear tire that's very common. Beyond that, they had low expectations of finding anything else of use because the vandal must've worn gloves."

"So there was nothing there?" I asked.

"Actually, we caught a break. The vandal left a crowbar buried under some debris. Sonny was able to pull some prints off of it. It was brand new and we hope he handled it some when he bought it. Either that, or we've got the prints of the worker who packed it or the hardware clerk who put it on display. Sonny put the prints in the AFIS database, but didn't get any hits."

"At least you've got prints to compare if you get a suspect," I said. "By the way, Hulda Packer says Vivien Swanson's grandson, Ronny, killed Alf."

Len thought for a moment. "Unless Ronny has escaped from prison, I think we can rule him out. But I would certainly include the children of the residents. They may have shared Alf's news about the hidden gold."

"With nieces, nephews, daughters, and sons, that leaves you a pool of several thousand suspects. Good luck with that, Len."

"Keep your ears open," Len said, rising from the chair. "Thieves are amazingly chatty."

"Sure," I said, opening the door for him. "I'm in contact with so many chatty thieves in my role as recreation director at a senior citizens residence."

"Looks like the contractors are done at Dolores's house. Did the work turn out okay?"

"What I saw looked fabulous," I replied.

He nodded. "I'm concerned about her. After all the gun incidents, I think her judgment is a little off and I don't think she should be living alone anymore."

"She's still sharp, she only takes a few medicines, and Jenny made sure that she's taking the correct dosage and on time. I think she's safe alone, if that's what you're asking."

"You're keeping an eye on her," Len said as he left, "otherwise, I'd ask the county to do a wellness check on her."

"She's touring Whistling Pines this morning," I said. "Let's hope she likes it here."

"Change of subject — Are the wedding plans going well?"

"I had to call my mother to tell her she couldn't host a groom's dinner in Duluth. It's too far away and too late in the evening. We're going to the VFW."

"I'm sure you did that tactfully."

"My mother doesn't understand the word," I said. "She's concerned about herself and everything else is secondary."

"Her heart was in the right place," Len replied.

"Yes, but sometimes her head and her mouth are unable to adequately filter the information."

CHAPTER 18
THURSDAY AFTERNOON

I was deep in thought when the phone rang.

"Peter," I recognized Amber's voice, "there's a truck at the dock to pick up furniture. They said you know about it?"

"I'll be on the dock in two minutes," I said as I logged off my computer.

There were two young men standing next to the liftgate of a large moving van. They shuffled nervously as they puffed on cigarettes.

"You're here for the furniture?"

"Yeah," they said in unison, throwing their cigarette butts to the ground and stepping on them. "Harry said you've got a whole apartment of stuff." They opened the back and took out packing blankets and two-wheeled carts.

I led them to Alf's apartment and opened the door. They looked around, talking quietly to each other. "Everything goes?" one asked.

"Everything," I replied. "There's cookware and dinnerware in the kitchen cabinets and even clothes in the closet."

The two guys cruised through the apartment, commenting to each other about their plans to load. I heard drawers opening and closing and they emerged from the bedroom looking focused.

Randy, according to the name on his shirt, was lean and sand-haired. He and Bob, who had dark hair and a beer belly that hung over his belt, finished their discussion. Bob walked over to me, rubbing his fingers.

"There's a weird dust all over the place. Are you sure it's safe?" he asked.

The question caught me off guard and I thought back to the housekeeping. "What kind of dust?" I asked.

He held out his fingertips, which were coated with a fine black powder.

"Fingerprint dust," I said. "The BCA was here taking fingerprints and looking for evidence."

Randy looked around nervously, then he sniffed. "There wasn't a stiff here, was there? I get creeped out when we go to a house where somebody was killed." He sniffed again. "It doesn't smell like anybody died here."

"He might've been kidnapped from here, but he didn't die here."

"Bob, you hear that? The guy didn't die here."

Bob nodded, but was busy upending the sofa and leaning it onto a two-wheeled furniture dolly.

"The BCA, huh," Randy said. "They done a pretty thorough job. They even turned all the old guy's pants pockets inside out." He surveyed the apartment one more time while Bob waited by the door. The sofa wasn't going through without some maneuvering. "We'll do the big stuff first," he said, mentally arranging the load in the truck. "Then we'll pack up the cupboards, take the small stuff. The clothes go last."

"Sounds like a plan," I replied.

"You gonna hang around to make sure everything is okay?" Randy asked.

"I don't see any point," I said, "as long as you guys don't need me."

"Naw. We'll let you know when we're done."

I left to pop popcorn and set up the Thursday afternoon

movie. As residents trickled into the recreation center they took bags of popcorn. I verified all the connections and set up Netflix to show *Out of Africa*. At exactly two minutes after two o'clock I started the movie, then walked up to Alf's apartment.

I heard the clatter of pots and pans as soon as I stepped off the elevator. The apartment was bare except for the two movers, who were loading cookware into boxes.

"Everything go okay?" I asked.

"Just fine," replied Randy. "The furniture is high quality and well-made. Most of what we get isn't up to IKEA standards and this stuff may have been Amish, based on the weight and construction. You're sure the family didn't want it?"

"They told me to dispose of it," I said. "Did you find any surprises?"

"The BCA guys did a good job," Randy replied. "They'd been in every nook and cranny. Most times we see a piece of jewelry or a watch that was overlooked when the family packed."

"We didn't even find lint in the pants' pockets," Bob added.

"Do you need anything else from me?" I asked.

"Who gets the receipt for the donation?" Randy asked.

"Give it to me," I said. "I imagine I'll see the family at the funeral."

Randy scrawled his name on a blank receipt and dated it. "There you go."

"Don't they need a list of the donated items?"

"Most people like to make their own list," Randy said with a wink. "I'm sure there were half a dozen Rolex watches in the top drawer."

"Really?"

"Really," he replied.

Back in my office I put the receipt into the drawer with the stamp collection. I briefly thought about giving the stamp albums to the drivers, but decided to hang onto them in case the family changed their minds and wanted them back.

The movie was over and the residents were leaving when I got back to the recreation room. I stood by the door as the credits rolled up the screen. Hulda Packer was pushing her walker, moving slowly with the crowd. When she got to the door she stopped and leaned close to me. I briefly wondered who the rumor mill was going to indict for Alf's murder this time.

"That was a terrible movie," she said. "Why don't you pre-screen them to save us from clinkers like this?"

"*Out of Africa* is a classic," I replied.

"It was so bad," she whispered, "that I didn't even feel bad when Robert Redford died."

"I'm sorry you didn't enjoy it," I said.

"If you choose to continue the Africa theme, perhaps you'll consider *The African Queen* next week. That's a real classic."

"We watched that last week," I said.

"That's the beauty of dementia," she said. "I can watch the same old movies over and over, and not remember."

As Hulda passed, Bette Kreul, one of the volunteers, leaned close. "Hulda can also hide her own Easter eggs," she whispered with a wink.

CHAPTER 19
THURSDAY EVENING

At five o'clock Jenny followed me out of the building. She looked bedraggled.

"Long day?" I asked.

"I'm busy and Mother is driving me nuts. She called five times today to tell me she'd made decisions about changes. I appreciate that she wants to keep me updated, but I finally told her that whatever she decides is just fine."

"Was that acceptable?" I asked.

"Of course not," she sighed. "She wants me to be part of all the decisions. This, after months of her deciding everything, we get down to the last two days before the wedding and suddenly she's nervous and wants my input. Argh!"

The director's car was parked next to Jenny's car. Hearing Jenny's complaint, in her calming voice Nancy said, "Your mother is stressed out and calling you is her way of dealing with the stress. Take her calls. Sound interested and supportive. It'll all be over in two days and life will move on."

Jenny nodded. "It's just . . . I'm stressed too, and I don't need her piling on even more."

"Take a deep breath every time she calls and smile," Nancy said as she opened her car door. "I'll see you tomorrow."

"Let's go to the VFW for pasties," I suggested.

"Anything, so I don't have to go home to a barrage of questions," Jenny said. She paused, then added, "You call Mother and tell her you're taking me out for supper. I can't face her right now."

———— ◆ ————

The VFW parking lot was half full, as was the dining room. As the World War II and Korean War vets died off so had the VFW's business, but Thursday night pasties were always a hit and we knew that if we didn't arrive early there was a chance they'd sell out.

We took a booth where it seemed like we could hide from the activity. Vern, the bartender who was working every night I'd ever been to the VFW, brought glasses to our table. "Jack and water for the groom and chardonnay for the bride," he said as he set the glasses on the table.

"Thanks," I said. "Start a tab for us. We're going to have pasties too."

"Dinner is on me," he replied, then walked away.

"You can't do that," I yelled. He waved without turning back.

"Are you as stressed out as I am?" Jenny asked.

I chose my words carefully. "I think the bride is always more stressed about the wedding. I mean, my life is changing, for the better, but the bride's family takes on the brunt of the wedding planning. It's got to be tough."

Jenny reached across the table and took my hands in her. "Let's elope. Let's drive to Duluth and get on a plane to Las Vegas. To hell with all the pomp and circumstance. I just want to be married and be done with it."

"It's supposed to be your big day."

"It's my big day all right. It's my panic attack and my mother's sudden insecurity. I'll be lucky to survive."

"You'll survive and it'll be a great day."

Len walked into the dining room and spied us. He dragged

over a chair and sat at the end of the booth. "I don't want to crash your party, but I thought it would look like I was snubbing you if I walked past and took another table by myself."

"Len," Jenny said, "you're always welcome at our table."

"I was hoping you'd say that," Len said, taking off his jacket and hanging it on the back of his chair. "I hate eating alone." I'd rarely seen Len out of uniform and the transformation was surprising. Swapping out his blue uniform for jeans, tennis shoes, and a green Minnesota Wild sweatshirt made him look like a different person.

"You came over for the pasties?" Jenny asked.

"I just needed to get out of the house," he said as he tried to get Vern's attention. He caught Vern's eye and made a drinking gesture. Vern nodded and drew a tap beer. "I heard that Dolores took a tour of Whistling Pines today."

"I saw Dolores and her friend eating lunch in the dining room," said Jenny. "I didn't have time to talk, so I waved and buzzed off."

"I think she's ready for the move," said Len as his beer arrived. "Thanks, Vern. I'm picking up Peter's tab tonight."

Vern patted Len's shoulder. "You'll have to get in line," Vern replied. "You're the third person tonight to make that offer. He nodded toward a table near the front door where two Iraq vets were sitting. They lifted their glasses in a toast. "They offered to buy too, but I told them the night was already on me."

"Looks like you're popular," said Len as Vern returned to the bar. "Everything ready for the big day?"

Jenny glanced at me, then took a sip of wine, not wanting to offer her opinion.

"There's a touch of chaos," I said. "Barbara is going crazy and she's sharing that with Jenny several times a day. Alf's murder has me distracted and there's the usual craziness at Whistling Pines."

Two pasties were delivered by Bertha, a heavyset woman in her seventies with bleached blonde hair and an endearing smile. She set them in front of Len and Jenny, then pulled a squeeze bottle of ketchup out of her apron and set it on the table. "I have a surprise for you, Peter," she said before retreating to the kitchen.

"I wonder what that's all about?"

A minute later she returned with another pasty and a steaming bowl of gravy. "Don't get used to this," she said, setting the gravy in front of me. "But your wedding is coming up so Vern and I decided to treat you with gravy instead of making you eat your pasty the right way, with ketchup." She stepped back and smiled broadly.

"Thanks. I hardly know what to say."

"You just enjoy that pasty. That's enough thanks," she said, turning toward the kitchen.

"Don't get used to this royal treatment," Jenny said as she watched me cover the pasty with brown gravy. "Come Monday it's back to macaroni and cheese."

Vern came back with another round of drinks and set them in front of us. "Courtesy of the couple in the back," he said, nodding toward an older couple sitting in the back corner.

"They are my folks' neighbors, the Andersons," Jenny said, waving thanks.

I looked at my still half-full first drink. "Vern, I think you'd better politely refuse anyone offering to buy another round. I have to drive home."

"Too late," he said. He nodded to the couple in the booth behind us. "Bob and Marie have already paid for the next round."

Jenny turned and thanked them. "She's my fourth-grade teacher," Jenny whispered.

"How many other people do you recognize here?" I asked.

She looked around the room, smiling and waving at the people around us. "I don't know the guy at the end of the bar, but I recognize almost everyone else."

"The joy of life in a small town," said Len.

"How many of them have you ticketed?" I asked Len.

"Too many," he replied before returning to his pasty.

"What are you going to do with Alf's stamp collection?" Jenny asked.

"I've got it locked in my desk drawer. Beyond that, I haven't given it much thought."

"Why do you have the stamp collection?" Len asked.

"Alf's son took the cards and letters, but told me to get rid of everything else. I told him that the stamps might have some value, but he had no interest in them and told me I could have them if I wanted."

"Are they valuable?" Jenny asked.

"They're old," I said, "but I have no idea what they're worth."

"Is there a stamp dealer in Duluth who could appraise them?" she asked.

"I've heard you get pennies on the dollar when you sell coins and stamps to dealers," said Len. "I know a guy in town who tries to tell me about his stamp collection about once a year when I'm eating at Judy's. You should call him. He might be able to help you estimate the value of the collection."

Len took a notepad and pen out of his coat. "His name is Larry Mohr," Len said, handing me the slip of paper. "He lives just west of the lighthouse. I'm sure he'd be happy to talk to you. To be honest, every time he starts talking stamps I yawn."

"You don't find stamp collections interesting?" asked Jenny.

"I'd rather watch grass grow," replied Len.

At the end of the evening we all had our bellies full of pasties and a healthy glow from the free drinks.

Len opened the door for us and whispered, "I can drive you home."

"Vern switched me to ginger ale after the second round. I'm okay," I said.

Len nodded. "Call Larry and ask him to look at the stamps."

"It's too crazy right now," I replied. "I'll call him after the wedding."

Jenny was buzzing from too much wine. Inside the car she started to shiver and couldn't stop. I put my arm around her and we sat in the car waiting for the heater to start producing warm air.

"Are you scared?" she asked.

"A little," I replied. "This is a huge step. I'm going to be a husband and a father. It's all uncharted territory."

"You and Jeremy get along great."

"I was wondering," I said, pausing to consider if my timing was right.

"What?"

"I want to adopt Jeremy," I said. "I'd like to be his 'real' father."

Jenny pushed away and looked into my eyes. "Really? Is this the alcohol talking?"

"I've thought about it a lot," I said. "I think it would make us more of a family."

Jenny pulled my arm around her shoulders and pushed against me. "Let's talk to Jeremy about it after the wedding. I think he'd like that."

"And you think it's okay?" I asked.

"It's better than okay. It's great."

CHAPTER 20
THURSDAY EVENING/FRIDAY

When I dropped Jenny off we were met at the front door by Barbara, who wanted to talk. She dragged us into the living room, then ran through the list of all the things that had to be done before Saturday. Most of the items were just double-checking things that had already been double-checked, like calling the photographer and florist to verify their timing and the plans. I'm sure they'd already heard from Barbara at least four times, and I cringed when she said there had to be one more call, "just to be sure."

It was nearly eleven when I climbed into bed. The buzz of the alcohol and transfer of Barbara's adrenaline rush kept me awake until midnight. I was tempted to hit the snooze button when the alarm rang. Looking at myself in the bathroom mirror I saw tired and bloodshot eyes. I showered, shaved, and wolfed down a piece of toast before starting my car. The five minutes of scraping frost from the windshield helped wake me up.

The phone was ringing when I stepped into my office. I threw my stocking hat onto the guest chair and picked up. I wondered who was calling at 6 a.m.

"This is Peter," I said.

"Peter, you said that Dad's Bible was missing. No one knows where it is?"

Caller ID showed a telephone prefix from the Twin Cities and G Paluzzo. "Mr. Paluzzo?"

"Yes. Yes. This is Gary Paluzzo. Do you know where the family Bible is?"

"It was missing when the police came to search your dad's apartment," I replied. "As I told you when you were here, we don't know where it is. What's the renewed interest?"

"My cousin called last night and told me the story about the letter Grandma sent. I called several times because you'd said there might be something in that Bible about the missing coins."

The message indicator was blinking on my phone display and it said there had been six calls since I'd left work yesterday.

"That was a theory I discussed with your father. As I recall, the letter said the answer was in something left behind and had something to do with the location of your uncle's death. Your uncle probably died on Guadalcanal in the Solomon Islands. The only things we could connect were the Bible and the Song of Solomon."

"Shit! And the Bible is missing."

"Unless the police have found it recently."

"Do you know if Dad ever figured out the clue?"

"The last time we spoke, he'd flipped through the whole Bible looking for a note, then he'd read the Song of Solomon, but nothing jumped out at him. I think he was planning to reread the Song of Solomon to see if he'd missed something."

"Were you helping him?"

"Other than hypothesizing about the Song of Solomon, no, I wasn't helping him. The last time I saw him he was very secretive and all he said was that he hadn't found the clue yet. The next time I was in his apartment he was missing and the place had been ransacked."

"Is there any chance he figured it out and the answer is somewhere in his apartment? Can I come up and look?"

"The BCA searched the entire apartment and the movers took all his stuff yesterday. The apartment is bare."

"Shit. Shit. Shit." He took a breath. "Okay, who picked up his stuff?"

"The Disabled Vets sent a truck. I have the receipt if you want it."

"Okay," he seemed to be writing a note. "And who did the search?"

"Two agents from the Northern Minnesota BCA office searched the apartment. Their names are Jeff Telker and Sonny Carlson."

"Okay. I've got it. Let me know if the Bible shows up."

Before I could answer I was listening to a dial tone. I took off my coat and hung it behind the door. I realized that my spare change of clothing was gone and I looked at the damp lump in the plastic shopping bag behind the door. In my haste to leave, I'd forgotten to take them home.

"I suppose it's too late now to try and get the stains out," I said to myself.

I had my coffee cup in hand and was stepping out the door when the phone rang again.

"This is Peter."

"Where is my father's Bible?" a shrill female voice asked.

"Ms. Paluzzo?" I asked, picturing the redhead.

"Yes. Where is my father's Bible? Is it in his apartment?"

"It was missing when the police came to search after he disappeared," I said patiently.

"You don't have it?"

"I don't understand the sudden interest. I had this same discussion with your brother moments ago."

"I'm asking again," she said, "do you have it?"

"I don't have it. It's missing. The police assume whoever kidnapped your father took the Bible."

"That's the story you're sticking to?"

"It's the only story there is. If you'd care to call the Two Harbors chief of police, I can give you his number."

"You are all bumbling incompetents! Your security sucks and you're imbeciles. I'll have my attorney call and maybe you'll respond to *his* inquiries." I was suddenly listening to a dial tone.

I took my cup to the dining room, where breakfast was in full swing. The chattering of dozens of senior citizens, most with some hearing loss, caused cacophony. I'd planned to swoop in, draw a cup of coffee from the urn, and swoop out, but Howard Johnson waved me over to his table.

Howard, Lee Westfall, and Bud Bloomquist had finished their breakfasts and were drinking coffee. Howard pulled out a chair for me.

"Tell me about Alf's Bible," he said.

"To the best of my knowledge, there's nothing new," I said. "It disappeared with Alf. The police think the killer took it. It's interesting that you ask because I've already had two phone calls this morning with the same question."

"It was a topic circulating while we were waiting for the dining room to open this morning," said Lee. "It's just more grist for the information starved rumor mill to throw about."

Bud jumped into the conversation, rolling up his sleeve. "Have you seen my tattoo?"

"You showed it to me yesterday. It looks less swollen today," I said, looking more closely.

Soon Jung started clearing the breakfast plates and Bud swung his arm over for her to see. "My grandson did this tattoo for me. It says 'samurai.'"

She looked casually at the tattoo and murmured something. Then froze. She looked at the tattoo more closely, giggled, then hurried off without clearing all the plates.

"That was odd," said Lee.

Bud cocked his head. "I wonder what's funny about a samurai tattoo?" He left his shirtsleeve rolled up, leaving the tattoo on his forearm exposed.

"Who called you about the Bible?" Howard asked.

"Both of Alf's children called. Apparently, their cousin from California called them asking about the missing clue to the gold coins and that's fueled their interest in finding the Bible and the clue."

Miriam, Connie, and Stacy all emerged from the kitchen and made a beeline for our table. "We'd like to see your tattoo," Miriam said.

Bud proudly held it out for inspection. "My grandson did it for me. It says samurai."

The women looked at the tattoo briefly, then started laughing before retreating to the kitchen.

"Something's up," said Howard.

Bud was suddenly uneasy and rolled his sleeve down, covering the tattoo. "Do you think there's something wrong with my tattoo?"

"I don't know how they'd know," said Lee. "None of them speak Japanese."

"Hang on," I said.

The women were gathered around Soon Jung in the kitchen, all with wide grins. They were chattering like schoolgirls. As I approached, the talking stopped.

"Is there something wrong with Bud's tattoo?" I asked.

They stood together, all stifling laughter. Finally, Miriam confessed. "Bud's tattoo doesn't say samurai."

"How would any of you know that?" I asked.

They all looked at Soon Jung, who was blushing. "It's wrong," she said.

"It's Japanese, and you're Korean. How can you tell?"

"Most Asian characters are variations of the same basic characters. Each language and dialect has added their own flourish to them, and the Japanese probably have the most complicated ideograms of all. We can't speak each other's languages, but we can sometimes read common writing."

"Doesn't Bud's tattoo say samurai?" I asked.

Soon Yung shook her head no.

"What does it say?" I asked. She continued to shake her head, but wouldn't speak.

"It says hemorrhoid," Miriam blurted out as the rest of the women started laughing.

Pushing a napkin to her and giving her my pen, I said to Soon Jung, "Draw me samurai and hemorrhoid."

With careful pen strokes she constructed two characters that looked almost identical, then held up the paper for me to see.

"Here. This is samurai," she said, pointing to the first character. "This other one is hemorrhoid. See the extra marks here, on the left side. They make this hemorrhoid."

"Uh oh," I said as laughter broke out again.

"Are you going to tell him?" Miriam asked.

"I think I have to," I replied. "Too bad the hemorrhoid has more marks. It would be easier to go from samurai to hemorrhoid than to erase the marks and change it back to samurai."

I took the paper and returned to the table where Howard, Lee, and Bud were still sipping coffee. I put the paper on the table and sat down.

"These characters look very much alike," I said, turning the paper so the three of them could see them. "This one on the left is the character for samurai. The other one, which is the same as Bud's tattoo, is for hemorrhoid."

The three of them studied the characters for a second, then Bud rolled up his sleeve. "Which one is samurai?" he asked.

I wrote "samurai" under the left character and "hemorrhoid" under the right. Bud held the paper next to his tattoo.

"Shit," he said, throwing the paper onto the table. "Who told you that?"

"Soon Jung said it's the wrong character," I explained as Lee started whooping laughs that brought everyone's attention to our table.

"Stop that!" Bud said, pulling down his sleeve. "I gotta talk to the kid. He'll make it right."

Bud got up and stormed out of the dining room.

"The kid isn't going to fix this, is he?" Howard asked. "He needs to take some ink off to make the correct character."

"Maybe he can get something to cover it up," Lee said, wiping tears from his face. "Maybe something tasteful, or nautical. Yeah, maybe a ship."

"I don't think Bud was in the Navy," Howard said.

"I wonder if Alf's kidnapper ever figured out the clue in the family Bible," I said, trying to change the topic.

"Was the Bible the only thing missing from Alf's apartment?" Howard asked, taking my cue.

"As far as we know," I replied. "Alf had a dusty box from storage and I didn't see everything in it. He talked about some letters and a stamp collection. They were still there after the kidnapping and when Alf's son came to pick up his stuff."

"And Alf hadn't found the clue?" Lee asked.

"Not when I last saw him. He was going to read Song of Solomon again."

"If Alf couldn't figure it out, I imagine the killer couldn't either," said Howard. "Especially if it was a special family code of some kind."

"Unless it was someone from the family who took it," Lee suggested.

"Both his kids called me this morning, asking about the Bible. I doubt they'd call if they had it. Someone already tore the old family home apart right to the studs and floor joists, so if there were gold coins they're probably somewhere else."

"Somewhere the Bible pointed to," Howard said.

"It was just a theory," I replied. "The letter from his mother said to look where his brother had been killed and he was a Marine in the Solomon Islands. That hints at the Song of Solomon."

"You said there was a book of stamps," said Lee. "Were they valuable?"

"I have no idea," I replied. "I'm not much of a philatelist."

"Maybe there's an upside-down biplane in the collection," Howard offered with a smile, referring to one of the most famous rare stamps in history.

———— ◆ ————

Back in my office I unlocked the drawer and removed the stamp albums. I flipped through the pages of the U.S. stamps and didn't see any upside-down biplanes. I decided to call Len's guy. And I remembered the name he gave me and searched for Larry Mohr online. Thirty seconds later I was talking to him.

"I'm Peter Rogers, the recreation director from Whistling Pines. I was recently given an old stamp collection and Len Rentz said you might be able to help me determine its value."

"Old Len yawns every time I mention stamps," Larry said with a laugh. "I'm surprised he even remembered that I was a collector. Tell me a little bit about the collection."

"There are five albums, each representing a different region of the world. As near as I can tell most of the stamps are really old, like pre-World War I. I don't even recognize the names of some of the countries."

"You've piqued my interest," said Larry. "I get an occasional call, but it's usually from someone who has a collection of late-twentieth-century U.S. stamps. I tell them that stamps of that vintage sell by the pound at stamp auctions. Most don't even return their face value. If you've got an international collection of nineteenth-century stamps, I'd be very interested in looking at them."

"Could we get together some evening?" I asked.

"Well, evenings end pretty early for us retirees. Can you come over during the day when I'm sure to be awake?"

"I can get away nearly anytime for a half hour. Tell me when it's convenient for you."

"Well, I can put off the noon nap I was considering if you could come over right now."

I checked my watch. It was nearly my lunch hour. "Sure. I'll be over in a few minutes."

Larry Mohr lived in a 1960's rambler in a tract of similar homes not far from the train depot museum. I parked on the street and was met at the door by an attractive sixty-something woman wearing a purple sweater with matching slacks.

"Come in," she said. "I'm Nancy Mohr. You'll have to excuse the mess, but Larry didn't consult with me before offering an invitation and I've got quilting pieces arranged around the living room."

"Not a problem," I said. "Actually, I feel a little guilty dragging these dusty stamp albums into your home."

"Don't worry about it," she said, taking my coat. "They're just like the rest of Larry's stamp collection. He stores it in the basement to keep that musty 'old stamp' smell out of the upstairs. Set your stamps on the kitchen table and I'll tell Larry you're here."

Larry was about the same age as his wife and as average as a man can be. He had thinning gray hair, but was mostly undistinguished. He was average height, weight, and complexion.

"It's not often that I get a willing victim to talk about stamps," he said, shaking my hand.

"Sorry, I'm not into stamps, which is why Len suggested that I talk with you." I pushed the stack of albums across the table to him. "They're roughly organized by continent, but there aren't many Asian stamps. The top album is the largest and it appears to be Europe."

He opened the leather-bound cover, exposing a yellowed page of paper with an assortment of stamps on it. One fluttered to the floor as the page opened. Larry picked it up and examined it through his bifocals.

"Well, this is definitely an amateur collection," he said, fingering the stamp. "Whoever put this together used hide glue to fasten the stamps to the paper. The glue has dried out and is cracking and releasing the stamps."

"I've never heard of hide glue."

"It's also called mucilage. It was originally derived from horse hides and hooves and was cheap and very popular. It used to come in a glass bottle with a tapered rubber stopper that had a slot that allowed a thin layer of glue to be applied as you dragged it across the paper."

"So, is that bad? I mean, did it ruin the stamps?"

"Well, it's devalued them," he said with a chuckle. "But let's face it, every stamp collector wants stamps that have never been detached from the sheet and were kept under controlled temperature and humidity. The reality is, particularly when you start looking at eighteenth-century stamps, virtually all of them were used for postage, so they were glued to an envelope and cancelled with an ink stamp. The values usually reflect that condition, and these are probably better than a lot of the newer collections I've seen where the stamps were affixed with cellophane tape. Don't get me wrong, Scotch Tape was a great invention, just not for the application of stamps in collections."

"I've never seen stamps like the ones on this page," I said, pointing. "They're in Kreuzen denominations, and I've never heard of that monetary unit. Is it from some obscure country that doesn't exist anymore?"

Larry smiled. "Well, the Austro-Hungarian empire doesn't exist anymore, but it's hardly an obscure country. In the late 1800s it was huge, encompassing most of central Europe, so the stamps aren't rare. I've seen them in many collections. But they're not common either. There probably aren't more than a handful of collectors in Minnesota that have the assortment of denominations and styles that are on this page."

"Does that mean they're semi-valuable?" I asked.

"Hang on for a minute. Let me get a catalog."

While he was gone I flipped through five pages of Austro-Hungarian stamps. I was looking at a collection that was rare by my standards, but I knew almost nothing.

He returned with a large book and opened the page to an array of stamps resembling the ones in the album. "These are the stamps you've got. As you can see, there are a variety of prices for each style. The different prices represent the varying degrees of quality. For instance, here's the stamp that fell out of the book. In mint condition, and I reiterate there are no stamps of this vintage in mint condition except in somebody's dreams, the book value is three-fifty, which means you might get fifty cents for it at an auction."

"But there are pages and pages of stamps. If each of them is worth fifty cents, the collection is worth hundreds of dollars."

Larry leaned back and looked at the stack of albums. "In a gross sort of way, yes, there are hundreds of dollars in individual stamps here. But that's only true in a gross sense." He flipped through a few more pages and stopped. "Here are Lichtenstein stamps. They're much rarer than the Austro-Hungarian stamps so are more valuable." He flipped through the catalog and stopped. "Now this is a pretty rare stamp," he said, pointing to a blue stamp. "The catalog value is six hundred dollars."

"Which means I might get twenty-five at auction?"

"Maybe fifty or sixty," he said with a shrug. "It depends on who shows up at the auction."

"So the bottom line is, what?" I asked.

"I can't give you a bottom line if you're looking for a value of the entire collection. Someone will have to catalog the collection one stamp at a time, assess the quality and value of each stamp, and then put a value on the collection." He flipped through more pages. "I can tell you that I've never seen a collection of nineteenth-century European stamps this complete. Looking at the scope of the collection, I'd say there's more value here than just the value of the individual stamps. Someone would bid a lot to fill their collection with these stamps."

"Are we talking thousands of dollars?" I asked.

"Without cataloging them, I hate to even guess."

"Are there any really rare ones in here?" I asked.

He leaned back and stared at the ceiling for a minute, then opened the album of South American stamps. He flipped through the pages until he stopped at a page of oddly shaped stamps. He smiled. "South American stamps of this vintage are much rarer than European stamps."

He turned the album so I could see the page from British Guiana.

"These are rare?"

"At auction, this page of stamps is probably worth two hundred dollars. That's a lot of money in the world of amateur stamp collectors."

My mind was overloaded. "How do I get these cataloged and priced?"

"I could loan you my catalog of stamp values, but there are lots of minute factors that grossly affect a stamp's value, from the number of perforations per inch, to the cancellation mark, to how they were hinged, to watermarks."

"What's a watermark?" I asked.

"Hang on," he said. He got up and I heard footfalls going down the stairs. Minutes later he was back with a magnifying glass, a stamp on a plastic tray, and a cloudy plastic squeeze bottle.

"Okay," he said. "Look at this stamp under the magnifying glass."

It was a British stamp marked in pence with a circular cancellation stamp cutting one corner. "I'm looking," I said.

He squirted some liquid on the stamp and an indistinct image appeared on the paper. As soon as the paper started to dry, it became invisible.

"Did you see it?"

"It's a hidden image that disappeared," I said.

"That's a watermark. It's in the paper the stamp is printed on. Many countries used them to prevent counterfeiting."

"How does that affect the value?"

"Only a few of the stamps on a sheet are over a watermark. And there are some counterfeit stamps. If you have a stamp with the watermark, you know it's genuine and rarer, so it's worth more than a stamp without a watermark."

"So, someone has to go through all of these stamps and test them for watermarks before we know how valuable they are?"

"Not all of them. Some stamps weren't made with watermarks, but some key ones are greatly affected by the presence or absence of the watermark."

I pushed myself back from the table and clenched my eyes shut. It was too complicated.

"I love it," Larry said. "I spend my winters in the basement hovering over the new stamps, counting perforations, and testing for watermarks. It's my own personal mystery investigation."

"If these albums were part of your collection, how long would it take you to examine and catalog all these stamps?"

"I'd be busy for years!" he said with a smile. "I'd be in heaven." He paused and his eyes got wide. "Would you sell them to me?"

"You said we couldn't determine the value until they're all examined. How would we set a price on the collection?"

He leaned back, considering the question. The doorbell rang and I heard Larry's wife walk across the living room and open the door. She gasped. I jumped up, turned the corner, and found myself staring into the barrel of a pistol wielded by a man wearing a ski mask.

In most of the country, a man wearing a ski mask would send the neighbors scurrying to their phones to call the police. In Two Harbors, more people wear ski masks or snowmobile helmets than don't. I knew no one in the neighborhood was dialing 911; Len was not going to come racing to our rescue.

"Give me the Bible," the male voice said, advancing toward me.

"What Bible?" I asked as I retreated toward the kitchen.

"The old man's Bible," the man said. "Give me the Bible and I walk away. No one has to get hurt."

Nancy Mohr had backed into a corner of the kitchen and was holding her hand over her mouth. She seemed safe. Larry hadn't seen the gun yet. I motioned for him to sit as the man in the ski mask walked into the kitchen.

"I don't have Alf's Bible," I said in my most non-threatening voice.

"I saw you carry it in here. Where is it?"

I pointed to the pile of stamp albums on the table. "I brought stamp albums, not a Bible."

The eyes inside the ski mask darted to the table and back at me. "Stamps?"

"Postage stamps."

"You carried a freakin' stamp collection here? What the hell?"

He turned to Larry. "Where's the Bible?"

Having no clue what was going on, he answered, "In the church?"

"Don't get smart with me. I came here for the old man's Bible."

"We aren't church people," Nancy said. "We don't have a Bible."

"You've got to be shitting me," the man said, becoming more agitated.

"The Bible was taken when Alf Paluzzo was kidnapped. No one has seen it since then. Really," I said.

"I know that. I want the other Bible. The one with the clue in it."

"There was only one Bible," I said.

"Flip those books open," the man said to Larry. "And you stay back," he said to me.

Larry slowly opened the stamp albums, one at a time, and flipped through the pages. "See. Just stamps."

The man rolled his eyes.

While the masked man was looking at the stamp albums, I studied his pistol. Something didn't look right about it, but it took me a few seconds to see the seam in the cast metal casing.

There was a chip in the black paint at the end of the barrel. I lowered my hands.

"Give me the gun," I said to him. "Mrs. Mohr, dial 911."

"You guys hold still or I'll shoot!"

"What the hell are you doing?" Larry yelled.

I reached out and put my hand on top of the gun and yanked it out of the man's hand. He spun around and took a step toward the door, but I stuck out my foot and tripped him slightly, causing him to stagger. That half step caused him to twist and his hip hit the corner of the sewing machine just inside the living room. He sprawled onto the carefully arranged quilting pieces. I heard drawers slamming in another room and Nancy Mohr's voice on the phone with the dispatcher.

Larry appeared at the hallway door with his own gun, a real Colt model 1911 Army pistol. He racked the slide and pointed it at the man's chest. "Get up and put your hands on your head, jackass," he said.

A siren whined in the distance and I heard Nancy answering the dispatcher's questions. I took a step forward and ripped the ski mask off the man's head, exposing Emse's grandson, Dan, our tour guide at the brewery. In the distance, a chorus of sirens wailed. I could hear Nancy explaining to the dispatcher that the masked intruder had been disarmed and her husband was holding him at gunpoint. I had a sudden vision of a policeman barging in, seeing Larry holding a gun, and shooting.

"On the floor," I commanded Dan.

"What?"

I grabbed him by the collar and pulled him to the floor. A spool of lace was next to my knee, so I tied his hands with it.

"Peter, you've either got guts or you're crazy," Larry said.

"It's a toy gun," I said.

"Peter, stand back. If he twitches, I'll shoot him."

"Don't let him shoot me," Dan wailed. "I won't move."

"Do you know this dirtbag?" Larry asked.

"I'm guessing he's the guy who killed Alf Paluzzo at Big Rock," I said.

"Let me shoot him. It'll save the taxpayers a lot of money."

"No shooting," I said, trying to keep myself positioned between Larry and the now-sobbing intruder. "He's got a lot of questions to answer."

"Bam!" The report of the gun inside the house was deafening and a spider-webbed hole in the front window above my head showed how close the bullet's path had been.

"Geez, Larry!" I yelled.

"Sorry," he replied, looking sheepish with the gun wobbling in his two-handed stance.

"I'll answer anything. Just don't let him shoot me," wailed Dan.

"How did you know about the Bible?" I asked.

"The old guy was blabbing to everyone about it. I overheard him telling a table of old men about it when they toured the brewery."

"How did you get Alf out of Whistling Pines?"

"I went to his apartment with the gun, but he started blubbering about not knowing where the gold was. When the fire alarm went off I grabbed the Bible and we went out the loading dock door while everyone else was going out the front."

"Why did you go to Big Rock?" I asked. "Did Alf tell you the gold was there?"

"Alf was driving me nuts." He hiccupped. "He was confused and said he couldn't figure out the clues. I strapped him in the car and we drove outside of town. When I stopped the car he was mumbling about the Bible and a jar under a rock. I figured he was talking about Big Rock swimming hole. There's always been rumors about gold being hidden there and I figured maybe that was what he was talking about.

"It was screwed up from the beginning. I was chipping at the mud under the rock when he started complaining about being cold and hungry. I was hot, sweaty, and angry. When he told me he didn't think the gold was at Big Rock, I lost it and hit him with the pickaxe," Dan said. "I didn't mean to kill him. He was just . . . just so damned irritating. He prattled on endlessly about the Bible, his house in Zim, and the gold. I was tired, frustrated from chopping at the frozen mud, and furious. I just wanted to shut him up."

"He really did kill that old guy?" Larry asked, his gun arm starting to droop from holding the heavy old pistol. I knew the cops would be at the door any second.

"Larry, unload your gun and put it in the kitchen."

"Can't I shoot him first? I mean, he's an armed killer inside my house. It's justified."

"Don't shoot me!" Dan wailed.

"He wasn't really armed. Put the gun away before a cop shoots you." I handed Larry the toy gun. "Put this by your Colt."

Seeing the first Two Harbors police car roll up in front of the house, Larry reasoned through my request and trotted into the kitchen. I heard the gun's slide rack and a live shell skitter across the floor.

Nancy Mohr stepped into the living room and froze.

"You used hand-tatted Belgian lace to tie him up? Do you have any idea how much that costs?"

A young Two Harbors policeman raced up the steps with his gun in hand. I met him as he hit the top step.

"The intruder is tied up on the living room floor." I held the door open wide and stepped back.

He stepped into the house and took in the scene: The ski mask was laying on the floor next to a man tied with lace. Larry, Nancy, and I were standing near the kitchen door.

"Who called this in?" the cop asked, staring at Dan, who was sobbing uncontrollably.

"I did," Nancy said. "This is my husband. He and Peter were talking about stamps when this guy barged into the house carrying a gun."

Len's cruiser rolled to a stop, blocking the first car. A county deputy arrived a moment later. They ran into the house together.

Len stared at Dan, shaking his head. Then he looked at me.

"What?" I asked.

"You seem to show up at all the wrong places," he said. "Tell me what happened while Officer Melin cuffs this guy."

"Don't cut the lace," Nancy commanded. "Untie it. I might be able to salvage some of it."

Melin looked at Len, seeking direction. Len shrugged. "Sure. Untie it after you latch the cuffs."

We went into the kitchen, where I pointed out Dan's toy gun. Nancy's adrenaline was wearing off and she started to shake. She rattled off the story like a machine gun. Len slowed her down a couple times, but he quickly got the gist of me bringing the stamps, the crazy masked man looking for a Bible, and me taking the gun out of the intruder's hand.

"You were one-hundred-percent sure it was a fake gun?" Len asked.

"The paint was chipped and I could see the seam in the metal where the halves of the casting didn't quite match. I was sure it was a toy."

Len looked at Larry. "Did you think it was fake?"

"I was kind of busy looking at the big hole in the barrel staring at me. I didn't have time to reason through the nuances of real versus fake guns."

Len rubbed his hand over his face and shook his head. "Peter, let me tell you this once, and only once. If you ever pull a stupid stunt like this again, I'll shoot you myself. The very last thing I ever want to do is knock on your door to tell your lovely wife that you're in the emergency room or, heaven forbid, the morgue. Are we clear on that?"

"It was fake, Len."

"I don't care if it was made of licorice. Don't mess with people bearing guns. Okay?"

"But."

"No buts. Nod your head yes and say okay."

I drew a deep breath and said, "Okay."

"Now, all three of you come to the police station. I'll have someone take your statements. Then you'll be free to go."

"One other thing, Len," I said. "Dan killed Alf."

"How do you know that?"

"He told us. He kidnapped Alf, took the Bible, and drove to Big Rock. He said he followed me here looking for another Bible, since he couldn't find a clue in the family one."

"Well, I'll call the BCA to let them know we'll have a set of prints heading their way that'll probably match the ones they recovered from the pickaxe and the house in Zim."

"I need to call Jenny and the director to explain why I didn't come back from lunch."

"We'll have to get your statement first," Len said, shaking his head. "What time is your wedding rehearsal?"

"Oh, crap," I said looking at my watch. "Just a couple hours. I have to go home and shower too."

At the police station we had to wait for Len to find someone who could record and transcribe our statements. Nancy Mohr was past the adrenaline rush and now into the horror stage. Larry was into the analysis of what had happened.

"You know, if he'd had a real gun, this would've been a whole different situation," he said.

"I know. I wouldn't have taken it away from him and he might've shot one or more of us."

"You think he might've shot us?" Nancy Mohr asked.

"Yup."

"Holy crap. That's scary!" said Larry Mohr.

"We shouldn't be talking about this before they get our statements," I said. "What would you like to do with the stamp collection?"

Larry got a silly grin. "I'll make you a deal. I'll go through the albums and put together what I think the book and auction values might be. It's going to take me a long time, maybe a couple years, but I'll have fun discovering the gems. All I ask is that you give me first right of refusal once I have a price. There are a lot of items that I'd like to put into my own collection. I could glean those stamps and still be able to sell the rest and break even."

"If you buy some replacement lace, too," I said sheepishly, "you've got a deal."

CHAPTER 21
FRIDAY AFTERNOON

As if the intruder at the Mohrs' house wasn't enough, there was still so much to do before the rehearsal. I was going through the list in my head and nearing home when my cell-phone rang. "This is Peter."

"Did you pick up the tux?" Barbara asked.

"Yes, I picked it up five minutes ago."

"You are planning to wear a suit to the rehearsal and groom's dinner," she said.

"I'm on my way home to change."

"Please try to be on time. Pastor Redmond made it clear that he goes to bed early and there will be lots of people who will want to wish you well," she said.

I bit my tongue, not pointing out that they'd all shake my hand tomorrow. "I should be there early," I replied politely. "All I have to do is shower, change, and run a comb through my hair."

I rounded the corner, half a block from my house, when I hit the "end" button. To my horror, Dolores was standing in her front yard shouting at a bull moose as she poked its nose with a broom. I locked my brakes as I got to Dolores's house and slammed the transmission into park.

"Step back, Dolores!" I shouted as I eased around the front of the car. As I spoke, the moose turned its head to look at me.

"He's destroying my shrubs!" Dolores shouted back.

"Just back away from him," I said softly, trying to de-escalate the confrontation. To his credit, the moose looked more curious than mad as he munched on the remnants of Dolores's shrubs. "Don't make him mad."

"I'm hopping mad," replied Dolores, poking at the moose again as he bent down for another mouthful of the shrub. "He's eating my arborvitae!"

I moved slowly, keeping my eyes on the moose, ready to run if he showed signs of aggression. He seemed more interested in the shrubs than Dolores, chewing idly as Dolores waved her broom at him. I was reaching for the broom when Dolores made a stab at the moose, poking him in the eye.

I grabbed the broom and put an arm around Dolores's waist, lifting her and backing toward her steps. The moose shook his head, blinking the irritated eye. His eyes locked with mine and I sensed the shift in his mood. The hackles rose on my neck. I dropped the broom and sprinted for the steps, setting Dolores on the top step. I heard a snort and bolted up the four steps. We would've been inside if Dolores hadn't stopped abruptly in the doorframe.

"You're not going to leave my good broom outside, are you?" she asked.

Before I could answer, a giant antler hit my side. I had no sensation of pain, I just seemed to float through the air in slow motion in an out-of-body experience, right up to the time I hit the porch railing, bounced, then slammed into the siding.

Seeing stars, I was suddenly back inside a Humvee that had been rolled by an exploding IED. People were shouting and I heard gunfire. I tried to get up but a searing pain in my ribs took my breath away. The jolt of pain brought me back to the present. The moose was standing at the bottom of the steps snorting and pawing the ground. Dolores finally understood the danger and had stepped inside the house, slamming the door behind her.

"Nice moose," I said softly. I felt somewhat secure being maybe twenty feet away inside the porch railing. The moose relaxed a bit, at least he stopped snorting, but continued to stare at me, cocking his head. "Go away, moose," I pleaded.

I tried to sit up, which brought another shooting pain to my ribs. "If it hurts now, I can hardly imagine how much pain I'll have when the adrenaline wears off," I said to the moose.

The moose no longer looked threatening, so I decided to just lay down. It felt better, and I rationalized that playing dead was a defense against a bear attack so maybe it worked on moose, too. The cold porch felt good against my ribs. I stared at the moose whose warm breath turned to steam that rose over his head. It fascinated me as I drifted into unconsciousness.

I'm not sure how long I was out but the moose apparently lost interest. I opened an eye and watched him meander across my yard and down the street. As he disappeared from my view, I heard the creak of rusty hinges. Dolores stepped onto the porch carrying what appeared to be a Civil War-vintage pistol with a ten-inch barrel.

"No!" I gasped as she tried to point it in the direction of the retreating moose. Luckily, the gun was so heavy that she couldn't lift it up to aim, even using two hands.

"He's going to get away," she said, obviously disappointed.

"Good," I rasped. "Could you dial 911? I think I need an ambulance."

CHAPTER 22
THE HOSPITAL

I opened my eyes and idly watched as ER personnel busied themselves with tasks around my hospital bed. "You're awake," a short, dark-haired nurse said. She was wearing green surgical scrubs. A surgical mask dangled around her neck.

"What happened?" I asked, trying to get my eyes to focus.

"According to the EMTs, you lost a fight with a moose."

"What's broken?" I asked. The pain was intense.

"Wiggle your fingers and toes," the nurse commanded. Her name tag became clearer, Mary Lu was her name.

"They all work," I said, wiggling my digits as directed. "But my ribs hurt like hell."

A coughing fit followed and each spasm caused incredible pain. When I caught my breath I was staring at a man dressed in blue scrubs and a white lab coat, with a stethoscope draped around his neck. Chet Billings, M.D. was embroidered on his chest.

"Peter, you're back again," he said.

"Listen, I'm supposed to be at my groom's dinner. What time is it?"

"You're not going anywhere until I get some lab reports and take a look at your X-rays." The doctor lifted my hand and ran his fingers over the scars. "Mary Lu, did I ever tell you about the guy from Whistling Pines who wrestled with a skunk?"

Mary Lu stepped to my bedside. "No, doctor. I don't believe you ever told me about that."

"Peter was here a few months ago. I treated him for skunk bites. Because we didn't capture the animal for rabies testing, we had to give him rabies shots, directly into his wound, in addition to sewing up his hand," said Doctor Billings. "The shots hurt like hell, don't they Peter?"

"That hardly describes the pain," I replied.

"Did the skunk spray you?" Mary Lu asked.

"I forget," I replied, hoping to move on to my newer injuries.

"Oh, yes," said Doctor Billings. "Peter came in and the stink nearly brought tears to my eyes. We had to incinerate his clothes. After treating his wounds we washed him with a mixture of hydrogen peroxide and baking soda, at the suggestion of our local veterinarian."

"Peter, how did you get into a fight with a skunk?" asked Mary Lu. "Most adults have more sense than that."

"That would be due to the unfortunate incident." Jenny's voice came from the doorway. "He took a load of senior citizens out for a trip. After lunch at Dixie's, he left the van door open when he went inside. When the residents came out to take their seats, someone cried 'Skunk!' and everyone rushed for the door. Hulda Packer got stuck in the rear of the van with her walker. Peter took off his jacket, threw it over the skunk, and carried it out of the van. The skunk wasn't particularly appreciative. He bit, scratched, and sprayed as Peter carried him away."

"So," the doctor continued, "Jenny retrieved a spare uniform from her car, which happened to be a set of pink scrubs with yellow ducklings. The pants fit his waist, but were way too short. His midriff was left bare and they hardly covered half his calves. That's what he was wearing when he was released."

"Yes," said Jenny. "Several of the residents had bumps and bruises in the rush to get out of the van. They were released at the same time as Peter. Hulda Packer grabbed Peter's arm and told him that the yellow duckie scrubs were unprofessional. She stepped close so she could see through her thick glasses, looked at the scrubs top, which was tailored to fit my bust, and added, 'Peter, you must stop wearing women's clothing. People will get the wrong idea.'"

"Did you ever get the skunk smell out of the van, or did you have to sell it?" asked the doctor, who was grinning from ear to ear.

"We had it fumigated," said Jenny. "It was out of commission for three weeks. By then it was cold enough that the skunks had all hibernated, but that hasn't stopped people from reminding Peter to keep the door closed when the van is warming up."

In the hallway I heard the approach of clanging bangles. "Oh," said Mother, who caught the end of the discussion. "Are you talking about the unfortunate incident?"

"Yes," said Jenny, as the medical staff stifled laughter. "Doctor Billings was just telling the nurses about it."

"Could you give Peter a tetanus shot and send him on his way?" asked Mother, who'd apparently already had a few glasses of wine at the VFW before arriving at the hospital. "He's late for his bachelor party."

Doctor Billings turned from the computer where he'd been entering notes. "Attendance at a bachelor party would be AMA."

"AMA?" Mother slurred.

"Against medical advice," I said. "Don't worry, it's a groom's dinner, not a bachelor party."

"What's the difference?" Mother asked.

"There won't be any dancing girls, pranks, or excessive alcohol consumption." Jenny said.

"It appears there's already been some significant alcohol consumption," said the doctor, looking at Mother.

"Why won't the doctor allow him to leave?" I heard Jenny's mother, Barbara, ask from the hallway.

"They were talking about the unfortunate incident," said Mother.

"Peter wasn't sprayed by a skunk again, was he?" asked Barbara.

"No," said the doctor. "He was butted by a moose and I'm waiting for his chest X-ray before I release him."

"A moose?" asked Barbara. "Where did you find a moose, Peter?"

"Dolores was trying to shoo it out of her yard with a broom."

"But they're dangerous. Why would she chase a moose with a broom?"

"What kind of moose?" I heard Jeremy's voice from the hallway.

"Could we break up this family reunion? You guys go back to the VFW. As soon as the doctor releases me, Jenny will drive me back."

Nurse Mary Lu directed the doctor to a computer station. "The X-rays are back."

He tapped a few keys and my X-ray popped up. "You're lucky," said Billings, studying the screen. "You've got a couple broken ribs, but they aren't displaced. Based on the bruising on your face, I'd say your head took quite a blow. I suspect you also have a concussion, so you should probably not drink alcohol, nor should you be left alone tonight."

Jenny came to the bedside and squeezed my hand. "I'll make sure he follows those orders."

"You're getting married tomorrow?" asked Billings as he keyed notes into the computer.

"Yes, at the Lutheran Church," Mother replied.

The doctor approached the bed and looked earnestly at Jenny. "I understand . . . um, tradition, but Peter will not be ready for any post-marital . . . gymnastics for at least ten days."

Jeremy's head popped up at the foot of the bed. "You were going to do gymnastics?" he asked.

"I think my gymnastics days are behind me," I said as Jenny blushed.

"Being a corpsman, you already know that there is not much I can do to treat rib injuries other than to tell you to take it easy. I advise against laughter, sneezing, or coughing for a few days."

"Or gymnastics," added Jeremy.

— ◆ —

It was nearly ten by the time Jenny and I arrived at the VFW. Jenny's father, Howard, was quietly sipping Scotch, neat. Barbara's tasteful dress looked a little worse for the wear after a long evening in the hospital and VFW. My mother was waving her arms, emoting as she spouted the solutions to the world's problems that primarily involved taxing the rich and giving money to the poor. Between sentences she gulped red wine. Barbara sat quietly, biting her tongue about the politics and sipping chardonnay.

"Oh, Peter," Mother said, digging in her purse. "I went to the bank yesterday. Here's the gift from your father. I got it out of the safety deposit box." She handed me a black velvet bag that was worn bare in spots. "It was your grandfather's."

Jeremy bounded across the room and pushed next to me, causing a sharp pain in my ribs. "What's in the bag?" he asked.

The small bag had little heft to it, so I knew it wasn't filled with gold coins. I untied the string and poured the contents into my hand.

"What is it?" asked Jeremy.

"It's a watch," I said, turning it so I could see the rectangular face.

"It's not even digital," said Jeremy.

I handed it to Jenny as I fought back tears, caused by a combination of emotion, exhaustion, and the pain pills.

"It's a very old Rolex watch," said Jenny, turning it in her hands and inspecting the leather band and the crown emblem on the stem. She handed it to Howard who carefully rubbed his thumb across the back.

"It's old, very old," Howard said, rubbing the face and back with his thumb. "I understand why it was in a safety deposit box."

"Howard, please take care of it," I said, grimacing. "I'm not sure I'm lucid enough to make sure it gets home."

"Is everything set for tomorrow?" Mother asked, in a sudden change of topic. "I suppose there are some things I need to do."

Barbara stiffened. Mother, being immersed in her own Duluth life, hadn't shown any interest in the Two Harbors wedding plans. It was totally in character that she would want to imprint her own twist on the ceremony at the eleventh hour.

"There's really nothing left to do," said Barbara, "Jenny and I have made all the arrangements and everything will go like clockwork. You really don't need to do anything but arrive at the church a half hour before the service for photos."

Mother, feeling the effects of the wine, which effectively removed what remained of any verbal filter, said, "I think it's so nice that brides with children from previous relationships can wear white gowns. In our day, those brides had to elope or at least wear an ivory gown. The world has come so far." Mother suddenly sat up straight, spilling wine on the table. "Peter, you can't have children for a while. I'm too young to be a grandmother."

"Mother, this is not the time or place for this conversation," I said. "Perhaps someone can give you a ride to your hotel." I threw a desperate look at Howard who set his drink aside and stood.

"But I want to make sure you understand," she slurred. "No grandchildren until I'm at least seventy!"

Barbara, having consumed more than her usual one glass of wine, saw an opportunity to make Mother squirm and patted her on the arm. "Audrey, you're going to have an instant grandson. Peter is adopting Jeremy."

"Noooo," Mother wailed. "I'm too young to have grandchildren."

Howard gently helped Mother out of her chair and guided her to the door. "It will be okay. Things will look different after the wedding."

"But I can't be a grandmother yet," Mother sobbed as she walked out the door.

I was putting on my coat when my cellphone buzzed in my pocket.

I didn't recognize the phone number, but it was local so I took a chance and answered, hoping it was too late for a telemarketer to call.

"This is Peter."

"Hi Peter. This is Larry Mohr. Your voice doesn't sound right."

"I had a little accident this afternoon and my nose is filled with cotton."

"Ouch. I hope you're okay. Say, I've been leafing through the stamps this afternoon and evening. There are some real gems in here."

"That's great, Larry. Can I call you on Monday? I'm a little tied up right now."

"Sure, we can talk on Monday, but there's something I've got to tell you now or I won't sleep tonight. I got to Australia, New Zealand, and the South Pacific section and I was floored. There were some stamps that weren't even in the catalog. I had to call a buddy of mine who does stamp auctions and he looked them up online."

"That's great. I really appreciate your hard work," I said, trying to end the call.

"No, wait. A lot of the South Pacific islands were colonies and most just used the stamps of the empire they were in. The Brits are into their stamps, think of the Boston Tea party. Anyway . . ."

"Can you get to the punchline? My pain pills are wearing off."

"Sure. The Solomon Islands were a British Colony and they started printing their own stamps in the middle 1800s. They printed very few and most were probably thrown away with the envelopes. Because of that, they are extremely rare. The collection you left with me has a corner block of four stamps with a watermark, and they aren't cancelled."

"They're valuable?"

"Peter, they're worth a fortune. Literally worth a fortune."

I was stunned.

"Are you still there?"

"Yeah, I'm trying to digest what you just said."

"You were talking about this old guy whose brother died on Guadalcanal and the hint he got about the family fortune being where he died. Well, I'm sitting here looking at his family's fortune. You were right about the Song of Solomon. But it was the Solomon Islands."

"Give me a second. I have to sit down." I sat on a barstool. "I'm sorry, but I can't process the information right now. Can we talk later?"

"Hey, I felt the same way. Call me Monday and I'll show them to you."

I dropped my phone into my pocket.

"Are you okay?" Jenny asked, putting her hand on my arm.

"Not really. I just learned where Alf Paluzzo's family fortune is."

"The police found the Bible and it led them to the gold?" Jenny asked.

"It never was in the Bible and there's no gold. It's the stamp collection."

CHAPTER 23

SATURDAY

After a call to Len Rentz to explain the stamp collection, Jenny drove me home and kept me under surveillance for the night. She slept on the couch and woke me every two hours to offer a drink of water and to assess my condition. By morning, neither of us had slept more than a few hours.

Jenny had dark rings under her eyes when she woke me at 9:00. I went into the bathroom and was shocked at the deep purple bruise covering half my face. I tried to take a deep breath, but gasped at the pain in my ribs.

Jenny watched from the bathroom door. "You're not going in the shower," she said. "I think you'd better shave, wash up in the sink, dab on some deodorant, and run a comb through your hair. I'm driving your car home to shower and dress. I'll have my dad pick you up at noon."

Shaving was nearly impossible on the swollen purple side of my face. I gave up after I'd cut myself a half-dozen times. As instructed, I washed up and then lay down on the bed in exhaustion. I was taking a catnap when Howard rang the doorbell and walked in.

"You look even worse today than you did last night," he said as I slipped on a pair of khaki pants. "How do you plan to deal with the pain today?"

I stood, grimacing from the searing pain in my ribs. "I have to take a Percocet."

Howard nodded. "I can see that you need it, but it's going to make your wedding day a blur."

I walked to the kitchen and took a Percocet tablet, then ate a carton of yogurt. Howard made coffee and when it was done he handed me a cup.

"You're going to need some caffeine."

"Oh, yeah," I replied, as I sat across from him at the kitchen table.

After a few minutes of sipping coffee, the "aah" moment arrived when the Percocet finally hit my bloodstream.

"Okay," I said, rising from the chair. "The Percocet is working."

I dressed in the rented tux and patent leather shoes. Howard was sipping coffee and reading the newspaper in the kitchen. "Let's go," I said, putting the bottle of pain pills in my pocket.

———— ◆ ————

The empty Lutheran church echoed. Pastor Redmond met us inside the door and shook our hands. "I'm honored that you asked me to perform the wedding," he said. "You know, I married Barbara and Howard, baptized Jenny and her son. I feel very proud to be able to perform this ceremony, marrying Peter and Barbara."

I cringed. Pastor Redmond was well into his eighties and during our meetings, I'd seen signs of early dementia, which included calling Jenny by her mother's name. "Pastor, I'm marrying Jenny. Barbara is the bride's mother."

"Oh, yes," he said, laughing off the slip. "Don't worry. I'll get it right during the wedding ceremony." He patted my arm, but I felt little reassurance. He noticed my bruised face. "Oh dear, did you have a car accident?"

"No, a moose head-butted me."

He laughed. "No, really, what happened?"

"A moose butted him," Howard replied.

"Well, I'm sure the bruises will make for memorable wedding pictures."

My mind recoiled. "Oh, no. I'd forgotten about the wedding pictures."

"Don't worry," said Howard. "I'm sure the photographer can Photoshop the bruises out of the pictures. It'll just take her a little extra time."

The door creaked as Wendy walked in with a folder of sheet music under her arm. She was dressed in a striking kelly green dress that showed a little cleavage, leaving a bit of a tattoo visible. "Good afternoon," she said. "I want to practice a bit before the guests show up."

Pastor Redmond introduced himself and stared unashamedly at Wendy's cleavage. "You have a tattoo."

Wendy, never one to shy away from attention, exposed a bit more of the tattoo, and her breast. "It's a teddy bear," she said, glancing at me. I shook my head. "But I think he has to stay in hibernation today."

"Wendy," said the pastor, obviously trying to make the name stick in his mind. "Wendy, I'll have to remember your name."

"You should come up to Hugo's sometime," she said. "I sing in a band."

"Oh, you play organ and sing. You're very talented, Wendy."

Wendy smiled. "Excuse me. I have to run through the music a couple more times before the guests arrive."

The pastor was mesmerized, watching Wendy walk away to the organ. "Wendy seems like an interesting person. And so talented."

"Yes, she is," I said. "But, I need to sit down for a few moments. I'm very sore."

Pastor Redmond pulled out a chair for me. "Your injuries are more extensive than just the bruise on your face?"

"He has a couple broken ribs, too," said Howard. "I think this is going to be a very long day for Peter."

Michelle, the photographer, swept through the creaking doors with bags hanging from both shoulders. A step behind was Barbara, who was dressed in a tasteful pink dress with a string of pearls.

"I thought we'd take pictures of the wedding party on the altar steps," said Barbara. "Will that work?" she asked Michelle.

The pastor walked past Howard and me with a nod, as Michelle set down her bags and considered the front of the church. As they chatted, Wendy started playing "Penny Lane." It was a standing joke between us that "Penny Lane" was a song suitable for all occasions, and she'd even played it at a funeral, much to the confusion of the elderly Whistling Pines residents. It was not one of the songs we'd chosen for the wedding.

Once she recognized the melody, Barbara rushed to the organ and quietly reminded Wendy of the song selections. Behind her, the photographer set up her equipment.

Jeremy, my best man, rushed into the church, followed by Jenny's high school friend, Betsy, the maid of honor, plus Kim and Cassie, Jenny's closest friends from work. Cassie, Kim, and Betsy were wearing ruffled mint green dresses that Jenny had described to me, but I hadn't seen before. They were chatting as they rushed past us to talk to the photographer. Behind them came one of the groomsmen, Vern, the bartender from the VFW who had befriended me when I came back from Iraq and suggested that I apply for the recreation director's job at Whistling Pines. He was a Vietnam veteran with a deeply creased face and chose to wear his graying hair in a ponytail. I was shocked to see him with a short, nicely combed haircut.

"Peter, what happened to your face?" he asked.

"A moose butted me," I replied. "What happened to your hair?" I asked.

"Your future mother-in-law hinted that she'd like to see me with a different haircut for the wedding."

"I've never seen you in anything but a ponytail," I said.

"I haven't worn my hair this short since I came home from 'Nam," he replied. "Barbara can be very persuasive."

Len, my other groomsman, walked in with a fresh haircut too.

"You got Barbara's message about haircuts too?" Vern asked.

"She just hinted that I was a bit shaggy and might want a trim."

I looked at Howard, who'd been listening. He shrugged and said, "Welcome to my life."

As we talked, Wendy played through the three songs we'd chosen for the wedding as well as the processional and recessional. As expected, she played flawlessly. When she finished, I noticed Pastor Redmond leaning on the organ chatting with her. It was obvious that she had a new fan. It struck me that he might be a candidate for residency in the memory care unit at Whistling Pines.

Michelle, the photographer, walked over and announced that she was ready to start the pictures. When I stood, she blanched. "Peter, let me look at your face." She gently put a finger under my chin and rotated my head from side to side. Barbara watched intently.

"I'm stumped," said Michelle. "It'll be nearly impossible to manipulate the images to hide Peter's bruising. We can set up so we're shooting his right side, but even then some of the purple will show through."

"Sit here," said Barbara as she took a makeup kit from of her purse. She gently layered lotion, foundation, and powders on my face. Then, she stepped back.

"That's not perfect," she said. "But it's the best I can do with what I have."

Michelle knelt next to me and rotated my chin again. "You're right, it's not perfect, but I can work with the lighting and I'll be able to keep the deepest bruises and swelling in the shadows."

Behind her I heard a low chuckle. Vern was covering his face, trying to hide his smile.

"What," I asked.

"I think you look pretty good with a little makeup," Vern replied. "Maybe you should wear some all the time."

I was about to make a profane reply when I saw Jeremy listening. "Thanks for your suggestion, Vern, but I think I'll go back to au naturel when the wedding is over."

"If you two are through," said Michelle, "let's take some pictures of the groom and attendants before his makeup gets smeared."

Michelle was arranging us on the altar steps when the back door creaked and the sound of jangling bangles echoed throughout the sanctuary. Mother entered the church without her usual flair. As she walked toward the altar I could see that she was suffering from the effects of her wine consumption. Her hair wasn't as fluffy as usual, there were bags under her eyes, and her usual sparkle was absent. She virtually fell into the front pew.

"I feel like shit," she said. "Does anyone have some Tylenol?"

Barbara sorted through her purse. "I'm sure I have some. And after you take a couple Tylenol, perhaps you'll let me touch up your makeup."

Mother swallowed the pills without water and, to my surprise, let Barbara apply makeup to her face. When they were done, Michelle pulled us all onto the steps and checked the lighting. The bridesmaids were chatting and Jeremy was regaling Vern with a story about school when the room went silent. We all looked to the back of the church where Jenny had entered, holding her father's arm. Her white dress and veil were backlit by the open door and she looked like an angel with an aura. I was stunned by her beauty and my pain disappeared.

CHAPTER 24

SATURDAY AFTERNOON

I watched the guests trickle into the church. I recognized several faces from Whistling Pines but most others were unfamiliar. I assumed they were Jenny's relatives or her parents' friends. A large group of senior citizens surged through the door when the Whistling Pines van arrived. Dolores came in behind them with three of her friends. None of them looked like they should be driving, a fact I chose to ignore.

The church was nearly full when Len tapped me on the shoulder. "It's time." We wandered into a small room hidden behind the altar. Jeremy, Len, and Vern shook my hand and were about to leave for their walk down the aisle with the bridesmaids when I leaned close to Len and said, "Please check Dolores's purse to make sure she didn't bring a gun."

"I've already checked," Len said with a smile. "She's not packing today." They disappeared down a side aisle.

"Peter," said the pastor as Len and Vern left, "you and I will walk out when the music changes. Your job is to stand quietly and smile. When we get to the vows, just repeat after me." With those words, the song changed and we walked out and stood in front of the altar. We watched silently as Jeremy and Betsy led the procession down the aisle, followed by the bridesmaids and groomsmen. Last were Jenny's cousins, Teddy, the ring bearer, and Megan, the flower girl.

I scanned the crowded church and saw smiling faces. All except for George Harvey, one of our newer residents, who was seated beside Howard Johnson. George, with beads of sweat on his brow, took several glances down the aisle throughout the procession of bridesmaids, ring bearer, and flower girl. As each passed he whispered to Howard. Each time, Howard shook his head no. I wondered if he was having some type of medical emergency, but I expected Howard to react if George's life was in any danger.

With all the attendants lined up on the altar steps, and the flower girl and ring bearer sitting with their parents, Wendy played "Here Comes the Bride." As the congregation stood, George stepped into the aisle with his cane and started hobbling toward the bride. Jenny and Howard stopped and waited. I looked at Barbara, whose expression went from confusion to anger. Halfway down the aisle George leaned over to one of his friends and announced in an outdoor voice, "I have to pee."

When George passed, Jenny and Howard started down the aisle. My mother was in tears and Barbara was holding a tissue to her eyes to protect her makeup from tears. Soon Howard offered Jenny's hand to me, then took his seat alongside Barbara.

"As many of you know, I retired from this parish a few years ago, but at the request of Howard and Barbara, I've returned to marry their daughter. I baptized Jenny thirty years ago, and I consider it a great privilege to preside at her wedding."

As the pastor made his comments, I saw George walk back down the aisle and slide/fall into the pew alongside Howard Johnson. He took a deep breath and leaned over to Howard, "That went well," he said, bringing a titter of laughter from the surrounding people and a glare from Barbara.

The pastor had to resort to his notes a few times, but was coherent and, at times, humorous. When he said, "And now we have a special song chosen by the bride's mother." He nodded to

Wendy, who shuffled music on the organ. Her Cheshire cat grin made me uncomfortable. She'd been reluctant to practice "O Promise Me." I looked at her and gave her the slightest head shake.

Wendy squared herself in front of the organ and burst into "If I Said You Had a Beautiful Body."

A titter broke out in the congregation and I could see Barbara shuffling through her program, trying to see if there had been a misprint.

Wendy forged on. Jenny closed her eyes and stifled a laugh.

The pastor was oblivious to the change and grinned as he looked across the smiling faces of the congregation, apparently unaware of the lyrics. When Wendy finished, the pastor nodded to her.

"I'm unfamiliar with that song, but the congregation seemed to enjoy it." I glanced at Barbara whose face was buried in Howard's shoulder. My mother was laughing, making her bangles rattle.

We stood through an overly long sermon that wasn't relevant to the wedding, or anything in the current century, before getting to the vows. Jenny and I faced each other and joined hands.

"Do you, Peter, take this woman to be your lawfully wedded wife?"

"I do."

"Do you, Barbara, take this man to be your husband?"

There was a collective gasp in the congregation and I saw terror in Jenny's eyes.

The pastor was looking at Jenny, expecting her response. I put my hand on his arm.

"Pastor," I whispered. I got a withering glare before he returned his gaze to Jenny, again looking for her affirmative response.

"Pastor, her name is Jenny, not Barbara," I said, just a little louder.

The pastor sighed and turned to me. He shuffled through the papers in his hands and unfolded one, holding it out to me. "I just filled in the marriage license. Look right here. It says Peter and Barbara Rogers." In his shaking hand I could see where he'd crossed out Jenny's name and written in Barbara, apparently correcting what he thought was an error.

"Barbara is Jenny's mother," I whispered, looking toward the front row, where Barbara was sitting, her pallor as white as Jenny's gown.

"Oh dear. Perhaps we should reschedule the wedding for another day so I can correct the license."

"Finish the ceremony," said Len, leaning close. "The paperwork can be corrected later."

"But this is a legal document," said the pastor.

"I'm the police chief. Keep going. We'll correct the license later."

"Well, this is highly irregular," said the pastor, looking suddenly confused. "Who is Peter marrying?" he asked, loud enough for the back rows of the church to hear.

Out of the corner of my eye I could see Vern glancing toward the congregation and trying to suppress a smile. I turned far enough to see Barbara with her face buried in her hands, apparently talking to herself. Howard was patting her on the shoulder and making reassuring sounds. Across the aisle, my mother was smiling and chatting with Nancy Helmbrecht, who was seated in the row behind her. They appeared to think it was hilarious.

I turned back to the pastor, who was studying the marriage license with obvious confusion.

"Pastor Redmond, I'm marrying Jenny," I said. "Please ask her if she'll marry me."

The pastor composed himself and smiled at the congregation. "Do you, Jenny . . ." He paused. "That's the right name, isn't it?"

I could hear Barbara sniffling and stomping her foot on the floor.

"Yes, she's Jenny," I said.

"Do you, Jenny, take this man to be your husband?"

"I do," Jenny whispered.

Redmond looked down at his notes and shuffled the papers. "Oh dear, we forgot the reading." He turned to Wendy and nodded.

I knew Wendy was supposed to read the verse from Ephesians 5. I also knew she didn't like it because it opened with the line, "Wives, submit yourselves to your husbands." She stepped to the lectern with a grin on her face and I knew she'd found an alternative reading. Barbara looked up. I grimaced.

Wendy arranged the paper carefully, looked at the congregation and said, "From Ogden Nash."

Barbara's jaw fell open.

I looked at Jenny, expecting her to have the same stricken look as Barbara. Instead, she was beaming.

"You knew," I whispered to her.

She nodded.

The poem ended with, "Whenever you're right, shut up."

This time the laughter was louder. Barbara's face was again buried in her hands. Howard had his arm around Barbara's shoulders, but he was grinning.

Wendy carefully folded the paper and returned to the organ bench.

The poem went over Pastor Redmond's head. He nodded to Wendy and turned back toward the congregation, smiling. "By the powers vested in me by the State of Minnesota, I declare you husband and wife."

Tears ran down Jenny's face and without prompting from the pastor, we embraced gently.

"Well, I suppose I'm introducing Mr. and Mrs. Rogers."

Len stepped past me and whispered something into the pastor's ear.

"Oh, dear," Pastor Redmond said, quieting the congregation. "It seems that in the confusion we forgot the ring ceremony. He motioned for Jeremy to bring the rings to him and he set them on his notes. He handed Jenny's wedding ring to me and said,

"Repeat after me."

I repeated "Jenny, accept this ring as a symbol of my unending love." I slipped it on her finger as tears glistened in her eyes.

When Pastor Redmond picked up the other ring it slipped from his arthritic fingers, bounced off his notes, clinked once as it hit the wooden step and quickly rolled under the pews. Jeremy was after it like a bird dog on a scent, skidding on the knees of his tuxedo pants as he ducked under the first pew and under Mother's dress. The guests started talking and shuffling their feet, as the ring rolled further into the sanctuary with Jeremy right behind, sliding under the pews on his stomach.

"Here it is!" yelled Brenda Olson, a huge woman who couldn't bend down in the narrow space between the pews.

"No! It's over here!" yelled a male voice.

I looked at Jenny, who was wiping tears from her eyes.

Barbara was wild-eyed as she watched row after row of people bend down to look for the escaping ring.

"Got it!" yelled Jeremy. He shuffled down the fifth row of pews, stumbling and stepping on toes as he went. He jumped into the aisle and ran to the altar steps, holding the ring up like a prize, oblivious to the dust that covered his tux.

Jenny broke out laughing, as did Len and Vern. Soon, the whole congregation, except Barbara, was laughing as Jeremy handed the ring to the pastor. Redmond was beet red. He took the ring between his fingers and quickly passed it to Jenny. Barbara was biting her finger and shaking her head in disbelief.

"Accept this ring as a symbol of my unending love," she said, pushing the ring onto my finger, still grinning. I hadn't seen the ring before. It was the simple, plain gold band I'd wanted.

"Now, let me introduce Mr. and Mrs. Peter Rogers," Redmond said.

We kissed, then stepped down from the altar as the congregation applauded.

As Wendy played a rousing recessional, we continued down

the aisle and arranged ourselves in the narthex to greet the guests. Barbara rushed to give me a discreet Lutheran non-touching hug and kissed me on the cheek. Before she released me, Mother tore me free and tried to give me a bear hug.

"No!" I yelled out in pain, holding her at arm's length. "I have broken ribs."

I held Mother's shoulders and pecked her cheek. She then started hugging everyone she saw. Jeremy avoided being seen.

As the guests paraded past, Barbara introduced their family to me. I mostly introduced Whistling Pines residents to her since my family representation was limited to my mother. When Dolores reached us, I fended off her hug, so she pecked me on the cheek. Breaking protocol, as only she could, she pulled Jenny over. "You've made such a lovely bride," she said. "Peter is very lucky to have you."

"Thanks," Jenny replied. It was obvious that Dolores had more to say, but Barbara discreetly took her elbow and steered her down the receiving line.

After hugging Jenny, Nancy tried to hug me, but I deflected her. "Broken ribs. I can't hug," I said for what seemed like the hundredth time.

"I'm so happy for you," she said, then she turned to Barbara, who was still rattled from the commotion during the wedding. "Barbara, it was a lovely and memorable ceremony and such a fun solo."

Barbara, the proper hostess who always had a gracious word to say in any situation, froze.

"There's no way you could've scripted the events during the ceremony," Nancy said, "but they made for the most memorable wedding I've ever attended. People will be talking about it for years."

Barbara got a deer-in-the-headlights look as she pondered the possibility of people repeating the story of the wedding for years into the future.

Wendy bounded up when the line was gone and hugged

Barbara. "You did a great job of putting this together," Wendy said. "I wish there was a video of the ring rolling off the altar steps into the crowd. It would go viral in a minute."

Barbara, overwhelmed by all the full-body hugs she'd endured, was gracious. "Thank you. You did a lovely job with the music," Barbara said as she tried to find a discreet way to peel Wendy away. I could see the twinkle in Wendy's eyes as she held Barbara, waiting to see how long the hug would go on. Barbara finally had enough and put her hands on Wendy's shoulders and gently eased her away.

"We should go down to the reception," Barbara said, trying to segue into a topic that didn't involve hugging.

"Is there an open bar?" Wendy asked.

"It's the church basement," replied Barbara. "There's no booze allowed."

"How'd you let that happen, sailor boy?" Wendy asked me with a grin.

She knew how little input I'd had in the planning and reveled in my discomfort as I searched for a politically correct answer.

"The caterers have prepared a lovely buffet," Barbara said. "We didn't think that alcohol would add to the experience."

"Lucky I've got a bottle of wine in the car," Wendy said, slipping away.

"She wouldn't ..."

"Probably not," I said. "She just likes to yank my chain ... and apparently yours."

As we ambled toward the stairs, Len took my elbow and pulled me into a corner, out of earshot from the remaining guests and wedding party. "I drove over to Larry Mohr's house this morning and looked at the stamp collection. He's convinced that the stamps from the Solomon Islands alone are worth a hundred thousand dollars at auction. The collection, in its entirety, might bring twice that."

"How ...?" I was at a loss for words.

"Alf's mother put a note in that section of the stamp album.

She explained that she had to sell most of the gold coins after Alf's father died to pay off their debts and move into town. Her brother Sid sold her the stamp collection for one of the last coins. He told her that some of the old stamps were very valuable. Larry Mohr told me that stamp collecting wasn't that big a thing until the 1950s, so Sid probably had no idea how extremely rare those stamps were or how much the value would climb as more people got interested in philately."

"So, Alf had the memory of the gold coins imprinted in his brain, and it never occurred to him that the treasure might be something else. He got fixated on the old Bible, probably because of me, and never looked at the stamp collection." I paused. "His son said I could have it. I suppose now that we know it's worth lots of money it will have to go back to Alf's son and daughter."

"I called Alf's son this morning and he's probably at Larry Mohr's house as we speak. I'd hardly hung up the phone when his daughter called, threatening me with a lawsuit if her brother took the collection without her permission."

"So you left it with Gary?" I asked.

"Alf's son showed me the will. He's the executor of the estate," Len explained. "It's his responsibility to divide it up as pre-scribed in Alf's will. It's not my problem. Or yours. You will not be the owner of the stamp collection. Now let's go down to the reception."

CHAPTER 25
THE RECEPTION

After Barbara's hours of planning and arranging, the church basement was tastefully decorated with silver wedding bells and white satin streamers. The tables were covered with linen tablecloths and each seat had a place card. As Jenny stepped into the room I could see the senior citizens moving names around on the tables. Barbara was a step behind us and I heard her gasp as she watched Hulda Packer pick up cards, study them, then move them to another location.

"What's she doing?" Barbara asked.

"Hulda has opinions," I replied.

"Stop her. We carefully planned the seating so the family groups were together."

Hulda gathered all the place cards from the table closest to the bride and groom, and replaced them with those of her deaf lady friends, who had been slated to sit closer to the rear. She pocketed the place cards set for Barbara's sister and her family.

"Kathryn and her family were supposed to sit there."

Howard patted Barbara's arm. "It's okay. Kathryn is able to talk with anyone and she doesn't need to be right next to the head table."

Hulda moved to the next table, removed the place cards, and

replaced them with the names of other Whistling Pines residents, again pocketing the original names.

"That was supposed to be for Robbie's family," Barbara moaned and turned to me. "Please stop her."

I looked at Hulda, who had shuffled to a third table and was exchanging place cards, and considered the possibilities. "It's not worth the scene she will make," I said. "She's not a quiet woman and she's quite vocal if she doesn't get what she wants."

Barbara buried her head in Howard's shoulder. He patted her back. "It'll be over soon."

The DJ was set up in the corner and he started playing some light jazz, signaling the end of the conversations. Jenny and I led the way to the buffet line, with Hulda pushing her way between the bridesmaids.

"It looks like chicken," Hulda said, leaning over the buffet. "It's always chicken," she muttered. "Chicken is cheap. I suppose if you cook it long enough no one will get food poisoning. There'd better not be any blood by the thigh bone. That's the hardest place to get done and all the salmonella collects in that part of the chicken."

"You should try some of the salads," Jenny said, trying to change the topic.

"Salads are okay, but it's hard to chew lettuce with my dentures. I haven't had an apple since they pulled the last tooth," Hulda said, scooping up a bit of macaroni salad. "Where's the pickled herring?"

"I don't think there's any pickled herring," Jenny said. Barbara was on the opposite side of the salad bar and she was emphatically shaking her head no."

"That's a shame," said Hulda. "December is the only time of year you can get decent herring. Is there a bowl of lutefisk down there? I need to save room on my plate for lutefisk."

"There's no lutefisk," Jenny said softly. "I think there's chicken and roast beef."

"Hmph," said Hulda. "I don't eat beef, not since that mad cow outbreak. You know they can't tell you've got that until they cut your brain open after you're dead."

"I'm sure this beef is safe," Jenny replied. I looked at Barbara, who was turning green with all the talk about food poisoning and mad cow disease.

"There's no tuna macaroni salad," said Hulda. She turned and hailed one of the caterers, who was dressed in a ruffled white shirt and black pants. "Hey! You forgot to put out the tuna salad!"

"There's no tuna salad," Jenny said softly as the caterer walked to the kitchen.

"The hell you say," said Hulda. "I suppose you're going to tell me there's no Jell-O salad either."

"We chose not to have a Jell-O salad," I said softly.

"What Lutheran ever put on a buffet without a Jell-O salad?" Hulda asked, even louder.

Barbara set her partially full plate on the buffet table and walked away.

"What's the matter with her?" Hulda asked. "Did she get food poisoning already?"

"I think she's just overcome by the joy of the wedding," Jenny said softly. "Would you like a roll?"

Hulda studied the basket of rolls. "I'll take a white roll. I can't eat those whole wheat ones. The seeds get stuck under my dentures and irritate the hell out of my gums. I'd have to take my plates out at the table and wipe them out."

Vern had stepped up into Barbara's spot across from us in the buffet line. Having braved the ravages of the Vietnam war and years of tipsy bar patrons, he found Hulda funny. I saw him run his tongue around inside his lips, and make a smacking sound. Len was behind him, laughing.

"Do they at least have some decent coffee?" Hulda asked, standing at the end of the line with her full plate in her hands. Both lines came to a stop while everyone waited for her to move on. "Where's the coffee?" she shouted.

One of the caterers magically appeared with a carafe and guided Hulda to her chosen spot near the head table. He turned her cup over and poured.

"Have you got some cream?" she asked. "I mean some real dairy cream, from a cow. Not those little cups of flavored crap that pretends to be cream?"

The caterer slid a silver creamer over to Hulda and stood back. With cream in her coffee and a plate full off food, I thought Hulda would be ready to go. As I chose a roll and put a pad of butter on my plate I watched her searching the table.

"Can someone push that salt shaker closer? I can't reach it."

Vern snorted. "What else can she want?" he whispered.

"Just wait," Jenny whispered back.

We took our seats at the head table just as Hulda blurted, "Has anyone got hot coffee? Mine's barely lukewarm."

A caterer rushed fresh coffee to Hulda as we ate and watched the rest of the guests make their way through the buffet line. A table in the back of the room was covered with presents wrapped in white and a small box was overflowing with cards. I knew Barbara's plan was to take all the presents back to their house where we'd open them the next day in a controlled environment so we could record the giver's name, address, and the gift they'd given. Everything was carefully orchestrated and controlled. One of the caterers stood watch over the gifts to make sure no one tampered with them.

Jenny and I stood and kissed when the guests clinked their knives on their glasses. We apparently exceeded the allotment of kisses because Barbara, who'd returned from the ladies' restroom during dinner, rolled her eyes after the fourth and fifth kisses.

After we'd eaten a few bites of dinner, cut the wedding cake, taken the requisite picture of Jenny feeding me a piece of cake and vice versa, and thanked the wedding party, Jenny and I walked around the room thanking the guests. In Hulda Packer's place-card shuffle, Mother had been seated next to Dolores and her friend Blanche.

I could tell that Dolores was uneasy and I wondered if it was due to physical discomfort or enduring too many of Mother's self-aggrandizing accounts of her charity work or her left-wing diatribes.

"Can we leave now?" Jeremy said, after rushing to us from the far side of the room.

"We have to thank the guests," Jenny said quietly. "Hang on for a few more minutes."

Jeremy wrinkled his nose, but followed along behind us, probably in the hope that his presence would move us ahead more quickly.

I noticed some commotion on the stairs. A man wearing lederhosen was backing into the basement with something clattering behind him. My view was obscured by the crowd, but he was apparently assembling some equipment. A moment later, he was followed by another man in a Tyrolean hat with an accordion strapped to his chest. My "Oh no," distracted Jenny from an earnest discussion she was having with an aunt whose name escaped me.

"What?" she asked. She followed my gaze to the far side of the basement just as a tuba emerged from the stairwell. "A tuba?" she asked.

"It's Brian," I said, "with an accordion player and drummer."

When the drummer started a beat, Barbara's head popped up like a prairie dog. Her eyes grew wide in disbelief as the accordion and tuba started playing "The Pennsylvania Polka." I waded through the suddenly silent crowd, and got to Barbara's side just as she was preparing to make a run for the musicians.

"Let them play," I said, pulling her close. "Look at the guests."

Everyone was facing the band and smiling. Two of my senior citizens got up and started dancing in a corner of the basement. A few people started singing the tune.

"This isn't the way I planned it," Barbara said, burying her face in my shoulder. "It's all out of control."

"Look at Auntie Lois and Uncle Freddie," Jenny said. The elderly couple had joined a growing crowd of people dancing in the corner. Two of the men were sliding back a divider to open a larger dance area and soon there were children dancing alongside octogenarians.

Barbara was shaking and on the verge of tears when Jenny embraced her. "This day couldn't have turned out any better."

Pastor Redmond was seated across the table. Seeing Jenny and Barbara embrace, he came over and shook my hand. "This is the most memorable wedding I've ever presided over. It's wonderful!"

Hearing the elderly pastor's words, Barbara turned and looked at the growing number of dancers as the band started "The Beer Barrel Polka." The entire crowd was laughing and clapping along with the music.

I felt Howard's arm around my shoulders. "I don't know how you pulled it off," he whispered, "but you just turned a stuffy reception into a real party." He was smiling from ear to ear.

We started wandering around, talking to our guests. When we reached Dolores's table she struggled to her feet, despite our requests that she stay seated. With the band playing "Hoop-Dee-Doo" in the background, she bent down and dragged her purse from under her chair. After hugging Jenny and giving me a handshake, remembering my ribs, she dug into her massive purse. I cringed until I remembered Len's reassurance that she didn't have a firearm. With her fist closed, Dolores pressed something into Jenny's hand and whispered in her ear. Jenny looked down, at first not recognizing what she had been given, then she threw her arms around Dolores.

Barbara and Howard joined us as Jenny continued hugging Dolores.

"Really?" Jenny asked Dolores. Tears were streaming down her face.

Barbara and I were almost ready to pry open Jenny's hand when Dolores turned to me and gave me a chaste hug that didn't come near my sore ribs.

"I'm moving into Whistling Pines," she said loud enough to be heard over the band. "I went to my lawyer Friday and had the house deed transferred to you and Jenny. I know you'll take care of it."

Jenny opened her palm and showed us the rusty skeleton key that probably hadn't seen the inside of the lock since the house was built.

"I've decided to pick up some new furniture for my apartment rather than moving all that dusty old stuff out. The contents are yours, too."

"But the doll collection, the Hummels, and the guns," Jenny said. "They're worth thousands of dollars."

"They're all yours. Do with them as you see fit." Dolores turned and walked to the door with Blanche trailing behind.

"What's up?" asked Jeremy, who couldn't hear over the booming drum, tuba, and accordion.

"We won't be moving into Peter's rented house. We have our own house," Jenny said as she hugged him.

After escaping the embrace, he asked, "Peter bought a house?"

"Dolores gave us her house," Jenny explained. "You can have your own upstairs bedroom."

"Cool!"

The polka ended and the accordion player, whom I recognized as the cook from Judy's Restaurant, stepped up to the microphone. "We were told that the bride and groom have a special song." He stepped back and at first I didn't recognize the song, having never heard it on accordion and tuba, but I was suddenly being dragged to the dance floor by Jenny. We were soon surrounded by a sea of people who were all singing the chorus, "If I said you had a beautiful body, would you hold it against me?"

With Jenny in my arms and the church basement full of friends and family, I realized I was the luckiest man in the world.

ACKNOWLEDGMENTS:

I want to thank my wife, Julie, who continues to put up with my daily writing and my distraction while developing a story. She always proofs the first version of the book, making corrections to the medical scenes, the assisted living scenes, and the characters.

Thank you, Larry Mohr, for bugging me until I added the stamp collection to this plot. Larry and Nancy Mohr allowed me to use their names as characters in this book.

My cousins, Jeff Telker and Sonny Carlson, add energy and fun to the BCA characters.

Tim Webb, a relative by marriage, is a funny, and more importantly, a highly competent craftsman, capable of all the home repairs mentioned in this book.

Brian Johnson provided me with an endless supply of tuba jokes. He is also the inspiration for the tuba player in the book and has become my muse when I write myself into a corner.

Dennis Arnold corrected the police procedures. He passed away between the first draft and the final version of this book. I miss his input and friendship.

There are several people who take my words and make them into a better piece of work. Pat Morris edits and corrects my manuscripts. Natalie Lund, Frannie Brozo, and Anne Flagge have proofread the manuscript. They have taught me that a manuscript full of red and blue marks is a good thing. Any mistakes in the final version of the book are usually items that I've added at the last second, and are there despite their efforts.

Thanks to the libraries and bookstores who support me and keep my books on their shelves. Thank you Sarah, Susie, Bert, Nancy, Devin, Kathleen, Kirsten, Jeanne, Mark, Kris, Jenny, Nancy, Amelia, Carolyn, Steve, Nina, Lisa, Sue, Heidi, Leo, Janie, and many others.

A special thanks to my readers who offer support and encouragement. It's you who keep me energized.

www.ingramcontent.com/pod-product-compliance
Lightning Source LLC
Chambersburg PA
CBHW051642260626
47170CB00004B/1295